NEVER HAVE I EVER

CAMPUS GAMES BOOK #1

STEPHANIE ALVES

This book is a work of fiction. Any names, places, characters, or incidents are a product of the author's imagination.
Any resemblance to actual persons, events, or locales is entirely coincidental.

Copyeditor: Amanda Oraha
Cover designer: Stephanie Alves

ISBN: 978-1-917180-04-7
Special Edition

This book contains detailed sexual content, graphic language and some other heavy topics.
You can see the full list of content warnings on my website here: stephaniealvesauthor.com

Happy Reading!

Also by Stephanie Alves

Standalone

Love Me or Hate Me

Campus Games Series

Never Have I Ever (Book #1)
Spin The Bottle (Book #2)
Would You Rather (Book #3)

To everyone who feels like they're never good enough, no matter what they do.
I see you.

Playlist

NEVER HAVE I EVER - Stephanie Alves

ANGEL - The Weeknd ♥

OVERDRIVE - Conan Gray ♥

INTO IT - Chase Atlantic ♥

HEAVEN - Julia Michaels ♥

STARGAZING - The Neighbourhood ♥

WHY - Sabrina Carpenter ♥

THINKING BOUT YOU - Ariana Grande ♥

STUPID - Tate McRae ♥

IMAGINE - Ariana Grande ♥

EYES OFF YOU - PrettyMuch ♥

HIT MY LINE - Plvtinum, Chase Atlantic ♥

LOVE IS (NOT) EASY - Chase Atlantic ♥

MESS IT UP - Gracie Abrams ♥

TEACH ME HOW TO LOVE - Shawn Mendes ♥

PARADISE - Chase Atlantic ♥

COMPASS - The Neighbourhood ♥

1

New beginnings

Rosalie

My eyes widen as I step into the frat house.

The place is crowded. Music blasts throughout the place as we step inside.

"Asshole," a girl yells at some guy who spilled his drink onto her. I take a step back, making sure I don't get caught in the crossfire. He shrugs her off and walks over to another girl, leaning down to kiss her before throwing her over his shoulder.

"I told you," Gabi says to my right. "Frat parties get a little crazy. Isn't that dress dry clean only?" she asks, raising an eyebrow.

I rub the fabric of my white silk dress between my fingers. "Yeah." I narrow my eyes at her. "But it's a party. I wanted to look good."

Especially because this is my first party. Ever. I don't mean the family gatherings my mother would host at the country club. I mean a real party. Drinks, guys, fun.

Tonight is my first taste of freedom, and I'm going to make the most out of it. If I do end up getting a drink spilled on my dress, I can always make another one. Though this is one of my favorite designs I have done.

"She looks good," Madi says to my right. "Besides, it's better to overdress than to underdress." Her red lips shoot me a smile. She's right. And Madi is dressed to perfection. Her dark, mahogany skin shines from the body oil she slathered on her body, which stands out in her tight black dress.

She flicks her long, dark brown hair behind her shoulder and leans into me. "Don't listen to Gabi. Her idea of fashion is a hoodie from Target."

"And I stand by that," Gabi says, running her hands down her black denim jeans. "It's a frat party. Not a gala or some shit."

"Dios," Leila mutters, laughing at the antics we're used to seeing between Madi and Gabi. "You two never stop arguing," my best friend since high school says before turning to face me. "C'mon, I need a drink if I'm going to deal with these two all night."

A laugh escapes me when Gabriella gasps. "Rude," she says, making Leila roll her eyes at her dramatics.

Leila links arms with me as we walk across the room through the crowd. Madi and Gabi follow us behind. I blatantly stare, gaping at the people playing beer pong. A guy stands shirtless as his friend pours alcohol on his body, and girls lick it up. My eyes widen as we keep walking across the house.

"Jesus, that was crazy," I breathe out when we enter the kitchen area. It's quieter here, but the music still blares in the other room, echoing through the door.

"You haven't seen anything yet. Halloween parties are insane around here." Gabi says.

My eyes widen. "Really?" I ask.

She nods with a smirk on her lips. "My sister used to go here. She would let me sneak in with her when I was still in high school. My poor little brain was exposed to things no one should see at that age," she muses, shaking her head.

Madi rolls her eyes. "You were sixteen," she says. "Your brain was probably already corrupted by then."

Gabi snorts out a laugh. "True. You know me so well." A smile spread across her face making us all laugh.

The door opens when someone walks in, and Leila curses. "Oh god," Leila says, crouching down behind me. "Hide me."

"What's wrong?" I ask.

"Tiffany just walked in," she whispers. "I'm going to end up in jail for killing her if I have to hear about her fucked up relationship one more time." She narrows her eyes. "I envy you. Living alone in a huge apartment."

I drop my eyes. For as long as I remember, I've felt guilty about my money. I come from a family who's never had to worry about anything. Everything I've ever wanted, I had. Even the apartment I definitely did not want.

My mother might have rented out that apartment and bought every piece of furniture there, but I'm not fooled by it. She doesn't support my dream of going to college at all.

What she really wants is to remind me of the life she has, of the life I could have if I just married rich. But I don't want that. I'm following my dreams by going to college and becoming my own person. I want to start a clothing line, and I'm not going to let my mother deter me from doing exactly that.

"Is she gone?" Leila asks when the door closes again.

I look around the room, not seeing Leila's roommate anywhere. I nod, and she exhales, lifting herself off the ground. She adjusts her purple romper, the material hugging her full figure.

"I can't believe you're living off-campus in a huge apartment, and you're only a freshman," Gabi says.

"Yeah, well." I sigh. "My mom said dorms are for crack whores and drug addicts."

"Guess we're crack whores," Gabriella says to Madi with a smirk.

"And addicts," Madi replies, making us laugh.

"I at least wanted to try it, you know? I've always imagined myself in a dorm when I thought of going to college."

Gabi shakes her head. "You aren't missing out on anything but annoying roommates and fear of catching infections in the showers."

"Uh… I'm your roommate," Madeline says, narrowing her eyes at her.

Gabriella grins; her eyes are on me. "My point exactly," she says.

"Like you're any better?" Madi says. "At least I don't bring people back to the dorm when you're trying to sleep."

Gabi faces Madi. "That was one time," she says, lifting a finger. "And in my defense, I thought you were asleep."

"If I was, I would have woken up," Madi adds, letting out a laugh.

Gabi rolls her eyes. "You're so dramatic. She left right after. Plus, she was quiet."

Madi scoffs. "But you weren't. I'm traumatized from hearing your sex noises when I was sleeping less than six feet away."

Gabi presses her hand to her mouth, trying not to laugh. "You're just strung out," she says, "you need to get laid."

"What I need is a drink," she says, holding out her cup. "Fill me up, Perez."

"Careful," Leila says, filling up Madi's cup, trying not to laugh. "Make sure you don't pass out like Gabi over here."

Gabi groans. "Not this again," she says. "Jesus, you pass out one time," she muses.

"You passed out?" I ask.

She shrugs. "I might have."

"She definitely did," Madi says.

"From one drink," Leila adds.

"You have no proof," Gabi says, crossing her arms.

"I definitely do," Madi replies. "The picture of you passed out on the floor is proof enough."

Gabi's mouth drops open. "You took a picture of me?" she asks. "What kind of friend does that?

"The kind who knows you're going to lie about it. Plus, you were passed out for like a minute. Calm down."

"You want to be my new best friend?" Gabi asks me. "Madi just got demoted."

"Thank god," Madi mutters, making Leila and I laugh.

Gabi links arms with me. "I'm a great friend." Madi snorts in the background, but Gabi ignores her. "And I have alcohol," she says, handing me a red plastic cup filled with the beer she poured. "Stick with me, and you'll have fun," she says, flashing me a wink.

I look down at the liquid and bring it to my mouth, taking a sip. My face screws up as the bitter taste burns my throat. But it's not completely horrible. I throw back the cup and down the rest of the drink.

"Woah. Slow down, Rosie," Leila says. "Have you ever had alcohol before?"

"Of course I have."

She smirks. "I mean, other than the wine they serve at communion."

I shake my head which makes her laugh. "Then take it easy. You're probably a lightweight, just like Gabi over here."

Gabi groans, pulling away from me. "That's it. I'm not taking any more of your shit," she says, walking away from us. The kitchen door opens as she walks away. "I'm leaving," she yells at us, looking over her shoulder.

"Goodbye," Madi replies. Leila and I smirk, trying not to laugh.

"Forever!" Gabi yells back, and then she's gone, muddled into the crowd of drunk college students.

I can't help but laugh at Gabi's dramatic exit. Madi shakes her head with a smirk on her face. She's always been like this. Since the day I met her, she's been a drama queen, which is funny considering Madi is the actress in the group.

"Should we go check on her?" Leila asks.

Madi sighs and downs her drink. "I'll go. If she ends up drunk and passed out somewhere, I'm going to have to drag her home."

She exits, and Leila links her arms with me. "C'mon," she says, opening the kitchen door and following Madi out. Noise fills the room as soon as we step out of the kitchen. My eyes scan the room, taking it all in. The music, the dancing.

"Hey." My head snaps to my side, and I see a guy smiling down at me. His teeth are bright as he grins, his blue eyes shine down at me.

"Hi." I smile back at him. He grins again, taking a sip of his drink. I turn my head, seeing Leila not so subtly wink at me and taking a step back, leaving me alone with this guy.

I look back at him, meeting his blue eyes as he does a once over, licking his lips. What do I say? If Leila were here, she'd touch his arm and flirt with him, maybe compliment him.

"I like your hair," I say, attempting to form a conversation with him. I don't know how to do this. This is all new to me. Should I flip my hair, flutter my eyelashes?

He chuckles. "Thanks," he says, running a hand through his dirty blonde hair. He lifts a brow and asks, "You new? I haven't seen you around."

"Oh, um. Yeah." I nod, trying not to fiddle with the hem of my dress. "I'm a freshman. I don't really go to these." I gesture around the room. "This is my first time here," I tell him.

"Cool." He grins, his tongue dipping out to lick his bottom lip. "I'm Ben, by the way."

"Rosalie," I reply.

"Rosalie," he mutters to himself, flashing me a smirk. "You want a drink?"

I lift my half-full cup at him. "Already have one."

"Right," he says. "Well, some of my friends and I are going to play beer pong. You want in?"

I look around the room and see Leila talking to a guy, laughing in the corner with him. "Uh… I'm here with my friends," I tell him. "Maybe another time?" I say, trying to placate him. He seems nice, but what do I know? I barely know the guy.

"No worries," he says. "Nice to meet you." He flashes me another smile while walking away.

I sigh, taking a sip of the cheap, bitter beer. My eyes catch on Leila as she walks toward me.

"So, how did it go?" she asks.

I shrug. “Okay, I guess. He asked me to play beer pong.”

“You didn’t want to?”

I shake my head. “I hardly know him.”

“That’s fair,” she says, nudging my shoulder, a smile on her lips. “You want to play Never Have I Ever instead?”

2

Angel on Earth

Grayson

All eyes turn as soon as I step into the frat house.

Fuck if I know why they're staring or what the new rumor is this week, and I don't give a shit. All I need right now is a drink to take my mind off it all.

I pick up a cup and fill it with whatever the fuck is in the bowl, downing it. I don't know why Aiden made me come to this dumbass party. Every week it's the same old shit. It's getting boring. The same music, the same drinks, the same girls. Nothing ever changes.

"Stop scowling." Aiden nudges my side, and I turn my head to look up at him. The dude is tall. He's a basketball player scouted right from high school. He stands out. I mean, he's 6'5, his head inevitably sticks out in the middle of the crowd.

"I'm not scowling," I tell him.

"You look like you're going to kill someone. Everyone's staring."

I glare at him. "You sure it's me they're staring at? You're not exactly hard to miss with your head almost touching the ceiling." It's an exaggeration, one that gets me a laugh from my best friend since freshman year.

"Dude, don't be jealous. It's beneath you."

I scoff. “Fuck you. I’m not jealous.”

His head shakes, laughing. Some of his teammates come to greet him as he walks deeper into the house.

I lean back on the wall, looking around the place. A group of guys play strip beer pong, and some poor girl is down to her skivvies while the guy is gloating in her misery of being almost naked at a party full of drunk, horny frat guys.

Guess that’s college for you. She takes another shot and misses. The guys around the table all cheer, and she looks terrified like she finally realizes she’s going to have to get naked in front of a bunch of strangers. She slowly reaches behind her back to unclasp her bra, but she stops and runs out.

Fucking Ben Reed. It’s the same thing every week. I swear he has a fetish for humiliating girls. He boos and his dogs follow suit, cursing at her as she races out of there, and I can’t help but roll my eyes.

“Grayson,” Aiden calls from the kitchen. “We’re gonna play some games. Wanna join?”

“Nah, I’m good,” I yell back, and he nods, but before he can escape, a swarm of girls surrounds us as they swoon over Aiden Pierce, the captain of Redfield’s basketball team.

Aiden's whole life is basketball. He lives and breathes it, and even though he came out tonight to party, he's going to be spending the whole night playing video games. I don't want to play. In fact, I don't even want to be here right now.

I need a smoke.

I lift off the wall, heading toward the back of the room, and pull out a cigarette. Lighting it up, I bring it to my lips and inhale. Shit, the only good thing I’ve got going at the moment is this smoke right here.

School's a dud. I want to kick myself for putting up with this. If I had another way of getting the fuck out of here, I would have done it by now. But this is the only way for now. Once I've got what I need, I'm leaving. Leaving these people, leaving my parents, leaving everything behind, and getting as far away from here as possible.

Redfield University is my ticket to freedom, my get-out-of-jail-free card, and once I graduate, or get enough money, I'm free to leave and do whatever I want.

I refill my cup and take a swig of my drink as I look around the room, the music blaring throughout the house.

I see so many faces I've seen before, all the same, every week.

Aiden's in a swarm of girls that are falling at his feet. I would hate to be in his position, but he has a huge smile on his face, so I guess he's not hating life right now. Even though he'd prefer to be down in the basement with his boys.

I couldn't deal with the attention he gets. I mean, I get my fair share of girls wanting a quick fuck, but nothing like Aiden. He can't go anywhere without being raided by a mass of groupies. I guess it comes with the territory of being on the run-up to becoming a pro basketball player.

I could see him being in the NBA. Aiden is good, like pro-level good, and he knows it. He takes advantage of his perks, I'm sure.

"Grayson." I cock my head to the side, seeing the douchebag I knew I'd run into if I came tonight. I knew I shouldn't have come. Parties like these are good for business but dealing with pricks like Brent isn't good for my temper. I bring the cigarette to my lips and blow out a cloud of smoke.

"Grayson," he says when I don't answer. "Hey, bro, I need another one."

I scoff. He's got to be kidding me. "After you duped me? The answer's no." I say, blowing out smoke to my side.

"I didn't have all of it last time, but I do now."

"Yeah, I've heard that before," I say, not bothering to look at him. I don't want to deal with another asshole who thinks the world owes him, and Brent is no different.

"I couldn't afford it," he tells me. Fuck, my stomach twists. I'm taking money from him, and he needs it. *You need it too.* Not as much as he probably does. But it was his choice; he chose to buy from me. I didn't force him, and I did my part, but he underdelivered on his.

"That's not my problem," I say, putting out the butt end of the cigarette on the table behind me. I start to walk away from him, but he grabs my arm. I look down at his hand wrapped around my arm and glare at him before he takes it off.

"Sorry, dude. I just… I need it. I can't get kicked off the team."

Brent is on Aiden's team. He's not as good as Aiden, but he's decent. I can smell the desperation coming from him right now. He needs it. Badly. I could take advantage of this, raise the price, knowing how much he needs it, but I don't. I can't.

I sigh. "Fine. But I want all of it, not one cent less." I tell him.

He nods and backs up. "You got it. Thanks, bro."

I leave the room, heading towards the living room, where it's quieter. A bunch of people huddle up, some sitting on the floor, some sprawled on the couch. I lift my brow at them.

How much do I want to bet they're playing Never Have I Ever?

"Never have I ever. This is how you play."

I scoff; of course, they are. Fuck it, why not. I lean against the wall, waiting for the game to start. I might as well drink now, these people are pretty tame, and I've almost certainly done everything they're about to say.

"Excuse me, can we come through?" A light voice comes from my side. My head turns, and I see an angel.

I blink twice. I need to make sure I'm seeing right. I see a vision of blue as her eyes look up at me, and then she smiles. A smile so beautiful that I become hypnotized, apparently because I do nothing but stare back at her.

She shifts uncomfortably and tries to squeeze past. My brain miraculously starts to work, and I move out of the way so that she and her friend can go past. She's so close I can feel her body heat as she shifts past me and walks into the room. They walk toward the couch and sit on the edge of it.

I can't take my eyes off her. She fans her long blonde hair behind her shoulders as she leans back onto the couch and adjusts her dress. A dress I've never felt luckier to be able to see. I always thought clothes were made to be ripped off. A dress is a dress, it's going to end on the floor at the end of the night. Hell, most girls here are wearing dresses, but none like hers.

The dress hits mid-thigh, showing off long legs that end in white heels. The white silk fabric flows off her body, making me wonder what she looks like underneath. Some girls here are barely dressed, I almost know what they look like naked—of course, some of those are from experience—but hers…

leaves everything to the imagination, and my imagination is currently running wild.

Who is this girl? I've never seen her here before, and I come to these parties a lot, mostly because Aiden makes me come with him. He says it's to be his wingman, but I highly doubt that. He didn't need my help back there, and he rarely ever does. They fall at his feet at the mere sight of him.

But I've never been more grateful to come tonight. I don't know who this girl is, but I need to find out. I can't look away. The way she sits, her back straight as she crosses her ankles. So poised, so… elegant. Who the hell is she?

She turns her head to speak to her friend and laughs. I'm socked in the stomach at the sight.

Her smile. Christ.

Her friend whispers in her ear, and I wonder what she's telling her. Has she heard about me? Or does the angel already know who I am? She didn't seem to when our eyes met, but I wouldn't know for certain.

"Let's play," I hear someone say.

Well, shit. If she didn't know me before, she's about to.

3

Never Have I Ever...

Rosalie

"Never have I ever had a threesome."

A sigh escapes my mouth as I drop my eyes. When Leila said we would be playing Never Have I Ever, I thought this would be fun. I would maybe even attempt to get drunk. I mean, it is a drinking game. But apparently, you have to have a life for that to be possible.

The game has been going on for over ten minutes, and I haven't taken one single sip. I think people are starting to notice, and that makes me shift in my seat a little.

"Never have I ever had a one-night stand."

I see nearly everyone around us take a sip of their drink, including Leila to my right. I cock my head towards her and raise my eyebrows. "You have?" I ask her.

She laughs. "My whole life is a one-night stand," she says.

My eyes widen. I know she hooks up a lot, but I always thought maybe it was with the same guy. I glance down at my drink, seeing the cup still full. I want to drink and have fun like everyone else, but I haven't done anything.

"Never have I ever got a tattoo."

Leila drinks along with three other people in the crowd. One of them being the guy that was standing by the wall earlier. He's covered in tattoos. His arms are scattered with black ink. I must stare a little too long because his eyes catch mine. I suck in a breath and turn to face Leila.

"You have a tattoo?" I ask her. She's quiet for a moment before she nods. "How did I not know that?"

"Because I wasn't going to show anyone. I can't have tattoos, it's in my modeling contract," she says, shrugging. "But I figured if I got a small one where they couldn't see, it would be okay."

Leila's been a model since I met her. At first, she was doing small commercials, but since she turned eighteen, she's done runway shows and worked for big companies.

She even models for me when I need her to, which I'm thankful for. Having someone at my disposal whenever I need makes my job so much easier.

"Where?"

She lifts her brown hair and turns her head. Behind her ear is a small black paw print. "A paw?" I ask her.

She covers it with her hair and turns to face me. "A tiger paw," she explains.

"Oh," I stare back at her. "Is there a meaning behind it?"

She shrugs. "Just thought it looked cool,"

I nod. "It does. It looks really good,"

She smiles, squeezing my thigh. "Thanks,"

"Excuse me," Madi says, walking past the huddle of people to sit on the couch next to Leila, Gabi coming right behind her.

"I thought you said you were leaving," I say.

"Forever," we all say dramatically.

We all laugh, and Gabi shrugs. "Yeah, well, I missed you guys."

Madi rolls her eyes. "That's a lie. She was about to hook up with some frat guy, and I dragged her back here before she brought him back to the dorm."

"She cockblocked me," Gabi says.

"Yeah, well, be thankful you don't wake up with a bunch of STDs tomorrow," Madi says back to her.

"You did that for your benefit, not mine," Gabi replies.

"Hell yeah, I did."

Gabi laughs, shaking her head, and turns to Leila. "What are we playing?"

"Never Have I Ever," Leila replies.

Gabi holds out her empty cup. "Then fill me up. I don't have the energy to go get a drink."

Leila pours half of her drink into Gabi's cup, and they sit back, waiting for the next one.

"Never have I ever stood someone up on a date."

Haven't dated, so I don't drink.

"Never have I ever kissed a friend's sibling."

Never kissed anyone, so I don't drink.

"Never have I ever gone skinny dipping."

Nope.

"Never have I ever had sex in public."

No.

"Never have I ever had a friend with benefits."

Nuh Uh.

"Never have I ever been to a sex shop."

Nope.

"Never have I ever sent a nude."

No. No. No.

I want the ground to swallow me up. I haven't done anything. All eyes are on me. They all know I haven't done any of it. Is this the part where they all laugh and throw things at me because they find out I'm a virgin?

My eyes meet with the tattooed guy. He's looking back at me, his face is blank, like he sees right through me, and maybe he isn't paying attention to me, but I've been paying attention to him. He took a sip every time. Everything they said, he's done.

I wonder what that's like. To actually live. This guy doesn't seem to have that problem. He seems to have done everything. It wouldn't surprise me if he's even killed someone before.

Our eyes lock, and I gulp. Neither of us has broken eye contact yet, and I don't want to challenge him, but I also don't want to stop looking. His eyes narrow as he smirks at me, making my eyes drift down to his lips. Those lips. Have kissed someone. I want to know what that feels like. Having someone's lips on mine.

"Why is Grayson Carter staring at you?" Gabi asks.

I wrench my head away from him and look at Gabi instead. "Grayson Carter?" I ask.

"Yeah. He's a sophomore. He's a drug dealer who sells drugs to support his mum's addiction."

I frown. "Is that true?"

Gabi shrugs. "I don't know, could be a rumor. It's what people have been saying since freshman year."

I glance back at him, and his eyes are still on me. Shit. I quickly avert my gaze and focus on my still-full.

"Never have I ever used a pickup line."

Most of the guys drink, and some girls, too, and to my side, I see Gabi sipping her drink.

"You've used a pickup line?" Madi asks her.

Gabi raises her brow. "Of course. Haven't you?"

Madi shakes her head. "No, but out of curiosity, what do you say?"

She smirks, clearing her throat. "I say, do you like to sleep? And they obviously say yes, because, duh, who doesn't? And then I say, me too, we should try it together sometime." She grins, taking a swig of her beer.

We all laugh at how ridiculous that is. "That's the worst pickup line I've ever heard," Madi says.

"But it works every time." She smirks.

"Even on girls?" Leila asks, skeptically raising her eyebrows.

Gabi scoffs. "Of course not. Girls aren't stupid."

"Never have I ever faked an orgasm."

Again… to no one's surprise, I don't drink.

I sigh, letting my head hit the back of the couch. "This is stupid," I mutter.

Leila turns her head to me, along with Gabi and Madi. "What is?"

I shrug. "This game. The fact that I haven't done anything at all." I frown. "Everyone's looking at me." I glance over to the group of girls staring my way, whispering to each other.

"Don't pay attention to them. They're judgmental bitches," Gabi says. "So, what if you haven't faked an orgasm or sent a nude? Who actually cares about that?" She turns her head and glares at the girls, and they stop whispering.

"I don't want to be the boring person who has no life," I tell them.

"You couldn't be boring if you tried," Leila says.

I try to smile at her, but it falls flat. "Still," I sigh, "I would have liked to join in. It's a drinking game, and I'm stone-cold sober."

I feel so out of place. I always knew I missed out on stuff. I knew I was sheltered, but this is just embarrassing. Sad, really. I realize now that I've missed out on so much more than I thought.

"Never have I ever skipped class," Leila says.

I turn to my side, seeing Leila smile down at me. I freeze for a second. I *have* done that. The first week of school, my mother showed up wanting to furnish the apartment and kept me up all night, making me miss the first class of the day.

She gestures to my cup, and I smile at her as I take a sip. Some people start to murmur, and a couple of guys even cheer. I don't know whether to laugh or to be embarrassed by it.

"There. You've done something," Leila says, and I smile back at her.

It's something small and not at all scandalous, but the fact that Leila did that for me makes me so happy.

I glance back at Grayson, and he's got the cup covering his mouth, but his eyes are on me. He takes a sip and brings the cup down. He swallows the drink, his Adam's apple bobbing while his eyes stay locked on mine. He wipes his mouth with the back of his hand, then he smiles at me and leaves.

His smile was quick and small, I probably imagined it. What was that about? Why would Grayson Carter smile at me?

The game continues, but all I can think about is Grayson Carter. Are the rumors about him true? And why do I want to know more about him?

4

Dirty List

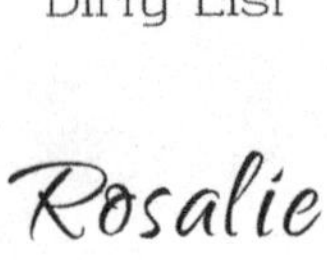

I think I’ve gone insane.

That’s the only explanation for why I’m on my way to Grayson Carter’s house.

I need to at least ask him. I can’t think of anyone else who would be more fitting to help me with a situation like this.

I want someone who’s done it all, experienced everything, and Grayson Carter is that man. The rumors I’ve heard about him speak for themselves. Drug dealer, playboy, sleeps around, drinks, smokes, steals. You name it, Grayson has probably done it.

I want to see what he’s like, what his life is like. I crave a life like his, I want it all. The fun, the danger, the excitement, and Grayson can give me that.

I’m curious about everything to do with Grayson Carter. The stolen glances I took last night whenever he drank to a question, the way my breath staggered when his eyes locked on mine. The way my stomach flipped when he smirked at me before he turned around and left.

I want to know what that means. He’s so different from any guys I’ve been attracted to. Dark hair, dark eyes, tattoos. It’s confusing. I’ve always been into preppy guys, blond hair, blue eyes, the kind you settle down with and marry, and Grayson definitely isn’t that.

I don't know what it is about him that makes me want to know him. It should terrify me that he's a drug dealer, and those tattoos should make me shiver at the mere sight of them. His dark eyes should make me run the other way, especially how intense they are, the way they burned into my memory.

But it doesn't. If anything, it makes me more intrigued. Who is Grayson Carter, and what would it be like to live like him? A life without rules, responsibilities, no expectations to be perfect. Just live and have fun.

He'd be exactly the type of guy my mother would hate, she would despise everything he stands for, and maybe that's why he entices me so much. Maybe that's why I feel drawn to him, and maybe that's why I'm currently on the way to his house, about to ask him to take my virginity.

Which brings me back to the conclusion that I've gone insane. I mean, I don't know him, not really. I know his name and his reputation. That isn't enough to know someone. I haven't even talked to him, except for a split second at the party.

The memory makes my palms burn. The way his lips parted, the way his dark eyes dominated his face as he looked down at me, almost shocked to see me. It etched in my mind, making me aware of him for the rest of the night.

Other than that, I don't know him, but I'm desperate. Desperate for fun and excitement in my life. Desperate to finally experience the life I've always wanted.

I've always felt like an outsider. With the girls from the country club that my mother forced me to interact with, I felt like I didn't belong. Even with my family, I felt like I was the odd one out. The one that was never good enough compared to my brother.

I have never once felt like I belonged, and maybe I still don't. Maybe I don't belong here, in college. Maybe my mother was right all along, and I was destined to follow in her footsteps, to be a housewife and nothing more.

But that's not what I want, and if my life is ultimately destined for a lifetime of despair and brunches at the country club, then I deserve this. Four years of doing whatever the hell I want and living my life how I've always wanted to.

The closer I get to his front door, the more I start thinking this is a horrible idea. What if he says no? I've never asked a guy out before. The one time I had a crush in high school, I was so nervous around him, I didn't know how to talk to him.

And at the party, I almost choked when Ben came up to me, wanting to talk to me. I'm not like Leila. She's confident, easy-going, fun. I remember seeing her talk to a guy at the party, laughing, touching his arm, smiling up at him like it was the most natural thing ever.

I wish I could do that. The whole flirting thing, it always scared me. Which is why I need Grayson's help. If I can't even talk to a guy, how will I ever date one?

But what if he rejects me? What if Grayson laughs in my face and turns me down? He doesn't have a reason to say yes. There's nothing in it for him. This is all beneficial to me.

I approach the door and take a deep breath, staring up at the large black door staring back at me. This is it.

I lift my hand and press the doorbell. I step back, waiting for someone to open the door, but there's no answer, so I press it again and wait.

"I'm coming, hold up," I hear from the other side of the door.

I push my shoulders back and wait for him to open the door. This is it. This is what I came here for. This is what I wanted, and I'm finally going to get it.

But when the door finally swings open, he's not standing on the other side.

"Yes? Can I help you?" The guy asks. I twist my neck up to look at him. Jesus, he's tall.

His hair is tucked underneath a baseball cap, and my eyes drift down his body. This guy is huge, in height but also in muscle. This definitely isn't Grayson.

I look up, and I'm met with a smile. I smile back. "Um… is this where Grayson Carter lives?" I ask.

He scratches the back of his neck and looks behind his shoulder for a second before he turns back to look at me. "Yeah?" He says, his brows scrunching a little. "Who are you?" He asks.

"I'm Rosalie Whitton. I need to talk to Grayson Carter. Can I come in?"

"Yeah. Sure," he says before he steps back, allowing me to enter.

I step inside the house. It's much nicer than I expected. There's a huge kitchen to the right, mostly black, with a chandelier hanging above the dining table and a staircase in front of me, with a black railing along the side. The floorboards are dark wood and shine underneath my heels. This house looks luxurious. How much do drug dealers make?

I twist my head to the left, poking my head through the door, seeing a huge TV. I'm guessing it's a living room. My eyes widen when I see four heads turn and all eyes on me.

These guys are just as big as the guy who opened the door. What milk do they drink?

Behind me, the door closes, and I jump at the sound, turning around and staring wide-eyed at the guy who opened the door for me, now leaning against it with his arms crossed over his chest.

"I'm Grayson's roommate," he says. "Aiden Pierce."

Aiden Pierce. Why does that name sound familiar to me?

I look over my shoulder at the four guys sitting on the black leather couch still staring at me. One of them is holding a basketball, and that's when it clicks.

"Oh," I say, realization kicking in. I turn back to face him. "Aiden Pierce," I repeat his name. "You're the captain of the basketball team?"

"Yeah," he says, nodding.

"I recognized your name. My friend watches your games," I say. Leila is crazy about basketball. She used to attend every game at our high school and now tries to drag me to the basketball games, which I decline every time.

"She does?" A smirk forms on his face when I nod, and then he gestures towards the couch with a tilt of his head. "These are some of my teammates."

I turn my head back and look at the guys. The whole group smiles at me, one of them lifting his hand in greeting. "Hey," he says.

"Hey," I reply, feeling my cheeks start to heat.

"You looking for Grayson?" another guy asks.

I nod. "Yeah." I turn back to look at Aiden. "Is he here?"

He gestures towards the stairs. "Yeah. He's upstairs. Is he expecting you?"

I shake my head. "No, he's not. He doesn't even know me." I let out a nervous laugh. "I came to ask for his help with something."

"Shit, I'll help you," one of the guys calls out, and a few of them laugh.

I feel another blush coming, so I focus on Aiden. "Can I go upstairs?"

He scratches the back of his neck again and nervously laughs. "Uh… he might be a little busy at the moment."

I shrug. "That's okay, it will only take a second."

He regards me with a scrunch of his brows and then blows out a breath. "Can I ask what you need help with?" Aiden asks me.

I shake my head. "It's… personal," I say.

"How personal?" One of the guys mumbles, and they all laugh under their breath. I freeze in place. Do they know? I tried to keep it as vague as possible. If anyone finds out about this, it will be so embarrassing.

Aiden nods. "Okay, and none of us can help you with it?"

They could. Any one of these guys is probably as experienced as Grayson, and they sound interested, but my mind goes back to Grayson. I need him.

I shake my head. "No, I need to see Grayson," I tell him and head for the stairs.

"He might be a little preoccupied right now," he tells me.

I sigh and sit on the stairs. "I'll wait then."

Aiden bunches his eyebrows together. He looks confused and possibly thinks I'm crazy, and maybe I am, for proposing this idea, but I've been held back for too long. I want to be free for once and experience everything.

"Are you thirsty? I could get you a drink," he asks me.

I shake my head. "No, thanks."

"Hungry?"

I shake my head again.

"Okay then, I'll be in here if you need anything," he says, gesturing to the living room.

He walks into the living room and closes the door behind him. I hear the deep sound of the guys talking through the walls while I sit on the steps, tapping my foot, waiting impatiently for Grayson to come downstairs.

The more time passes, the more I think this might be a horrible idea. It seemed like the perfect plan two nights ago. I came home from the party, sober and upset about how the night had ended and made the list.

I blow out an exasperated breath. Where is he? I clutch my hand on the railing and take a deep breath in. I take a step forward and climb the stairs.

What if he doesn't accept? What if he says no? This is embarrassing enough. I sound desperate. I am desperate. After last night, I don't want to live like I have been for the past eighteen years. I need this.

I take a deep breath when I reach the top of the stairs, looking down the hallway. All of the doors are closed, and I have no idea which one is his bedroom.

Maybe I should just leave, he wouldn't even know I was here in the first place, and I could forget about this whole thing. It's insane that I'm asking a guy I don't even know to sleep with me. But I came here for a reason, and I'm not leaving without at least asking him.

I knock on the first door and wait for a reply or movement from behind the wooden door, but there's no response. I walk further down and knock on the next door I find.

"I'll be down in a second."

I suck in a breath at the sound. That's him. Well, I think. I've never actually heard his voice before, and maybe Aiden and Grayson have a roommate.

I have no idea what possesses me to do what I do next, I know that I should wait for him to open the door or come out, or that it's wrong, but that doesn't stop me from reaching for his door handle.

I'm really about to do this. I'm about to ask Grayson Carter to take my virginity.

Here goes nothing.

I twist the door handle and push the door open.

"Dude, I said I'd be—"

His eyes lock with mine.

Oh, it's his room, alright.

Except, Aiden was right. He is busy. With another girl's tongue down his throat.

I gasp at the scene and slam the door closed.

5

Good girl gone bad

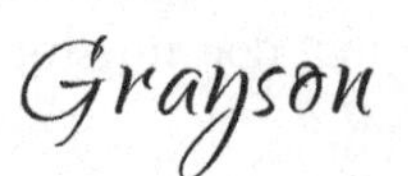

It's her.

I'm rigid for a moment, unable to move, staring at the wooden door that she closed behind her. She rushed out of here so quickly, I barely had time to look at her, but it was definitely her.

I can't believe she's here. Why is she here? In my house, in my room? After Friday night, my mind filled with thoughts of the angel I saw and never thought I'd see again.

Part of me thought I had made it up, made her up in my mind, made up the way she would keep looking back at me all night. But she was just here, in my room.

"Who was that?" Brianna asks. She sits back on my thighs, eyebrows scrunched as she looks down at me. She's still straddling me, her arms wrapped around my neck as all my thoughts are consumed by the girl who just ran from me.

"Huh?"

"The girl," she clarifies. "Who was that?"

Your guess is as good as mine, I want to say. I never saw her before the party, and now I've seen her twice.

"I have no idea," I say honestly.

"Was that your sister?" she asks.

My expression drops as I glare at her. My sister? In what world would she be my sister? She's blonde with blue eyes.

Whereas my hair is dark, my eyes are dark, everything about me is dark, and the complete opposite of her.

"Does she look like my sister?"

"So, what, is she just another skanky whore?" she says, raising her voice as she backs off my lap and stands above me with her arms crossed.

I groan. She's jealous, that's not a good sign. "Another?" I ask. "Are you calling yourself a skanky whore?"

She scoffs. "Ugh. You know what I mean."

I shake my head. "I think it means you're leaving," I say, getting up from the bed.

"What?" she yells.

I open the door and turn back to face her. "You heard me. I need you to go." And quickly. She's probably gone by now, and I don't even know her name, let alone where to find her.

"Why?" Brianna asks.

"Well, first of all, I'm not in the mood anymore."

"I can help with that," she says huskily before grabbing my junk outside of my pants.

I grunt at her touch and take her hand off me. "Yeah, no."

She looks like I just slapped her in the face. Her eyes are widened as she backs away. "Is it because of her?" she asks.

I don't know how to answer that. I don't even know that girl, but since she walked in on my make-out session, all I want to do is run out there and find her.

"Second of all," I say, ignoring her question. "Don't call girls skanky whores, especially girls you don't even know. It's tacky, even for you."

"I didn't mean—"

"Third of all. I told you what this was. A hook-up. I'm not your boyfriend, and I will never be. I never gave you any inclination that this was something else."

"Yeah," she says, nodding. "I know, I just thought you'd change your mind." She sighs. "I mean, we've been hanging out a lot more recently."

Yeah, that's probably my fault. I know girls get clingy, especially if you see them more than a few times a week. They start thinking it's something other than what it is and get false expectations.

Brianna's a nice girl, she's fun, but she's probably the kind of girl who believes in love and wants a relationship and all of that bullshit. That's not me, or ever will be, so I've got to cut this off now.

"I think it's best we end it," I tell her.

She nods, dropping her eyes. "Yeah."

"Are we good?" I ask her.

She shrugs, picks up her bag from the desk, and slings it over her shoulder. "I guess."

I nod. "You know your way out?"

"Yeah, I'm fine," she says.

I rush out of the room. I scan the hallway, but she's not here. I can't rack my mind for any reasoning why she would be here.

My mind floods with memories of Friday night's party when we were playing Never Have I Ever. I looked at her. The whole night I kept my eyes on her. My angel is a good girl. She didn't drink once.

She seemed upset by it. The slight frown on her face whenever a new question was asked was obvious, but probably only to me since I was looking at her all night long.

But she looked at me too, a lot. Her eyes caught mine multiple times. I even held eye contact for longer than necessary, expecting her to back down, to shy away, but she kept looking, continued her stolen glances at me, and now she was in my house. Except she wasn't, not anymore.

She probably got scared at the sight she walked in on. From the very revealing questions last night, I can only assume that she's as innocent as she looks and has probably never had a sweaty make-out session with someone, and the thought of that makes me want to find her even more.

Maybe it's because of how different she is from me and everyone else I've seen, but I want to know more about her. I'm intrigued, and I need to find her.

I rush down the stairs, looking for blonde hair, but she's not here.

Aiden walks out of the living room, and I walk over to him. "Have you seen a girl? Blonde hair."

He furrows his brows a little, and then his eyes widen. "Oh, you mean Rosalie?" he says.

Rosalie. Jesus, even her name sounds sweet.

"Yeah, she ran out of here," he says, laughing. "Seemed like she couldn't get out of here any faster. What did you do?"

Of course, he'd assume I did something to make her run out. She looked shocked to see me with a girl on my lap. The little sound of her gasp knocked the breath out of me, only seeing blonde as she slammed the door. Maybe she hasn't heard about my reputation around here, but why was she here if she doesn't know about me?

I don't even answer him, I open the front door and look down, seeing blonde.

There she is, sitting on the front steps. I shut the door behind me as quietly as possible, not wanting to scare her away.

"Were you looking for me?"

She gasps at the sound of my voice and turns around, stunned to see me. She gets up from the steps and brushes her skirt back into place. My eyes drift down her body; she's wearing white again. A white skirt and a white tank top covered by a light pink cardigan around her shoulders. She looks heavenly, like an angel. I smirk; the nickname I gave her is very fitting.

My eyes drift lower, down to her hands, seeing her clutch a piece of paper. "What's that?" I ask her, stepping closer to her.

"Oh, um. I came here to talk to you." Her voice is like sugar. A light, sweet melody comes out of her lips when she speaks.

"Okay," I say, waiting for her to explain because I have no idea what she wants to talk to me about or why she would be looking for me specifically.

"I need your help," she says. That shouldn't make my palms twitch, but it does.

"What do you need help with?" I ask her.

She stares at me for a while, letting her eyes shut slowly and pulling her bottom lip between her teeth. "I thought this would be easier," she says, hushed and low.

She's nervous. She should be. I have no idea what's on that note or why she came here looking for me, but I'm glad she did.

"Can I see the note?"

Her eyes snap open, and she blushes, the red tint filling her pale complexion as she tucks a strand of her blonde hair behind her ear. She nervously reaches out and hands me the note, and I take it from her, my fingers slightly touching hers.

I take the note in my hand and open it up. Scanning down the list. What the hell?

1. Get drunk (ask Leila for other options besides beer)
2. Kiss someone
3. Go on a date
4. Go to a sex shop (do they still have those or is everything online now?)
5. Go skinny dipping (maybe in the summer so the water isn't cold)
6. Have an orgasm
7. Lose my virginity!

"Are you serious?" I ask her in disbelief.

She nods.

"This is what you need help with?"

She nods again.

I smile, she's so nervous she can't even speak. "I think I'm going to need more of an explanation than a nod, angel."

Shit. The nickname just slipped out of my mouth. Her eyes widen at the term, but then her eyes soften as she smiles. Thank fuck it didn't freak her out.

She stands straight and licks her lips. "I want you to take my virginity," she admits. She sounds confident, more so than before, but I can see her throat bobbing as she swallows nervously.

I start to laugh. I don't mean to, but I choke out a laugh, she frowns a little, so I clear my throat, steadying myself. "You're serious?" I ask her.

She nods, clamming up again.

"That isn't much of an explanation," I say, raising my eyebrow at her. She can't be serious. Is this a joke?

"I said I needed your help," she says.

I smirk. "That's a little different than taking your virginity. I'm going to need a little more from you. What exactly do you need help with?" From her list, it's pretty obvious, but I like to see her squirm.

Which she does. She shifts on her feet as she fidgets with her hands. Color reaches her face once again. I like seeing her blush, nervous, and shy around me. Most people assume they're better than me and look the other way.

"Everything," she admits.

"That's a big spectrum."

She nods and looks towards my hands. I've still got her note filled with a dirty to-do list, and I can't help but wonder why she asked me. Does she know who I am around here? If she did, she wouldn't want to be around me, let alone ask me to help her with this list.

"Why do you want to do this?" I ask her. "It's okay to not do everything in a Never Have I Ever game. It doesn't make you less of a person because you're not… active."

Her eyes meet mine, and her brows furrow; a line forms between her soft eyebrows. Shit, I didn't mean to upset her. I just wanted her to know, if anyone pressured her into thinking she had to do any of these things, that she doesn't have to if she doesn't want to.

"I want to be like you," she says.

My eyebrows raise. I step back in shock, wondering why the hell she would say that. "No one wants to be like me."

"I do."

I'm confused. I'm so confused about why this girl thinks she needs my help, why she says she wants to be like me. She's pure and sweet, and I'm everything but that. I'm tainted, corrupted, and I ruin everything I come into contact with. She'd be right to run the other way and never speak to me again.

"Why?" I ask her.

"Because," she says, taking a step closer. "You have lived."

I'm only more confused by that statement. I have lived? She thinks being me is living?

"What do you want from me?" I ask her because this is a completely different explanation for why she's here. The list feels like just the tipping point for what she really wants.

She sighs. "I want to see the world like you do. I want to go crazy and forget about rules for once in my life," she breathes out, blinking at me before continuing. "And I want you to teach me how to do that. I want you to teach me everything. How to not care, how to have fun and…" She tucks her hair behind her ear before her eyes meet mine. "I want you to teach me about sex. All of it."

"Do they not have sex education wherever you come from?" I joke. She can't possibly be serious. She wants me to corrupt her, to make her everything she's not, when that's the first thing I noticed about her. How honest and pure and kind she is. Not a chance.

She blinks slowly, her eyes locked on mine. "I want to learn from you," she husks out.

Aw hell. This is the worst form of temptation. I can't do this. It would be like I was taking advantage of her, and it wouldn't feel right. The only reason she's asking me is because she has heard the rumors, and she thinks I'm the complete opposite of what she is, good and happy.

If it were anyone else, they would jump at the opportunity, but seeing her standing at my doorstep, asking to ruin her goodness, I can't do it.

6

A deal's a deal

Rosalie

"What do you mean you can't do it?"

I narrow my eyes at him, but he's not meeting my eyes. His head is down, eyes locked on the paper still in his hands. My face heats up, my body flushing with heat at the thought of him staring at that list, knowing he just rejected me.

He finally meets my eyes, and his brows knot together as he sighs and drops his head again, shaking it. "I'm sorry. I just can't."

I don't get it. I thought he would have no issue with it. He's done everything on this list, so why can't he help me do the same?

"But… why?" I ask.

He doesn't answer. He doesn't even look at me while he takes out a pack of cigarettes and lights one up. I stare dumbfoundedly at him, watching as he brings the lit cigarette to his lips, inhales, and then turns his head to the side and blows the smoke out.

He's avoiding the question. Avoiding looking at me. I don't understand. From what I've heard about him, he doesn't care about anything, let alone have morals, so why is he rejecting me?

Unless… "Oh," I say. "Are you not…" I breathe out a nervous laugh. "Are you not attracted to me?"

This finally gets his attention, making his head snap up, his narrowed eyes on mine as he stares at my face, frozen in place. "What?" he asks.

I take a step back, feeling my whole body shiver as embarrassment floods me. I don't know why I just assumed he'd be up for it. "I didn't think," I whisper, wanting to slap myself for coming up with this yesterday. "I just assumed. If you're not attracted to me, it's fine. I'm sorry for bothering you," I mumble, turning on my heels and rushing away.

"Wait."

I don't. I can't. I know my face must be all blotchy and red by now. I walk faster, my feet barely hitting the ground as I reach for the gate.

"Rosalie. Wait."

My hand stills on the metal gate. I slowly look behind my shoulder, seeing Grayson standing behind me. "You know my name?" I ask.

He nods, gesturing with his head to the house. "Aiden."

"Right."

He blows out a breath, starting to shake his head again before I can even say anything. "Rosalie," he husks out. "Look at me." I slowly lift my eyes until they meet his. "It's not that I'm not attracted to you," he says, taking a step closer to me. Strands of his black hair fall onto his face as his dark eyes look down at me. "I am."

I suck in a breath. He is? "Then why won't you help me?"

He lifts his head, his eyes closing as he runs a hand through his hair, looking exasperated.

Realization dawns on me. "Was that your girlfriend?" I ask him. From what I've heard about him, Grayson doesn't do the girlfriend thing. It seems like he's a hook-up kind of guy, perfect for what I'm asking for.

"No," he says. "I don't have a girlfriend. I just… This doesn't seem like it's you."

I narrow my eyes at him. "You don't even know me." This is the first conversation we're having. He just learned my name less than ten minutes ago, and now he thinks he knows who I am?

"Well? Am I wrong?"

I let my eyes fall, pulling my bottom lip between my teeth. "No," I whisper. He's not wrong. This isn't me. But that's exactly why I want to do this. I don't even know who I am anymore. I need this.

"Then why do you want to change that?" he asks.

A sigh escapes my lips as I think about everything I wrote on the list he's got in his pocket. "I feel like I don't belong," I tell him. "I feel… left out. Like I'm not in on this huge joke. Everyone our age has done these."

"It doesn't mean you have to," he replies.

"I want to," I say, lifting my head to look at him.

His brow raises in questioning. "Do you?" he asks. "Because if you're just trying to prove it to someone—"

"This isn't about anyone else. I want to prove it to myself."

"Prove what?" he asks, furrowing his brows,

"That I'm more than this. That I can be like everyone else," I say, shrugging. "I want to do what I want for a change instead of doing what my mother expects of me."

"And what does this list have anything to do with that?"

"I want more, Grayson," I tell him, loving how the side of his lips lift in a small smirk at the sound of me saying his name. "I want to get drunk, go to parties, have some fun and danger for once in my life. I've missed out on so much that normal teenagers do, and I don't want to miss out on anymore. I want my college life to be as eventful as I can make it before I'm forced to marry a rich husband and have kids that will be raised by maids." I let out a breath, letting go of everything I've kept inside. Everything I wanted to say.

He blinks, staring back at me for a while. "That's what this is about?" he asks.

"Yeah."

He's gone back to being quiet. I don't know what he's about to say, but I have a feeling he's going to say no again. I regret coming here. Making that list and spilling my guts to a stranger was a mistake. I don't know what else I can say to convince him. How can I get him to agree?

"I can pay you," I blurt out.

He raises an eyebrow. "I'm not a prostitute."

I clamp my mouth shut. Jesus, I'm a trainwreck today. "I… I know it's just." I sigh, shaking my head. "I'm sorry. I know there's nothing in it for you, and you don't even know me, so why would you possibly—"

"I'll help you."

My eyes widen. "You will?"

"This might be a mistake," he says with a smirk. "But I'll help you." I can't help my face heating up as a smile spreads across my face. He smiles too, but then it drifts as he sighs. "But."

"But?" I ask him warily.

"No sex."

"What?"

"I'm sorry," he says, shaking his head. "I can't do that. It would be like taking advantage of you."

I erupt into laughter. “Taking advantage? I’m asking you.” I’m practically begging him to do everything on that list.

“Yes. But you’re naïve. You don’t know any better.”

My face drops as I take a step back from him. “I’m not naïve.”

“Shit. Rosie,” he says, closing the distance between us again. “I didn’t mean… I don’t want you to sleep with someone just to check it off and toss it as an experiment. You should do that when you’re ready. You should wait until there’s someone you trust and like, not just ask the first guy you see just because you think he’ll do anything without a second thought.”

A frown forms on my face. “I’m sorry,” I whisper. I thought he’d be up for it. I never actually thought he’d care about my feelings in all of this. “I thought—”

“I know.” He nods. “I get it. But that doesn’t mean I’ll do it. Those are my terms,” he says. “I’ll help you with all of the other stuff you want to do.”

He’ll help me. Even if he won’t do everything, he’ll help me. “Okay,” I say. “I accept.”

A small smile appears on his face. “Do you have your phone with you?” he asks.

“Yeah, why?”

“I’m kind of going to need your number if we’re going to be seeing each other for these… lessons,” he says, his lips upturning at the last word. I guess he’s like my life coach.

“Oh, right,” I say, handing him my phone.

He puts his number in my phone and then reaches for his phone, putting my number into his. Then, hands it back to me, my fingers brush his, and I love the feel of it. They’re rough and feel completely different than my soft hands. I wonder what his hands would feel like on other parts of my body. I know now that will never happen, but it doesn't hurt to imagine it. "Thank you. For helping me."

He smirks. "No problem, angel."

My breath hitches. *Angel.* He called me that before. I loved hearing it.

I reach for the gate and make my way out. I have no idea when I'll see Grayson again, but I can't wait. I wonder what he's going to teach me first, what we'll do.

My phone rings from my bag, and I pause. I reach for my phone, and my smile drifts when I see the name flash on my screen. I pick it up and bring it to my ear. "Yes, mom?"

"Rosalie," she snaps. "That is not how you answer the phone."

I sigh. "Sorry. Hello, mother." I roll my eyes.

"That's better. I've been running all day with Tilly trying to get this event planned. How have you been, still being a college girl?" she says those last words like it's all a joke to her.

My mother didn't go to college. She got married straight out of high school and moved in with my father at eighteen.

"I'm good," I tell her. "Busy with classes."

"Hmm," she mumbles on the other end of the phone. She probably didn't even hear what I said. "I spoke to Beth last week; you remember Beth, right?" I want to say no, but I can't because she doesn't let me answer. "Well, she said her son is about your age, and he's single."

I sigh. "Mom, please stop trying to set me up with people."

"A young lady needs a husband. When I was your age, I was already engaged."

Always the same story. I should mention that, before this, she had never allowed me to date or have a life of my own. "Mom, I've got to go to class," I say. I wish I could talk to my mom about something else. I'm sick of hearing her talk about marriage and how much of a mistake I'm making by deciding to be my own woman and attending college.

She hums disapprovingly. "Are you sure this is what you want?" she asks me. "You could drop out, and we'd reimburse you for the tuition you paid without so much as even asking us first," she spits out. My mother hates that I'm straying away from the life she wants for me.

I shouldn't have to ask her anyway. It was the money they happily gave me, so it's my choice to do with it what I want. "Mom, I don't need your money," I tell her. "I've got to go."

"Wait, Rosalie. I still need to talk to you."

"What about?" I ask skeptically.

"The event I'm planning. We're having a charity event on Saturday, and I'm expecting you to come."

I snap my eyes closed. I don't want to attend another gala which is nothing more than a cesspool of people fighting over how much money they have. I want to be done with that life, those people.

"Mom. I told you—"

"It's on a Saturday," she interrupts. "There's no reason for you not to come."

I sigh. I know I've lost this battle. "I'll think about it."

"You will come, or I will fly out there and drag you back myself."

Heat rises to my face. She's still treating me like a child. "I'm eighteen," I tell her. "I'm an adult."

She laughs. "You are a naïve child, and I am your mother. I know what's best for you."

That word. Naïve. Grayson called me that before, and now my mother. Does everyone around me think I'm foolish and immature?

"And marrying someone I've never met is the best for me?"

"He's a hotel owner and ready to settle down with a woman. It offers you security, Rosalie. Financial freedom."

Money. It always comes down to money.

"Even if I don't love him?" I ask.

"You haven't even met him yet. He's not your only choice. There are plenty of eligible men that will be here next weekend. You can change your mind." That's what she ultimately wants. She wants me to change my mind about my wants and desires and instead live her life.

"Fine. I'll go," I concede. "I've got to go now. Bye, Mom."

"Okay, I expect to see you here this weekend."

I sigh as I hang up the phone.

Another event that I'm being forced to attend. I can't escape it, or this life. I thought being eighteen and going to college meant I could finally get my mother off my back, but that's not the case.

The only thing that makes me feel a little better about this situation is the thought of seeing Grayson again.

7

Late night drive

Grayson

This girl wants to live like me.

Fuck knows why. But she asked me for help, and I said I'd help her.

I can't stop thinking about the list full of dirty things she asked me to do with her, to do to her. And if she were anyone else, I would have done it without hesitation.

I almost laughed in her face when she thought I wasn't attracted to her. Ever since I laid my eyes on her at the party, I haven't been able to stop thinking about her.

Something about her intrigued me. I wanted to know more. And then two days later, she came to my house, looking for me, asking me to corrupt her, to make her into everything she's not.

I keep picturing her blonde hair, her white dress, how she smiles, how sweet she is, how delicate her voice is.

Fuck. I groan, feeling my dick harden in my pants. Jesus, I think about her voice, and I get hard. I wish I knew why this girl, in particular, has me doing things I'd never even think of doing, like turning down sex to *help* her.

I feel the heat travelling to my groin, and I curse under my breath. I can't do this to the thought of her. I tuck my dick in my waistband and try to forget about her blue eyes staring up at me, begging me to teach her every dirty thing on her list.

Shit. It isn't working. I need some fresh air or a smoke or something. I get up from my bed and walk over to the bathroom. Turning the faucet, I splash some cold water on my face to try and divert any thoughts of Rosalie out of my mind.

Even if she did come and ask me for those things, even if she said it wasn't taking advantage, it still feels wrong. No matter what people at this school think of me, I can't do what she asked me to or even think about her in a perverse way.

It's been a week since I last saw her. I haven't texted, and I've been trying to forget her. School's been keeping me busy enough, and my sales have gone down this month. I haven't had time to think about her.

Not to mention that my mother has been breathing down my neck every damn day. Phone calls, texts, emails, the whole joint. It's not like I can avoid her. I need to be on my parents' good side, or else I won't get what I need. I'd be attending this school without a purpose because the only reason I'm here is because of them.

The only thing easing my mind is the thought of seeing Rosalie. Teaching her how to be me. How do I even go about doing that? I can't turn her into a fuck up like me. But I can show her what I do for fun, what makes me feel like nothing else in the world matters.

That's what she asked for, after all, and that's what I'll show her. I pull my t-shirt over my head and open my dresser, pick out a fresh shirt, and throw it on.

My phone lights up, and I reach for it, seeing a text from my mother. I let my eyes drift closed in frustration. God damn it, I can't escape them. No matter what I do, they'll always be on my case. I can't take back what I did, and they see me completely differently because of it.

It doesn't matter that it wasn't my fault. They'll always view me as a deviant, an aberration, and a disappointment to the family.

I swipe away from her message and unlock my phone, searching for Rosalie's name in my contacts. My finger hangs above the call button. I stare at her name on my phone screen for what seems like forever. I shouldn't be around her, but I offered to help her, to do this favor for her. She said nothing was in it for me, but she doesn't know how wrong she is. Just the thought of seeing her again has my pulse racing, and that should scare me.

But instead, I say fuck it, and I press the button and bring the phone to my ear, hearing the line ring.

"Grayson," she says on the other line. Fuck. I forgot how breathy and angelic her voice is. I start to harden again and curse silently. I run a hand through my hair and tell myself to focus.

"Hey, angel." I smirk. She seemed to like it when I called her that, just as much as I like calling her that.

"Hey," she responds with a light giggle.

This is the second conversation we've had. I hope it's one of many because hearing that voice does things to me that I don't want to think about.

"How do you feel about a lesson today?" I ask her.

It's a Friday night. Aiden has already invited me to go to another dumbass frat party with prospects of hooking up with one of his groupies. I just scoffed at him and left. He couldn't pay me to sleep with one of these girls again. It happened one time during my freshman year, and the girl was cute and seemed interested.

But when we finally got down to it, she wouldn't stop asking me about Aiden. I get it. He's a jock. Girls fawn over him all the time, and I'm his best friend, so I would know the most about him.

But when she started asking how big Aiden's dick was or calling me Aiden, that's what made my balls crawl back into my body and far away from her.

And when I told Aiden that, he cracked up, laughing like it was the funniest thing he had ever heard. But he still doesn't let up on passing his groupies onto me, which I reject every time.

So, no. I don't ever want to hook up with one of Aiden's groupies again, or anyone else at that party.

Right now, I've got an angel on the phone asking me to take her on adventures, to corrupt her, and sadistically, I'm enjoying it.

"Today?" she asks, sounding a little panicky.

"Uh, yeah?" Shit. Has she changed her mind? I thought she'd be down for it. It's been almost a week since she came to me, and tonight seems like the perfect opportunity to show her how I live. "If you don't want to do this anymore, that's fine."

"No, it's not that. It's… ugh." She groans, clearly frustrated, and I take a minute to collect myself. Even when she's angry, she sounds heavenly. "I'm supposed to be flying out to New York tonight."

"Oh?" I say because I don't want to make it seem like she has to come with me, and I don't know if this is just an excuse she's using to blow me off.

"Yeah." She sighs. "Long story, but my mother is basically forcing me to."

We may have more in common than I originally thought. I recall her telling me about wanting to be more than her mother's expectations, and she sounds exasperated, so maybe she isn't blowing me off, and that makes me smile.

"I thought you said you wanted to escape your mother," I say, remembering that was one big reasoning for the list in the first place.

"I did, but—"

"Then come out with me tonight. Forget your mother."

"I can't," she says, sounding defeated.

My eyes shut closed. I really wanted to see her again. I need a distraction tonight, and she sounds like she needs the same. "Rosie. Come on. You said you wanted fun, so let's have fun."

She's quiet for a while, and I think she's going to decline again. I start to lose hope that this arrangement will ever work if she can't take one weekend away from her mother, but then she surprises me.

"Okay."

I smirk. "Yeah?"

"Yeah." I hear a small laugh from the phone, and I can't help but close my eyes and smile, imagining what that laugh would look like if she were here.

"Will you be ready in ten minutes?" I ask.

"Maybe?" she says, sounding more like a question than an answer. "What should I wear? Where are we going?"

She's asking me for fashion advice? My lips twitch in amusement. I've only seen her twice, but both times I couldn't stop staring at her, at the way clothes fit her like they're made for her.

"We're going for a drive," I tell her instead because I couldn't care less about what she wears. I know she's going to look hot in whatever she puts on.

"A drive?" she asks skeptically.

"Yep."

"Okay," she says after a second. "I can do that."

"Great." I waste no more time. I grab my keys from my nightstand and rush out of the door. "Where do you live?" I ask her. "I'll come pick you up."

"Over on Lincoln Road," she says, her voice muffled and sounding far away.

My brows furrow. "What are you doing?"

"Getting dressed."

I groan at the image of her undressing. Jesus, I need to control myself. I don't want to show up with a hard-on and scare her away. "Okay, I'm going to hang up. See you in ten."

8

Smoke and mirrors

Grayson

Ten minutes later, I'm outside her apartment.

I pull out a cigarette while I text her, letting her know I'm here. When she walks out, I freeze. God damn, I forgot how pretty she is. Her cheeks are pink as she smiles at me, walking closer to my car. I smirk at her, letting my eyes scan down her body. I smile, a small laugh escaping my lips. How does she always look this good?

"What?" she asks, frowning a little. "Should I go change?"

I stop laughing, wiping my mouth with my hand, composing myself. I don't want to make her feel like I'm laughing at her. I'm definitely not. I'm laughing at myself. I'm an idiot, turning her down. "No," I say, bringing the cigarette to my lips and taking one last smoke before I throw it out the window. My eyes lift to hers. "You look gorgeous," I say, because why the fuck not. It's true.

I'm glad I do. Her eyes light up at the compliment, her lips raising in a cute little smile.

She takes a step closer to me. "Nice car," she says, trying to avoid meeting my eyes, but I already saw her not so subtly checking me out.

I nod, grinning at her. It is a nice car. "Do you know anything about cars?" I ask, lifting a brow.

She shrugs. "Not really, just looks nice. Suits you," she says.

I smirk at her answer. "It's an SRT Demon," I tell her, knowing it will mean nothing to her, but I'm proud of this car.

She snorts. "How fitting."

I laugh, running a hand through my hair. "Get in, angel."

She makes her way around, getting inside my car. I look to my left and see her sitting in the seat. I like her there. She looks fucking beautiful in a blue dress covered with a denim jacket; her legs are out and smooth. I glance at them again, seeing her pale skin get a little red. It's pretty cold out, and when I asked her to come with me for a drive, I expected her to wear some sneakers and a sweater or at least some pants, but I'm starting to think this girl doesn't even own a pair of pants.

She looks gorgeous, though. Her blonde hair flowed in the wind, half pinned up with a blue clip to match her dress. She still looks like an angel without the signature white.

I turn on the radio as I pull onto the road, letting the music fill the car. She taps her foot to my music, making me smile at the sight. Jesus fuck, I've become a sappy shit around her. I can't help it, though. Seeing her in my car with me makes me twitch.

Every time I see her, I get more and more confused. What's her story? Why does she think she needs to be like every other girl in here when she's the complete opposite? That's what I like about her.

I raise the volume, letting the music fill the car, and she turns to face me. My eyes meet hers, and she smiles at me. I grip the steering wheel firmly, wanting a hold on my emotions. That smile is like nothing I've ever seen before. It's intoxicating.

I rip my eyes away from hers and focus on the road.

"Where are we going?" she asks me.

"For a drive," I reply.

She's quiet for a minute, but then she finally speaks up. "That's it?"

"Yeah, I did tell you."

I glance towards her again, and she's frowning. A small downward curve to her lips makes my jaw clench. She's disappointed. Of course, she is; that's all I ever do. I let people down. She shouldn't have confided in me or asked me for help. I don't help. All I do is destroy.

"I thought we were… you know, going somewhere."

"Like a date?" I ask her, anticipating her answer. I have to let her down gently. If she thought this would end up with us in love and shit, I need to let her know that's never going to happen.

"No, I mean… no?" She sighs. "I don't know what this is exactly. Like, what are we doing here?"

She's just confused. That I can deal with. "We're friends," I tell her. "We're not dating or sleeping together. I'm just helping you." I hope that didn't sound too harsh. I don't want to hurt her. She's too good for that. I don't want her to get false expectations, wanting something that's never going to happen between us.

"Okay," she says. "So we're really just going to drive?"

I smile. "You see the handle up there," I say, pointing to the ceiling handle.

"Yeah?"

"Use it," I tell her and press my foot down on the accelerator.

"Grayson!" she yells as the car speed up, faster and faster, through the street.

We're on a highway, and it's pretty empty around this time of night, so we won't be crashing into anyone.

"What the hell are you doing?" she gasps. Her eyes are shut, and one of her hands holds on to the handle while the other clutches my arm as if she needs to hold on for safety.

I'll keep her safe. I promise. I never want to hurt her. I just want to show her a little fun.

"You said you wanted to see how Grayson Carter lives," I tell her, raising my voice above the music and the wind blowing in through the window. I press my foot harder on the acceleration, feeling the car move faster and faster down the highway.

The euphoric feeling of adrenaline crashes into my veins, making me feel alive. This is what I needed, and I'm sharing it with Rosie. She's no longer screaming, which makes me smile. Her eyes are still closed, though. Her mouth moves as she mumbles under her breath, probably praying.

I can't help but laugh. "Open your eyes," I tell her, but she shakes her head and grips tighter on the handle. I slow down a little, and her grip loosens. "Open your eyes, angel," I say.

She does this time. Her eyes snap open as she focuses on the road in front of her, the blurry view from the side rushing past as the car moves. I press my foot down on the accelerator, making it a little faster, and she gasps.

"You're going to kill us," she says, but she's not closing her eyes.

"Come on, Rosie. I'll keep you safe. I promise. Live life on the wild side with me."

She laughs at that. The sound hits me right in the chest, making me tear my eyes off the road to glimpse at the pure joy on her face. Her eyes are wrinkled, and her smile is wide as she continues to laugh and laugh and laugh… until she's crying.

"Fuck." I ease my foot off the accelerator and slowly bring the speed down. She's crying. I fucked up, I always do.

"Rosie," I say, reaching for her hand. "Angel, I'm so sorry. I didn't mean to scare you."

She's shaking her head, her tears streaming down her face. "You didn't." Huh? I'm even more confused. Why is she crying then? She wipes her tears with her hand and then turns to face me. She's smiling. Her smile is wide and so beautiful. "I'm crying because I'm happy. I'm so happy. Thank you."

I let out a breath of relief. Thank fuck I didn't scare her. I should be focusing on the road, but I can't help but look at her face as she smiles at me and looks at me with adoration. She shouldn't be. I'm a mess, a fuck up, and she's looking at me like I'm her savior right now.

I reach over and grip her small, delicate fingers in my hand. Interlocking our hands and squeezing. She lets out a small gasp, and I turn to face her. "You have nothing to thank me for," I tell her because it's true. I haven't done anything special for her. I just took her to experience a little danger and some adrenaline.

I realize how thankful she is for this small gesture when she squeezes my hand back and sighs. For me, it's small, but for her, it's huge. She let go and lived in the moment, which I'm sure isn't something she's ever done.

I pull my hand away from hers and grab the steering wheel, taking the exit to a familiar location.

I keep driving along the road, the view making me gulp. I haven't been here in so long since…

And now I'm taking her here with me. It won't mean anything to her, but it means something to me. Bringing someone else here feels a little weird, but at the same time, I couldn't imagine anyone else I'd want to bring here.

The road narrows as the ground gets higher and higher. Rosalie's looking out the window, seeing as the view gets farther away the higher we go. She looks back at me, questioning where we're going, but she doesn't ask, and I don't answer.

When we reach the top, I stop the car and pull the handbrake up.

"This is it?" she asks.

"Yep."

"Is this the part where you jump, and I'm an accomplice in your suicide?" she jokes.

I laugh. "You're funny."

She smiles. "So… what do we do?"

"We chill." I turn to face her, and the look on her face makes me chuckle. She's confused. Her brows are furrowed, and her lips are pursed, which makes me glance down at her lips. They're pink, and they look so soft.

I tear my eyes away from her lips and instead bring something else to my mouth. I take out my cigarettes from my jacket and light one up. Her eyes stay focused on the movement of the cigarette as I bring it to my lips.

"I thought there'd be more, you know, with your reputation and all."

I snap my eyes toward her. "Don't believe everything you hear."

"So, it's not true?" she asks.

I shrug. "Some of it is, some of it isn't."

"And the drug dealer part?" she asks.

I'm not up for discussing what I do or don't do in my free time. She doesn't need to know about it, and it doesn't concern her, so I don't say anything. I inhale the cigarette and blow the smoke out of the window.

She sighs loudly. "Can I try?"

That catches my attention. I look at her as her brows raise. Her hands are out and open, waiting for something

"Try what?"

She points at the cigarette hanging out of my mouth. "That."

"That?" I ask. "Do you even know what it's called?" I joke.

"Can I smoke?" she asks.

I lift my brow at her. "I think you've had enough excitement tonight, angel."

She frowns a little but then shakes her head. "Please?"

Jesus, I can't say no to her. She looks like a little puppy dog. I take the cigarette out of my mouth and hand it to her. She picks it up between her thumb and pointer finger. I laugh. "Have you ever done this before?" I know the answer. Of course, she hasn't.

"No," she admits. "Will you teach me?"

I smirk. "That's what I'm here for."

I grab her hand in mine, relishing how different we are but how well her hand fits in mine. I put the cigarette between her pointer and middle finger and bring her hand to her lips. "Open."

She opens her mouth and stays like that, waiting for me. I bring her hand closer to her face until the cigarette is inside her mouth. She tentatively closes her mouth until her lips are wrapped around it, and now I'm thinking of her lips wrapped around something else.

Christ.

I need to focus on the task at hand and not get carried away with how I could teach her so many things other than smoking.

"Now what?" she mumbles with the cigarette between her lips.

I grin. "Suck."

Yeah, this no longer sounds like I'm teaching her how to smoke, and definitely sounds more like I'm teaching her something completely different.

She must have caught on because her cheeks redden as she blushes, but she complies. She sucks, inhaling the cigarette until she's coughing uncontrollably.

I can't help but laugh. "That's enough, newbie," I tell her, reaching for the cigarette.

She bats my hand away. "Teach me, then."

I almost laugh again. She's eager to learn. "Okay, try again. This time, inhale and hold it."

She nods and brings the cigarette back to her lips, trying again. She sucks and inhales, keeping the smoke there for a bit before she blows it out and coughs.

"Much better," I tell her. "You did so well."

Her eyes light up at the praise, shining as she smiles at me.

"You're not wearing white tonight," I tell her, taking the cigarette from her and bringing it to my lips.

She laughs. "Nope, no white. I didn't want to get dirty."

I inwardly groan. Heat floods my groin at those words, and I swallow the temptation to reply with something less than friendly.

"So, New York?" I say instead.

She sighs, and I instantly feel shitty for bringing it up when she was trying to forget it and her mom.

"Yeah. My mother invited me to some charity gala event and basically threatened to drag me back there if I didn't go."

"And you didn't want to go?"

She shakes her head. "No. She wanted to set me up with her friend's son, a hotel owner who wants to find a wife."

My eyes widen. "A wife? Aren't you eighteen?" I assume she's a freshman since I hadn't seen her before last week.

"Yeah, but according to my mother, I'm running out of time. 'these are my prime years.'" she says, using air quotes.

"Jesus." I can't imagine marrying anyone at eighteen. Hell, I can't ever imagine marrying at all.

"I just want to get through college and live my life how I want. Even if it ends up in a loveless marriage and a rich husband who's always on business trips."

I scoff. "Isn't every marriage loveless?"

Her head snaps towards me. "You don't believe in love?" she asks.

"No," I tell her, honestly.

"Why?"

"Why do you?" I retort.

She shrugs. “Because love is beautiful.”

I lift my brow. “Have you ever been in love?”

“No,” she admits.

“Then how do you know what it’s like, or if it’s even real?”

She crosses her arms over her chest. “Have you ever been in love?” she retorts.

I inhale the cigarette and blow the smoke out the window. “Obviously not.” I almost laugh. “Because it isn’t—”

“Then how do *you* know it’s not real.”

“Because I do. Love isn’t real, angel. Hate to break it to you. There’s attraction, lust, but love is bullshit.”

She shakes her head. “You’re so cynical. What happened for you not to believe in love?”

I shrug, looking away from her. “Don’t really want to talk about it.”

“Oh c’mon.” she says, “It can’t be worse than me coming to your house asking for you to take my virginity.”

I snicker, looking over at her. “That wasn’t so bad,” I tease, loving how her cheeks turn red as she tucks a strand of hair behind her ear. I sigh, feeling my jaw clench. I don’t feel like talking about this right now, but she’s right. She’s been opening up, might as well give her something. “My parents,” I tell her.

“They don’t love each other?” she asks.

I laugh. “Oh, they do. At least that’s what they say, but underneath, it’s a complete disaster. A whole mess of lies.”

She looks almost worried. The line between her brows is begging me to smooth it out with my thumb, but I don’t want to touch her. She’s too close to me already, and I’m sure I’m not her favorite person right now after admitting that I don't believe in love.

"Why?" she asks.

I blow out a breath. "My father," I say. "I don't know if my mom knows or if they have some sort of arrangement, but he cheats on her. Often."

"Oh."

I'll never forget when I walked in on him and his assistant in his office at work. I was only thirteen, and if my dad hadn't been screwing around that day, maybe what happened later wouldn't have happened. Maybe he would have helped me, and it wouldn't have ended the way it did.

"Yeah, so sue me for not believing in love when the two people I looked up to all my life turn around and cheat."

She lifts her hand and places it on top of mine. Squeezing it lightly until I look up at her. "I'm sorry that happened," she says. "But you can't use one example to reference every other relationship."

I know that, but my parents aren't the only ones to cheat, and they won't be the last. So how could love exist if people could do that to those they claim to love?

She shuffles in her seat, and my eyes drift down to her heels. The sight makes me smile, making me forget for a minute about my parents.

"You look good in heels," I say, seeing her smile and tuck her hair behind her ear, flushing. She reaches down, takes off her heels, and props her legs onto the dashboard.

I like seeing her comfortable, like she can be whoever she wants to be around me, and I won't judge her. I love finding out new things about her, her quirks and likes, and what she believes and doesn't.

Every time we talk, I figure out how different we are. She doesn't know much about me, but I'm letting her in slowly because I want to get to know her. I want to get to know more about her every time we hang out. I wish I knew why, but she captivates me.

My eyes drift from her feet up her legs, seeing her dress raised higher on her thighs from propping her feet up. I tear my eyes away. I shouldn't look at her legs or how her dress has ridden to the point where I can almost see her panties. Nope.

"Let's go," I tell her, opening the car door.

"What? Where?" she asks, dropping her legs and turning to face me.

I get out of the car and lean on the door, looking at her from the window. "Come on, angel. I won't bite." I smirk at her. "Unless you ask me to."

9

Your secret is safe with me

Rosalie

I step out of the car and close the door behind me.

Grayson stands in front of the car, holding a blanket. He opens it up and places it on the floor, sitting on it. I step towards him and sit next to him.

I know he said this wasn't a date, but this feels a lot like a date. I won't bring it up, though, especially since he seemed relieved when I accepted this wasn't a date.

He's looking out at the view. It's gorgeous from up here. I don't even know what part of Pennsylvania this is, but it looks like something out of a painting. We're high up on this hill, and it looks out onto a patch of green. So much grass. I've lived in New York all my life. All I have been subjected to are buildings and skyscrapers. I have never seen something so beautiful as this.

"Wow," I say. "It's so beautiful here."

He nods, taking out another cigarette from his pocket. I'd hated the taste when I'd smoked. It burnt my throat and made me feel fuzzy. I don't know how he does it. "I used to come here a lot as a kid."

It's one of the first things he's told me about himself. I soak it up like it's a rare commodity to know anything about Grayson Carter. I'm starting to think he doesn't share much about himself with anyone, and I feel grateful that he's willing to let me in.

"With your parents?" I ask.

I don't know much about his relationship with his parents, other than that he caught his dad cheating on his mom, which is awful.

He shakes his head but doesn't elaborate. He doesn't say anything else other than take another smoke. I guess sharing time is over. He's shut down again.

"So, why did you bring me here?"

He blows out smoke and shrugs. "I don't know, honestly," he says. "I saw the exit and figured I'd come here, and you were with me, so..." he exhales. "I haven't been here in a while."

I expect him to tell me something else, but he doesn't. I get it. We don't really know each other, so it's not like I expect him to open up to me about everything in his life. But I've been telling him about mine. Whenever he asks, I tell him everything.

I guess I am naïve in a way. I had no problem getting into his car and letting him drive me wherever he wanted. At least he brought me somewhere with a nice view. It really is beautiful up here.

I should be more wary. After spending so long being trapped in my house, I should be scared to be out with someone I barely know, but I'm not. I crave to spend more time with him, for him to teach me everything he knows and bring me into *his* world.

"Can we keep this a secret?" I ask him. His eyes widen as he looks at me. "I mean, if that's okay with you? I don't want anyone to know about this." I laugh nervously. "It's a little embarrassing."

I look up at him, seeing his throat bob a little. "Who would I tell?" he asks before a small smirk forms on his face. "Don't worry. Your secret is safe with me."

I nod, loving how I'm in on this big secret that no one else knows. It would be way too hard to explain exactly what Grayson and I are doing. Sometimes I don't have the answer myself. My friends have no idea, and I don't think his friends have any idea either.

Who are his friends? I know he and Aiden Pierce are close, being roommates and all, but does he have any other friends?

From what I've heard, Grayson has a lot of friends of the opposite sex, but not many girlfriends, or any for that matter. Maybe it's because he doesn't believe in love, which would explain why he wouldn't want a relationship.

I know if it was any other girl asking him for what I did, he would have no reservations over it and would say yes in a heartbeat. So, what is it about me that's so different? He's said before that he's attracted to me, so why did he say no? I should ask him, I should ask why he doesn't want to be with me in that way, but he's willing to help me with everything else.

I mean, there is nothing in it for him. He gets nothing out of this arrangement, and I get everything out of it. I get the college experience I have desired ever since I left my mother's house and came to Redfield. I get to live life like Grayson Carter and forget that I'm Rosalie Whitton, even if it's just for a minute.

"Why did you agree to help me?" I ask him.

He furrows his brows. "What do you mean?"

"I mean… you get nothing out of this. I offered for us to do something else that would be beneficial for both of us," I say, feeling heat rise to my cheeks. "But you refused. So why help me at all?"

He laughs under his breath, shaking his head. "I don't know. Let's just say you surprised me."

"Surprised you how?"

He shrugs. "In a lot of ways. The way you're so good and kind, yet you want to live the life of someone who's not." He blows out smoke and stares out at the view in front of him. "You want to live like Grayson Carter," he muses. "I don't even know what that means."

"It means I want to live life," I tell him. "You do that. I mean, look at you."

His head snaps towards mine, his lips pulled in a side smirk, he looks amused at my answer. "Look at me?" he repeats.

I nod. "Yeah. Tattoos, smokes, sells drugs, hooks up with every girl he sees…" Well, not every girl. Apparently, he has morals when it comes to me. "You get the picture."

"And that's living to you?" he questions.

I smile weakly. "Compared to my life for the past eighteen years, yeah."

"What was your life like? Enlighten me."

I sigh. "You really want to know?" I ask him.

He raises one eyebrow. "I wouldn't ask if I didn't."

I nod, stretching my legs out onto the blanket. I can feel the rocks underneath the thin cotton, and my legs are red from the cold. It's late out, way past midnight, and if I had known we'd be coming to a mountain, I would have worn something warmer.

I left my heels in the car, as per Grayson's request, so my toes are freezing cold, but I get it. The surface here is rocky and rough, and heels wouldn't be the easiest to wear.

"Well, most of my life, I was raised by strangers," I tell him. "Maids my mother would hire. They changed often, but they were somehow all the same. They followed my mother's rules, and didn't step out of line, even when I bribed them with money."

Grayson laughs, and I appreciate him listening to me ramble on about my life. Even if he doesn't care, he's here listening.

"My mother was always busy with her country club and hosting events, she never had time for me. The maids I grew up with were nice enough, they seemed to care about me, but that could be because they were getting paid to." I shrug.

"My father was never around," I continue. "I only ever saw him on weekends, and sometimes not even then. He was always out of the state for business. I don't even know what he does exactly. I know it has something to do with stocks, but other than that…"

Grayson laughs, shaking his head. "Sounds like the life of a rich girl."

"Yeah. I know. First world problems." I feel a little guilty ranting about my life when his is completely different. From what I've heard about Grayson Carter, he grew up with an addict for a mother and now sells drugs to support his mother's addiction.

He must think I'm so vain for thinking my issues warrant a second thought when his must be ten times worse than mine.

"I never had to worry about there being food on the table or a roof over my head. I get it," I tell him. "But I did miss out on so much. I didn't even have my first friend until Leila."

"Is that the girl you came with, at the party?"

I remember wondering if he even remembered seeing me at that frat party, and now I knew. He had.

"Yeah. We met my sophomore year of high school. I was homeschooled until then, and she was my first-ever friend." And I couldn't have asked for a better one. "Before that, I had to 'bond' with the bratty girls from the country club. So, I suppose they were my first friends? Except can you call them friends if they hated me? They bullied me, even."

I sighed. "I don't know why. They just despised me. And when I got to college, I wanted to experience everything like a normal freshman would. Crappy dorm rooms, having to wear shower shoes, having roommates, I wanted everything. But my mother got me an off-campus apartment, so that dream was taken away."

He laughs, blowing out smoke. "Your dream was to live in a dorm room? I don't know anyone who wants that," he says.

I look out towards the green below us, focusing on the patches of grass covering the ground. "I did," I tell him. "And for the first couple of months of college, I did nothing but catch up on work."

He throws out the cigarette and blows the smoke from his mouth before turning to face me. "You're a freshman. I'm sure there wasn't that much work you had to do."

"You're right," I say. "But I came to college to study fashion. That's what I want to do. And whenever I have any free time, I work on my designs. So, I was learning how to juggle doing classes and focusing on my designs at the same time. I hadn't even gone to a party before last weekend."

His lips turn upwards, flashing me a smile. "You really are an angel," he says.

"Why's that?"

"You're so innocent, Rosie."

I look away, feeling my face heat up. "Stop saying that. It's not a good thing."

"It is to me," he says.

I turn my head towards him. "It is?"

He nods. His eyes don't leave mine as we stare at each other, lying on our sides on this thin blanket, feeling the gravelly ground beneath us.

"How?" I ask.

He smirks. "Because it makes me want to corrupt you."

Heat rises to my cheeks, feeling them redden, and I look down at the space between us.

His hand lifts, reaching out and swiping his thumb across my cheek. I suck in a breath, and he smiles. "You blush so easily," he says, laughing under his breath.

"It's embarrassing," I say, feeling my cheeks get hotter under his touch.

He shakes his head. "It's cute."

His eyes drift to my lips, making me do the same. His lips are parted as he breathes heavily. This is heading somewhere we both know is out of bounds. This wasn't what we agreed on, but it seems like he doesn't remember the deal we made, but I do.

I swallow as I back away from him slightly, putting some distance between us. "So, tell me about your family," I say.

He sighs and falls on his back, head tilted up, looking at the night sky above us. "Not much to tell, really."

I wonder if the rumors I heard about him are true at all. He doesn't seem like the guy they all said he was, but I guess I'll never know unless I ask him. "Is it true?"

He turns to face me. "Is what true?"

"The rumors about you selling drugs," I say, swallowing.

He turns his whole body to face me. "What do you think?" he asks. "Do you believe them?"

I shake my head. "I don't think so." I've known Grayson Carter a lot less time than some of the people who have told me these things about him but having spent today with him, I don't think that is true.

"That's good to know."

We stay quiet for a moment, hearing the wind crash against the trees and the sound of crickets. But other than that, it's silent. Peaceful.

He gets up and walks over to his car. He jumps on the hood of his car and sits on top of it. I look back at him, and he's looking back at me. He smirks and taps the hood next to him. "Join me."

I smile, get off the ground, and walk over towards him. He reaches his hand out, and I take it, pulling me up until I'm seated next to him on the hood of his car.

I look up, seeing the sky pitch black with only a handful of stars filling the sky. "What time is it?"

He laughs. "Want to escape from me already?"

"No." I laugh, shaking my head. "Just wondering how long we're going to stay here."

I know there will be fallout for disobeying my mother today, and I want to be at the apartment when she ultimately comes to reprimand me for not going to New York like I told her I would.

"Well," he says, "Do you want to stay and watch the sunrise with me?" he asks before clearing his throat. "I can drive you back if you want."

I should go back and wait for my mother to call or fly here. But right now, it doesn't seem to matter. All I want to do is stay here with him. I nod. "I love watching the sunrise," I tell him, remembering how I used to wake up early and sit on my balcony to watch the sunrise. "Even more than the sunset."

He smiles. "Well, that's good because the sunset's long gone, angel."

10

Number 1: Get drunk

Rosalie

Is it bad that I smile when I see Grayson's name on the screen of my phone?

It probably is. I might be getting a little too attached to him, and it's only been a couple of days since I've seen Grayson, but I honestly can't wait for the next time. It was a rush being with him, experiencing that adrenaline and freedom. It was honestly one of the best moments of my life.

Grayson:

Hey

Rosalie:

Hey

I press send, staring at the phone in my hand, waiting for his reply. I snuggle up on the couch, burying myself in the blanket, and try to focus on the tv instead of anticipating his response.

When the phone buzzes, I rip my eyes from the tv to my phone.

Grayson:

What are you doing?

Is this a booty call? Sounds like one. But he made it very clear nothing like that will ever happen between us, which makes me a little confused.

Rosalie:

Watching TV

I press send and put my phone down. But a second later, when it buzzes again, I check it instantly. I can't help it.

Grayson:

I'm downstairs. Your concierge won't let me come up

Rosalie:

I'll be right down

I press send and get up from the couch, fixing my hair in the mirror. I wish I didn't care what I looked like in front of Grayson. It doesn't really matter, it's not like we're ever going to hook up, so I shouldn't care how he sees me. However, that doesn't stop me from changing from my pajamas to a white crop top and pleated pants.

I grab my keys, shut the door behind me, and leave my apartment, heading downstairs. The elevator doors open, and I see Grayson standing in the lobby, leaning on the counter. His head turns when he sees me in the lobby.

A smile spreads across his face as he turns his head back to the concierge. "You see. I knew she would want to see me."

The concierge, Sergio, ignores him, grumbling under his breath, and then turns to face me. "Miss Whitton. I apologize for the disturbance. This man said he knew you."

"Yes, Sergio. I know him. It's fine."

Grayson stands, meeting me halfway. He looks down my body, and his breath stills. He's checking me out. He finds me attractive. That's good to know. I just wish he would show it. I wish he would let me practice everything on him.

"You look beautiful, angel," he says.

Sergio scoffs, and Grayson scowls at him before taking my hand in his and pulling us outside.

"You ready to go?" he asks.

My eyes widen a little. "Now?" Honestly, I was ready to crash into bed, but I guess the plans have changed. When Grayson calls, I know I'll have fun.

"Yeah," he says, shrugging. "You ready for another lesson?"

A smile breaks out on my face. I love the sound of that. A lot. I nod, grinning at him. "Yeah."

"A bar?" I ask, stepping out of his car.

He wouldn't tell me where we were going. I'm a very curious person. As much as I love surprises, I'm also the kind of person who tries to guess everything, the kind who shakes the present to see if I can figure out what's inside. I'm impatient. And the whole ride over, all he told me was, 'you'll see.'

"Yep," he says, locking the car once I've closed the door behind me.

This bar is close to campus, so he must come here a lot. I start to wonder if he's ever picked up girls here. I want to ask, but I don't. Instead, I smile up at him as we walk inside.

The place is packed. I guess a game had just ended tonight, given that the whole football team is here, cheering and drinking. The whole room fills with their deep voices.

"You want a drink?" Grayson asks, leaning down to speak in my ear.

"I uh… I can't drink," I whisper.

He furrows his brows. "Why not?"

I shrug. "I'm not twenty-one."

He laughs, his breath hitting my skin. "I can get you a drink, don't worry."

I pull back a little to look up at him. "You're twenty-one?"

He shakes his head, smirking. "Not yet," he says, "But I've got a fake."

"Oh," I nod. "Right."

"So, do you want a drink?" he asks again.

I nod. "Yes, please. Something tasty," I tell him.

He laughs again, the sound making my stomach drop. I love the sound of his laugh. "I got you," he says. He pulls back and leads me to a table that's secluded at the back of the bar. "Stay here."

He walks off, and I look around the bar. My eyes catch on the football team, all of them surrounded at one table, a group of girls around them. Some of them on their laps, giggling, flirting with them. They make it seem so easy.

My eye catches on a guy who seems familiar. His head turns, and our eyes meet. Ben. The guy from the party last week. He grins when he catches me, and the next thing I know, he's walking toward me.

He flashes me a smile. "Hey, Rosalie," he says when he approaches my table.

"Hi, Ben," I say, smiling back at him.

"You following me?" he jokes, grinning.

I shake my head, letting out a laugh. "No, just here with someone."

"Someone, huh?"

"Yep. A friend," I say.

He smirks, sitting down at the table. "I've been thinking about you."

My brows lift. "You have?"

"Hmm," he mumbles, running a hand through his short blonde hair. "You ran away from me last Friday."

"Oh." I laugh. "I didn't run away exactly. I just didn't want to ditch my friends."

He returns with a laugh of his own, leaning back on his chair. He fills the space, the muscles of his arms accentuating when he drapes his arm across the back of the empty chair. "I just ditched my friends for you."

I smile. "Then I promise next time I'll say yes."

His smile widens. "Next time, huh? So, I'll be seeing you again?" he asks.

I shrug. "Let's leave it up to fate." This guy makes it hard to say no. He's attractive as hell, flirty, and fun.

He leans forward. "Fate doesn't get me a date with you, gorgeous."

I smile at the compliment. He's leaning against the table, his face not that far away from mine. Is he going to…

"What the fuck are you doing?"

I snap my head to my right, seeing Grayson scowling at Ben.

Ben laughs and stands up from the table. "This is your friend?" he asks me.

Grayson's frowning at me, and Ben's got a cocky smirk on his face. I have no idea what I just walked in on, and I don't know what the right answer is. "Um, yeah?" It comes out sounding more like a question than an answer.

"Word of advice," Ben says to me. "Get some better friends." He shakes his head and laughs again. "I'll be seeing you around, Rosalie," he says with a mischievous smile before turning around and walking back to his table.

"What the fuck was that?" Grayson asks while placing the drinks on the table. "I go for five minutes, and now you've got a date with Ben Reed?"

"It wasn't a date," I tell him, "He just came over to talk to me for a few minutes."

Grayson scoffs and sits opposite me. "Trust me, that slimy motherfucker wants in your pants." He takes a swig of his beer.

He seems familiar with who Ben is. Maybe he's heard rumors and assumes the worst, which is shitty of him. Here I am with him, even though everyone has warned me off of him. "You know him?" I ask.

He waves a hand. “Yeah. From back home,” he says before narrowing his eyes at me. “Question is, how do you?”

I shrug. “I met him at the party last week.”

“Rosie.” He sighs, shaking his head. “Stay away from him.”

I laugh. “You can’t be serious.”

“I am,” he says, no humor in his tone. “He’s an asshole.”

I lift my shoulder in a shrug. “He seemed nice.”

He groans, running a hand down his face. “I don’t want to talk about him anymore. Drink up,” he says, pushing a drink in front of me.

“You trying to get me drunk?” I tease.

The previous scowl is wiped clean as he smirks. “Yeah. It was on your list. Number 1. Get drunk.”

My stomach flutters. It happens a lot around him. “You remember the list?”

He laughs, low and manly. I really do like that laugh. “Kind of hard not to,” he says.

I feel my face heating as I blush, remembering everything I asked him to do to me, with me, for me.

“You’re so cute when you blush.”

I ignore him, trying not to turn into a tomato, instead picking up the drink he gave me and taking a sip.

“How is it?” he asks.

“Good.” I take another sip. “What is it?”

“Margarita,” he says, taking another sip of his beer.

I tilt my head. “Is that the James Bond drink?”

He shakes his head, laughing. “That’s a martini, Rosie.”

“Oh. Well, whatever it is. I like it.”

“Knew you would.”

I lick some of the salt around the rim, keeping my eyes on him. He shuffles in his chair, his hand gripping the glass tighter as he clenches his jaw.

"I'm sorry," I say. "Was I not supposed to do that?"

He clears his throat, shaking his head. "No, that was… um." He fists a hand through his hair. "That's fine."

I smile, licking more of the salt and finish the drink in one sip. He laughs. "Easy, newbie."

"The point is to get drunk, right?" I say.

He shrugs. "You're right. Drink away."

I pick at the pretzels on the table, loving the salty taste mixed with the sweetness of the drink.

"How did it go with your mom?" he asks.

I groan. "I don't want to talk about her."

A laugh escapes his lips, making my eyes dip to them. "That bad, huh?"

I shrug. "Don't know," I say. "She never called."

I admit, I found it odd when I woke up the next morning with my head still intact. I was half expecting her to crash my apartment in the middle of the night and drag me home, but she didn't. She hasn't even called yet to give me what I can only expect will be a scolding of a lifetime.

"So, you're wearing pants," he says. I silently thank him for moving on from my mother.

"Yeah?"

He shakes his head, a small smirk on his face. "Didn't think you owned those."

"I prefer dresses," I tell him. "I've got great legs. Why not show them off?" I say, bringing another pretzel to my mouth.

He nods. "And you're wearing white tonight."

I smile. "I am. You're very observant."

He lifts an eyebrow. "Was that for my benefit?"

"Nope," I lie, knowing he liked seeing me in white at the party. "Just a lucky coincidence."

He smiles. "Lucky me."

"You could be."

He snorts. "I think the alcohol's affecting you already."

I shake my head. "Not nearly enough," I say, taking his beer and downing half of the glass. Even though I'm not a fan of the bitter taste, the whole point is to get drunk, and I will find a way to do that. "You mind?" I ask him once I've already had half of his drink.

He laughs, rubbing his jaw. "Not at all. Go crazy."

"I'm planning on it."

11

Bridal style

Grayson

She's hammered.

I don't know whether to be worried or laugh. She gets up and grabs my hand, pulling me up from the table. She starts dancing around me, and I'm drinking her in. She looks so happy, so beautiful as she dances like no one is watching.

But everyone is watching her, looking at her. They can look all they want, but tonight she's mine. I'm here with her, making her let go and have fun like she asked me to. I won't fuck this up. She needs me, and she asked me to help her. I will do everything to make that possible.

She swivels her hips to the music, getting dangerously close to my groin, so I back up, clutching her hand so she doesn't fall to the floor. She had two drinks and half of my beer. It's almost funny how drunk she is.

She turns around unexpectedly, spinning on her heels, and then trips, crashing into my chest. I groan as our bodies make contact, but she just laughs, letting me hear that heavenly sound of how happy she is, and wraps her arms around my neck.

My hands drift to her waist, holding her up. She feels so good in my hands, I want to relish this moment right here, knowing she feels comfortable with me.

She sighs, resting her head on my chest. Her movements slow down, and I feel her relax in my arms.

"You want to go home?" I whisper in her ear.

She nods. "With you."

I laugh. This fucking girl. "Okay, angel, let's go."

I take her hand in mine, pulling her out of the bar. She's tired. I wonder if she enjoyed herself. She looked happy in there. She looked like she was having fun. I love being the reason for that smile. The one who can make her forget for a little while.

I drop her inside my car, and she closes her eyes, resting her head on the headrest.

The whole way home, she's got her eyes closed, and I steal glances at her. Her lips are parted, and her head laid back. She's asleep. If I had known she got drunk so easily, I wouldn't have gotten her that second drink.

When I get to her apartment, I turn the car off and look at her for a while. I find myself tracing her features with my eyes. Seeing how her chest moves when she breathes, how her lips are plump, and her skin is flushed from the alcohol. She's so goddamn beautiful. Fuck, I'm an idiot.

I stroke her cheek. "Rosie," I whisper. "We're here."

She mumbles, blinking her eyes open.

"Hi," I say.

"Hey," she says and then lets out a hum. "I had fun tonight," she tells me.

I like the sound of that. "Yeah?"

She nods. "Thank you."

I shrug. "That's what I'm here for, angel."

She sighs, closing her eyes again. "I like when you call me that."

"Me too." I open the car door and get out, walking over to her side. I open the door, and her head turns to face me. When she makes no move to get out of the car, I laugh. "You want me to carry you?"

She nods, holding out her arms.

Shit. I was joking, but it seems like she's serious. Fuck it. A beautiful girl wants me to carry her in my arms. Who am I to say no?

I lift her off the seat, carrying her bridal style to her apartment. The concierge looks at me sideways, and I get it. What is a fuck up like me doing out with a girl like her? I don't get it either.

"What's her apartment number?" I ask him.

"It should be on her key, he tells me, not even glancing up at me, typing away on the computer.

I look down at Rosie in my arms, her eyes are closed again. "Rosie," I whisper. "Do you have your key?"

"Hmm," she hums. "In my pocket."

I reach for her pocket and pull out her key. 305.

I don't even look back at the concierge and walk towards the elevator, taking her to her room.

I find apartment 305 and manage to get the door open without dropping her on her feet. I head through the apartment, finding her bed. I place her on the bed, taking off her heels. She starts to kick her feet, trying to cover herself with the sheet.

I pull the covers back, getting her under them, but she shakes her head. "Pants," she mumbles. "Off."

I freeze. Is she serious?

"What?" I ask, in case I heard her wrong.

"I want them off." She starts to fumble with the buttons, and I don't know where to look. I can't look at her, right? I turn around, giving her some privacy, and run a hand through my hair, trying to think how in the hell I got here. Rosie groans, sounding frustrated. "Help me," she says from behind me.

I curse under my breath, and then I turn around. She mutters those two words, and I do anything she says. Who the fuck have I become? I stare dumbfoundedly at her as her pants are hanging halfway down her legs. I pull them off her and cover her with the sheet. Thank God she didn't ask me to take off her top too.

"You'll be okay, Rosie?" I ask her.

She nods, her eyes already closed.

I want to stay here with her, but I can't. So, I back up from her. "Call me if you need anything," I tell her from her bedroom door.

I leave her apartment, shutting the door behind me, wishing I would have stayed with her. But I can't do that. I told her we'd be friends. Sleeping in the same bed would confuse things for her. Things are already starting to confuse me. Lines are starting to blur, and I don't know what to do about that.

12

Roommates and thongs

Rosalie

"Alright, you're all set. Is there anything else I can help you with?"

I take the bags from her hand and smile at her. "No thanks. We're good."

The woman at the register smiles back and calls for the next person in line.

I glance back at Leila, whose hands are filled with shopping bags. She's waiting for me at the storefront, struggling to find room on her arms for all of the bags she's holding.

"Jesus, Leila," I say, laughing when she tries to get her hair unstuck from her lip gloss. Ultimately failing when she can't reach due to the mass amount of shopping she did.

"Don't just stand there, help me," she says, and I quickly make my way to her, picking off her dark hair that's practically glued onto her pink lip-gloss.

"You went a little overboard," I tell her.

She shrugs. "I just got paid. Thought I'd treat myself." She looks down at my hands, and her eyebrows raise. "You barely got anything. Who are you, and what have you done with Rosalie Whitton?"

I laugh. I have one shopping bag, which definitely isn't something Leila is used to seeing. I never went shopping with friends. My mother got me everything I needed, and the rest I made myself. But Leila always bared witness to all the new outfits I bought.

Every time I'd come into school wearing one of my new outfits, she'd first ask how much, which would shock her every time I told her the price.

So, of course, when Leila wanted to go shopping, I couldn't pass it up. Except all I had bought was jeans. I guess if Grayson is going to be taking me on mountain tops and for late-night speed racing, I could at least buy some pants that don't cost a fortune. I always preferred dresses or skirts. I love feeling the breeze on my legs, not to mention that my legs look good. I might only be 5'5, but I have long legs and like to show them off.

"God, I needed this." Leila sighs. "I needed some time away from my psychotic roommate."

"Tiffany, right?" I remember Leila mentioning her roommate on many occasions. Apparently, she was the roommate from hell, and now I was feeling a little more grateful that I had my own apartment. "What did she do this time?" I ask her.

She scoffed. "What didn't she do?" She grimaced. "She nearly set the dorm on fire."

My eyes nearly pop out of my sockets. "What?"

"Yep. I walked in on her cutting up and burning her polaroids. I'm guessing she broke up with her boyfriend, and I hope it's for good because if I have to hear them argue again, I will kill them."

Maybe I was being presumptuous in wanting to live in a dorm since this sounds like a horror story

"And that's not even the worst part," she continued.

"There's worse?"

"Well, I yelled at her and told her to put it out, so she grabbed the first bottle she could see, which was vodka."

I gasped. "Oh my god."

"I nearly died. If I did, I'd bring that hijueputa with me," Leila says.

I don't know whether to laugh or be worried for my best friend's safety. "That's… insane," I said, shaking my head in disbelief. "How has she not gotten kicked out?"

She groaned. "I complained to the housing department, but they said I have to wait until next semester to check If there are available rooms."

Once again, my money makes me feel guilty. Leila has to deal with a dangerous roommate, and I live alone in a big apartment. "If I had an extra bedroom, I'd let you move in," I tell her. "Unless you want to sleep on the couch?"

She sighs. "I'm tempted. I'm really tempted," she says, but then her eyes drift to the one bag in my hand. "Why did you barely get anything?"

I shrug. "I didn't need anything new, really."

"But you needed jeans?" she asks, laughing. "I've never seen you wear jeans, Rosie."

"I needed a change."

"Yeah. About that. Where have you been lately?"

I look up at her, furrowing my brows. "What do you mean?"

"You haven't been hanging out with us. I've seen you maybe once this week, and now you're buying jeans because you need a change. What's that about?"

"Where are the girls?" I ask her.

"Madi is at an audition, and Gabi's at dance class. But stop avoiding the question. What is going on with you?" she asks.

I don't know how much I should tell Leila about Grayson. I should tell her. She's my best friend, and it would be fun to have someone to talk to about this. But what if she judges me for doing this? She won't understand why I need this, why I need Grayson.

"Nothing much," I tell her.

"Nothing much?" she questions, laughing. "Sounds like something, and you just don't want to tell me."

I ignore her comment, and my eyes lock on the store across the street. The woman in the window storefront makes me wonder what I would look like wearing something like that. "Let's go in there," I tell her, already crossing the street.

Leila scoffs. "You know I could just get you some for free, right?"

"You get clothes for free?" I ask her. "Then why are you buying the whole damn store?"

"I get some clothes for free, but Bare Lush has been trying to get me to do an underwear shoot, so they're bribing me with free lingerie," she says.

"And you don't want to do it?" I ask.

She shrugs. "I don't know."

Her voice quiets when she answers me, so I don't push her on the subject.

"Let's go," I tell her instead, walking her over to the store. "You can help me with this."

This is one of the things I can learn from Leila. I would die before asking Grayson about lingerie, but then I remember that I already asked him for sex, so how embarrassing would that really be?

We enter the store, and the amount of choices overwhelms me. There are so many different types of underwear and bras I don't know where to start.

"What exactly are you looking for?" Leila asks.

"I don't know," I tell her, honestly.

"Well, what do you normally wear?"

I laugh. "Not these," I say. She raises her eyebrow, and I explain. "I wear briefs. I told you I wanted a change."

She smiles. "Nothing much, huh?"

I feel my cheeks start to blush, and I sigh, picking up a lacy blue bra from the counter. "Will you help me or not?"

She laughs, shaking her head. "Come on," she says. "I know just the thing for you."

13

Don't look in the bag

Rosalie

Maybe I was wrong to ask Leila for help. She definitely knows something's different with me, as if asking her to help me buy lingerie wasn't suspicious enough. The pair she picked out for me is cute, though. I wonder what it will look like on me.

It's not like I have anyone to wear it for. Maybe if Grayson hadn't rejected me, I'd have worn it for him. I can't help but think of his reaction to me wearing this. Would he be shocked, turned on? I don't know.

They barely cover anything, but I guess that's the point. Looks over comfort.

I can't help but feel deflated over the fact that no one will see them. I could buy it for myself to make myself feel sexy, but that's not the point of lingerie. It's to make you feel what it does to the other person. Having their eyes on you like you're a meal they want to devour, that's what I want.

And Grayson is reluctant to give it to me. Even though he's willing to help me with everything else I asked him, this one thing he won't give me.

"Hey, angel."

I snap my head up, seeing Grayson Carter leaning against his car door, smirking at me as he finishes off his cigarette and throws the butt end away.

Did I summon him with my thoughts?

Leila and I separated when she went back to her dorm room. Thank God. Because I didn't really want to explain to her why in the hell Grayson Carter was talking to me and why he just called me angel.

What would I even say? That I practically begged him to sleep with me, and he said no, so now he's helping me let go of the girl I was raised to be? How would that even go? I'm not embarrassed to be seen with him, but I'm okay with keeping this a secret.

I did a lot of recon on Grayson after the night of the party. I wanted to know everything I could possibly know about him and what he was like. I needed the right person, and Grayson seemed to be that.

And so far, he's done well. He took me drinking for the first time. I can't say I was fond of the hangover I got yesterday morning, but knowing I finally let go and was happy for once made it all worth it. I kind of wish Grayson had stayed. I wish I'd woken up with him next to me.

I still remember waking up by his side last Friday night when he shook me awake at four in the morning to watch the sunrise. We slept on the hood of his car after talking mindlessly for hours. Which isn't the most comfortable place to fall asleep, but I had never been happier than I did at that moment.

I felt a twinge of sadness when he dropped me off at my apartment that same morning. I wanted to spend more time with him, even though we had spent the whole night together, and he took me on my first 'lesson,' I wanted more.

I loved the feeling of the adrenaline rush that he gave me when he pressed his foot down and made me fear for my life.

But for one second, when he told me to open my eyes, and I focused on the road blurring past me as he sped up faster and faster, I didn't care about it. I didn't care about anything other than that moment. Living in that moment with Grayson by my side, feeling the wind on my skin and the rush of the speed, not knowing what would happen later, just living in that moment.

And when Grayson said he would never hurt me, I believed him. I knew deep inside that he'd never hurt me, and that was the scariest thing. I gave my life up on a platter at the hands of a stranger.

But whenever I spent time with him, he didn't feel like a stranger. He felt like freedom and liberation. I loved spending time with him, so when I see him outside of my apartment, I can't help but smile.

"Hey," I say. "What are you doing here?"

He shrugs. "I figured I'd come look for you but it looks like you've been busy." He smirks, looking down at the bags in my hands.

He approaches where I'm standing, but then his eyes land on the bouquet of flowers in my arms, and he frowns.

"Who bought you flowers?" he asks.

"Oh… well, no one. I bought them myself."

His eyebrows scrunch. "You bought yourself flowers?" he asks me. "Why?"

I avert my eyes from him and look at the flowers in my arms. They're huge daisies that fill out the bouquet so beautifully, and the sight of them makes me happy. "I love flowers," I tell him. "And I don't have anyone to buy them for me, so I buy them myself." I shrug.

Maybe it's weird to buy myself flowers, but I love how they look in my apartment, and it's not like I have a boyfriend to get them for me, so I'm the next best thing.

"I guess it's a little pathetic," I tell him, feeling my cheeks start to heat.

I look up at him, and my eyes instantly lock with his. I look into his dark eyes, wondering how the hell this guy with jet-black hair, dark eyes, and tattoos all over his body makes me feel like this, especially when the sides of his lips turn up into a smile.

He's right in front of me. We're so close, and I don't want to look away, so I don't. I keep staring back at him until he clears his throat and takes a step back, putting some well-needed — but unwanted — distance between us.

His eyes drift to the bags in my hand. "What did you get?"

"It's girl stuff. You don't care about this."

He scoffs. "When it comes to you? I do."

He reaches into one of the bags and opens it up, laughing at what he finds. "Jeans?" he asks.

I shrug. "If we're going to be sleeping together on mountains and the hood of your car, I'd better come prepared." I smile. His eyes widen, and he smirks. Realization dawns on me, and I quickly correct myself. "I meant, sleeping… together. Not sleeping together."

He laughs, shaking his head. "Yeah, Rosie. I got it. Don't worry."

I let out a breath of relief, and his hand travels to the next bag. I remember what is in that bag and snap it closed. "It's just clothes," I tell him, not wanting him to see the lingerie that I bought with him in mind.

"Rosalie," he says. "Let me see."

I smile. "Hey, that rhymed."

"What are you hiding in there?" he asks, narrowing his eyes.

"It's nothing, really. Just dumb stuff."

"Then you won't mind if I see it."

He picks up my hand that's clamped shut around the bag and holds it in his hand while his other hand opens the bag. I did say I wanted someone to see it, and while I wasn't really planning on Grayson seeing the underwear in the bag, it's as good as it's going to get.

His brows furrow as he looks inside the bag, confused about what it is. His hand reaches inside, and he picks up the bra, lacey and white. His eyes widen when he realizes what it is, and he drops the garment back into the bag. "Oh," he says, clearing his throat. "That's why you didn't want me to see it."

I nod, and his jaw clenches as he keeps staring down at the bag, looking at the lacey underwear inside it.

"Who did you get them for?"

Did he just ask me that? "Just for myself," I tell him.

His eyes narrow at me like he sees through my lies. "It's none of your business, really," I say. "You said we weren't ever going there, so I found someone who would."

"Someone?" he asks. "Don't tell me it's Ben Reed."

He's angry. His jaw is clenched, and his fists are balled up by his side. He doesn't like the thought of anyone else seeing me in this underwear, but he doesn't want to see me in it, either.

I turn on my heels and start walking away from him.

"Don't walk away from me."

I look over my shoulder, seeing him approach me. "You sound awfully jealous for someone who doesn't want anything to do with me."

A hand wraps around my arm, and he twists me around, crowding me until I can feel his breath on my skin. "Don't put words in my mouth, Rosie. I never said I wanted nothing to do with you."

"You said you didn't want to have sex with me. Same thing."

He groaned, wiping a hand down his face. "I'm still helping you, Rosie. I'll still do that for you if you want, but we just… Fuck," he curses, running a hand through his hair. "I can't. Not with you."

My face starts to redden, not because I'm embarrassed but because I'm sick of his excuses. "Why not? What's so different about me that you won't sleep with me?"

"Is this really how you want to lose your virginity, Rosie?" he asks me. "With some guy you don't even know, who, according to you, has a fucked-up reputation."

"I do know you," I tell him. He's more than the rumors and reputation around here.

He shakes his head, scoffing. "You don't know me, angel. Not really. And you definitely didn't know me when you walked in on me and another girl, proposing the idea of us sleeping together all for some dumb list!"

My eyes widened as I stepped back from him. I confide in him, and he throws it in my face. I thought he would help me without judgment or restraints, but instead, he just reminded me that he'd sleep with anyone, just not me.

I laugh bitterly. "This," I gesture between us, "was a mistake. I shouldn't have asked you for anything." I pull my arm out of his reach and continue walking toward my apartment.

"Wait."

I ignore him. I keep looking forward, walking toward my apartment, when I feel his hand wrap around my wrist again. He doesn't twist me around this time, just holds me there like he doesn't want to let go.

"Please. Don't walk away from me, just let me talk. Let me explain why we can't have sex."

He'll give me the same talk he has for weeks. That he just can't. Well, that's not an explanation. It was stupid of me to think I could do this. It's not who I am, no matter how much I want it to be. No matter how much I wanted to step out of being Rosalie Whitton and become someone completely different, I'll never be able to have that.

Grayson was my first and last choice. I confided in him when I shouldn't have. I know that now. I won't repeat the same mistake.

"We can't have sex," he starts. "I want to. You have no *idea* how much, but we can't."

"Then why don't you?" He has nothing to lose. I'm standing here asking him to take me, to teach me, to let me experience what it's like, and he still won't.

"Because, Rosie. You're a virgin. And call me a dumb fuck for saying this, but I can't get involved with a virgin, especially not one like you."

One like me? "What does that mean?"

"It means that you're innocent. I'm guessing you haven't been on a date or been in a relationship." I look at the floor, knowing he's right. "You'll just end up getting the wrong idea."

I furrow my brows. "Wrong idea?"

He nods. "I know girls. They get attached. They catch feelings and convince themselves they're in love, especially with the guy who took their virginity, and I can't do that to you. This will never go anywhere, and I don't want to hurt you. Ever. So, we can be friends, but we can't get involved like that."

"But you sleep with girls all the time, and you're never in a relationship."

He sighs. "That's different."

"How?" I ask him. "How is asking you to sleep with me, to teach me, different than you hooking up with those girls?"

"Because they know what this is. They know it's just sex. No feelings or any of that bullshit."

"You don't even believe in love, so what are you so worried about?"

He runs his hand through his hair, shaking his head. "I'm worried about *you*."

"Me?"

He nods. "Yes. You believe in love. And if we get involved, you'll confuse what it is, you'll confuse attraction for love, and you'll end up getting hurt. I don't want to hurt you. You're too good for that."

"Oh my god. Stop."

He looks taken aback. "Stop what?"

"Stop saying I'm too good or too pure or whatever else you think. I want to learn, and I want you to teach me. I want to do this."

"Rosie…"

I hold my hand up. "Let me finish." He nods, and I take a deep breath before continuing. "I know what this is. I know it would be just a hookup, and I won't get feelings for you or fall in love with you. Yes, I'm attracted to you, but my life is already set out for me. I won't end up with someone like you. I'll end up with someone with money who comes from a good family, most likely picked out by my mother. Some hotel owner or whoever else she wants to set me up with, and I'll ultimately go along with it because, like you said, I'm naïve, right?"

He shakes his head, taking a step closer to me. "Rosie, I didn't—"

"It's okay," I reassure him. "I get it. I am naïve. I've been sheltered all my life, and I want you to help me step out of the shade. To show me the rain, the good, the bad, and the ugly. All of it, and I want it with you."

He's quiet for a while, but then he blows out a breath. "Fuck, Rosie. I don't know."

I reach out and grab his hand. I clutch it in mine, feeling the coldness of his skin mix with the heat of mine. "Please, just say you'll think about it?"

He lets out a breath and shakes his head. He looks down at me, staring into my eyes. "I've done nothing but think about it," he admits.

"Then give it a chance. I just want to learn. Please. I trust you."

He drops his eyes, frowning a little. "I can't, Rosie. I just can't." He lets his eyes drift closed, pain etched in his brows. Why is he fighting this so hard? "I understand if you don't want me to help you anymore, I get it just—"

"No," I interrupt him. "I still want your help. I had fun the other night, and last weekend was… I loved it."

His lips curve upwards in a small smile. "Yeah?"

I nod. "It was the best. And I like spending time with you, even if it's just as friends."

He lets out another breath. "Me too."

My chest clenches. I'm so glad he likes hanging out with me because he's become the one thing I have looked forward to recently.

"Then don't say no. Not yet. Just think about it. That's all I ask."

I look up at him, waiting for him to agree to at least think about it. I get it now, he doesn't want me to catch feelings, and I won't. I can handle them.

He sighs. "Okay."

"Thank you."

His phone rings, and he pulls it out of his back pocket, cursing when he sees who's calling him. "I've got to go. But I'll call you soon."

"Okay."

He gives me a small smile, then turns around, gets in his car, and leaves.

I make my way into the building, unlocking the door once I get to my apartment. I kick off my heels and drop my bags on the couch, wandering into the kitchen to find a vase. I pull out one of the crystal vases my mom bought when she furnished the apartment. I fill it up with water and drop the daisies inside. The flowers make the apartment look so much brighter than before.

Maybe Grayson was right. He isn't willing to give me what I want. Even if it ends up being just sex. I think I'll always want more, eventually. I want to know what it's like to fall in love. If I do end up with someone I don't love, at least I'll know what it was like, once in my life.

And Grayson can't give me that. He's made it clear that if anything happens, I need to understand it's nothing more than just another lesson. But I can find someone willing to give me everything I want. Love, feelings, the whole lot.

14

Cock blocked

Grayson

I look down at the screen. Waiting for something. A call, a text. I just want to see her name on the screen.

She won't call. I know that. She never calls. I told her I'd call her, but I haven't. Ever since I last saw her, I can't stop thinking about her, looking at her name on my phone. I even found her social media to see what she's been up to.

She threw me off guard the other day. She asked for the one thing I can't give her again. She asked me to take her, to brand her as mine. I let her down as gently as I could, but she won't give up. I don't know how much longer I can hold out, either. I've tried. The more those baby blue eyes stare up at me and beg me to teach her everything I know, the more I want to accept.

The things I could teach her. I could learn her body, make her learn mine. I would have so much fun with her. I already do without the sex. I can only imagine what it would be like if I just gave in and took all of her.

"How was that?" Aiden grunts.

"Huh?"

He groans, lifting the bar off his chest and placing it back on the rack above him. "Dude. If you're going to be my spotter, you can't just stare into space."

I blow out a breath. "Sorry."

He sits up on the bench, drying his sweaty face with a towel. "What's going on with you anyway?" he asks. "Is it your parents again?"

Aiden's the only one who knows about my parents— to a certain extent. He's been my best friend since I met him in orientation freshman year, and he's a loyal motherfucker, so I know he won't be running his mouth.

"No," I tell him. "They call, I ignore. It seems to work out fine."

That's a lie. It's not working out. I can't get them off my back. They don't trust me and probably never will, but I can't change what happened, and I'm here, dammit. I'm here trying to prove to them I'm willing to do whatever the fuck they want me to do until I get what I need, and I can leave.

"Then what's up?" he asks.

Rosie and I agreed to keep it a secret. She probably feels embarrassed to be seen with me, knowing she's too good for me. So, I don't want to ruin her freshman year by letting everyone assume she's with me.

She needs the freedom, the space to discover who the fuck she is without her parents breathing down her neck. Who would have thought I'd be relating to Rosalie Whitton?

"C'mon. You can tell me," Aiden says.

I run a hand through my hair. "I can't,"

He scoffs. "Dude. It's obviously bothering you. You haven't stopped staring at your phone since we got here."

I groan, running a hand down my face. "Fine, but I swear to God, if you tell anyone about this, I will break your kneecaps."

He snorts. "Like you could reach. Just tell me and stop whining."

I can't help but laugh. "Jesus. You're a cocky bastard. Fine, do you remember that girl who came to our house two weeks ago?"

He uncaps his water bottle, downing half the bottle, and then wipes his mouth with the back of his hand. "You're going to have to be a little more specific. I've seen many girls come in and out of our house."

Not from me, he hasn't. I haven't been with a single girl since Rosie walked in on Brianna and me. Fuck knows why. Maybe it's the fact that I haven't stepped foot in a party since I saw her that night, or maybe it's because I haven't been able to get her off my mind to even start thinking about another girl.

I glare at him. "Blonde hair. White skirt. Ran out of there?"

"Oh. Rosalie, right?"

"Yeah."

"His eyes widen. "You slept with her?" he asks. "You?"

My eyes narrow at him. "No, asshole. What do you mean by that? You don't think I could get with her?"

He laughs. "She's not exactly your type, is all. And you don't seem like her type,"

He's not completely wrong. Most of the time, I'd end the night with a dark-haired girl, tattoos, piercings. Girls who I knew wouldn't turn this into more. The more fucked up, the better. We matched. We made sense. But nothing makes sense between Rosalie and me.

"That doesn't matter. We're not sleeping together."

"Who said anything about sleep?" He smirked.

"Fuck off. You know what I meant."

He laughs. "Then what's the problem?"

I sighed. "She asked me for, um… help."

Aiden snorted. "Is that code for sex? Because you just said—"

"No." I wipe a hand down my face. "She asked me to show her how to live like I do."

He nods. "So, she wants to run away from her problems by pretending to be a fuck up?"

"Fuck you. No one's pretending," I tell him.

"Oh really?" he asks. "Because you let those rumors about you fly by when you could shut it down if you wanted to. But you don't want to. You want everyone to think you're a poor boy whose mother is addicted to drugs." He laughs humorlessly. "I've got to tell you, it's not as cool as you think it is."

"I don't think it's cool," I tell him. "I just don't give a fuck what they say about me."

"It's the fucking worst," he continues. "Having to stand by and watch your mother rot away. Not having food for a week. Having to sleep on a dirty mattress. Do you have any idea what that's like?"

Yes. I want to tell him. *I've seen it before.* But all I can do is stare back at him, seeing his eyes darken at me. "Fuck, bro."

"Yeah." He scoffs. "Fuck, bro."

"Shit, Aiden." All I can think of is Aiden living in those conditions. "That's just what they assume," I tell him. It's not like I started those rumors.

"But you don't say any different. You let them think it."

"Because I don't want anyone to know."

"Know what? That you have two loving parents who are richer than most people here. What a fucked-up life you have."

"Aiden. It's not like that."

He doesn't hear me, though. He looks right past me. "If it was me, I'd be flashing my money around to get them to shut the fuck up."

"I don't have any money. I'm doing this for you," I grit out.

He stiffens, meeting my eyes. "Fuck," he mutters, wiping a hand down his face. "I know." He sighs. "I just… I got carried away. I let my fucked-up life get the better of me and took it out on you." He blows out a breath, "I'm sorry."

"It's fine," I tell him. "Don't worry about it." He has every right to be mad over the fact that what people are saying about me is his reality.

"It's not," he says, shaking his head and dropping his eyes.

"Aiden," I say, making him look at me. "It's fine."

He nods, swallowing. "So, what's the problem then? With the girl?" he asks me.

His eyes soften, making me remember why I don't care about the rumors. I would do it all over again. "She asked me to show her how to live like a regular college kid," I smirk, remembering her at my doorstep.

"What makes her not a regular college kid?"

"She's rich," I tell him, rolling my eyes when he snorts. "Yeah, I get it. We have that in common. You can drop it now."

"Fine. So, what's the issue."

"She wants me to give her the college experience. Drinking, parties, all of that. And um…" I rub the back of my neck. "She asked me to…" Fuck, am I really going to tell him this? "She asked me to teach her about sex. She wants me to take her virginity."

"Fuck."

"Yeah."

"You can't do it," he tells me.

"What? Why not?"

"Girls like that are too vulnerable. Too emotional for casual sex. She'll end up getting feelings for you and cling to you like a wet dog."

"Yeah. I figured." That's exactly what I told her the other day. He's right. I know he's right.

"You've got to end it with her."

My head snaps up, looking right at him. "What? No," I tell him. "I can still help her without getting in her pants."

He raised his brow at me. "Really?"

"Yes." I glare at him. "I've done it already."

"And you didn't touch her? He asks suspiciously. "Not even kissed her?"

"No. I can control myself, you know." I don't tell him how badly I want to kiss her every time I see her. He doesn't need to know that.

"This isn't going to end well," he says. "I'm telling you now, you'll end up giving in, and she'll get attached. You're better off just backing away from her."

I know what he's saying is true, but I don't want to stop seeing her. Even if we can't fuck, I still want to help her. I can't imagine someone else taking her to places, teaching her everything they know, taking all of her firsts. I hate the idea of that being a possibility.

"I'm not going to stay away from her," I tell him. "Nothing's going to happen between us. I help her, that's it."

He shakes his head, laughing under his breath. "Good luck with that."

I scoff. "I don't need luck. I can control myself; I'm not an animal."

The door opens, and the gym fills with noise as Ben Reed and his band of assholes follow. I curse under my breath, rolling my eyes. I hate this fucking guy. Ever since we went to school together, this asshole has gotten on my nerves. He's the kind of douchebag who thinks he's better than everyone else. The kind who flashes his daddy's money and spits on poor people.

He's had it out for me since the beginning. I know he was the one who started those rumors; he told me so. Even though he knows the truth, he still acts like I'm gum on the bottom of his shoe.

"Look who it is," Ben says as he catches me.

Aiden groans when he sees him. He doesn't like Ben either. Freshman year, Aiden tried to pledge to be in the frat house. He told me it was cheaper than a dorm room. Ben tried to get Aiden to snort a line of cocaine as one of their hazing rituals. He quit the pledge, and I told him he could move in with me.

"Ben, why don't you fuck off?" I spit out.

"Where's that virgin of yours?"

I freeze. My eyes drift to Aiden, and he lifts his eyebrows in question. He's probably wondering how Ben knows that. I sure as hell didn't tell him.

"What did you just say?"

"You don't think I know?" he says, laughing. "That girl screams virgin."

My jaw clenches and my fists ball up. God, I want to punch him.

"Do you want to bet who gets that sweet pussy first?" he asks. "I bet it's me."

Fuck this. I close my eyes and try to calm myself down. I can't get expelled. I need that money.

He laughs. "You know, I can be so kind. She'll be screaming underneath me in no time. She won't even see it coming."

That's it. I can't fucking stand here and listen to this bullshit. I stride towards him, but Aiden beats me to it, pinning him against the wall. "Say that again. I dare you."

"Aiden, what the fuck." I pull him off of Ben. He doesn't have money like my parents do. He can't get out of this.

"I'm not going to let that asshole say that shit."

I don't know whether to thank him or punch him. He stood up for Rosie, but he also risked his future here.

I turn to look at Ben, and he's got a scowl on his face, breathing hard. "You stay away from Rosie, or I will fucking kill you myself."

"Fuck you," he spits out. "That bitch isn't worth it," he says before he and the other two dicks, who follow him around, leave the gym.

"What the fuck was that?" I ask Aiden once they're gone.

He shakes his head. "I hate motherfuckers who speak about women like that," he says, running a towel down his face and cleaning up the sweat.

"You could have gotten suspended. Or expelled," I tell him.

He breathes out like he just realized that. "Fuck."

My phone lights up on the bench beside me, and I pick it up.

Brent:

I'm here.

"I've got to go," I say, looking up at Aiden. "Are you going to be ok?" I ask him.

He shakes his head. "Go. It's fine." He stands up from the bench, walking over to the treadmills. "I'm gonna do lower body. Calm myself down."

I nod, pick up the duffle bag, and walk out the door. Telling Aiden about Rosalie was a mistake, even if he protected her from that asshole. I needed a second opinion, but I didn't need someone else to cockblock me. I've been doing that just fine. I know I can't go there with her, I know that, but now he's suggesting I stay away from her completely? I can't do that.

No matter how hard it is for me to keep things friendly between us, I want to keep seeing her; I want to help her.

I see Brent leaning against the wall outside the gym. He's looking around, panicking while he's got a joint in his hand. He's paranoid; I can see it in his face, the way he keeps looking around him. If he doesn't calm down, he's going to call attention to himself.

The closer I get to him, the more I can smell it. The smell hits me like a brick, and I tense. I hate the smell of pot, and it's everywhere I turn. He sees me approaching and walks toward me.

He lifts his head in greeting when he approaches me, but he keeps looking behind his shoulder.

"Could you be any more obvious?" I snap between clenched teeth. I take it out of my duffle bag and hand it to him.

In a second, there's a waft of cash shoved in my hand as he hurries away.

I start to count the cash, making sure he didn't stiff me this time.

"Hey…oh."

My head snaps up at the familiar voice. She's walking away. Her head is down as her feet rush away from me. I don't give a fuck about the money right now. I shove it inside the bag and head towards her.

"Hey, wait up."

She looks behind her shoulder and stops at the sight of me. She slowly turns around as I get closer to her.

"Hi," I breathe out when I get to her. "Were you running away from me, angel?"

"Hey," she says quietly. "I'm sorry I interrupted you. I didn't…" She tucks her hair behind her ear before leaning in. She's on her toes and still can't reach me. I'm taller than her, so I give her a hand and lean down until her mouth is resting next to my ear. "Was that a drug deal?" she asks.

I snap my eyes closed at the breathy sound of her voice in my ear. I hate that she thinks I'm selling drugs. Aiden's words come back to haunt me. I should tell her that none of those rumors are true. Instead, I take her hand in mine and start to pull her away.

"Where are we going?" she asks.

"For another lesson."

15

I'll do it

Rosalie

"I have class." I almost gasp when his hand wraps around mine and pulls me away.

"C'mon," he says, slowing down his steps so I can catch up with him. "You've skipped class before. That's nothing new to you."

I have skipped class before, but how does he know that? "How do you… oh my god. You remember that?" The party. It was the only thing I drank to that night.

He turns his head to the side, stopping abruptly and staring right at me. "I remember everything about you, angel."

My heart hammers against my chest so loudly I think he might be able to hear it, especially when he smirks and then lets go of my hand. He opens the car door and climbs inside. I walk around to the passenger side and open the door, getting in the car with him.

Fashion technology can wait because nothing in the world could stop me from getting into this car with him. He starts the car and speeds up, pulling out of campus and onto the road.

"Where are we going?" I ask him.

"I don't know."

"So, we're just driving?"

He shrugs, running a hand through his hair. “Where do you want to go?” he asks.

I don’t care. I don’t know where we’re going or what we’re doing, but I don’t care as long as I’m here with him. I just want to be here with Grayson, wherever that is.

“I want to live like Grayson Carter,” I tell him.

He lets out an exasperated breath, shaking his head. “I don’t want to be Grayson Carter right now.”

My brows furrow, and I frown. “Why not?”

He shifts the gear, and my eyes drift down to stare at his hand around the stick. Why does Grayson make driving a stick look so hot? “Just be with me, Rosie,” he says, his eyes looking out at the road. “Forget about who you think I am or who you’re trying to escape being. Just be with me. Right now. Right here.”

Something’s up with him. He wants an escape from his daily life, and I understand that better than anyone. “Okay.”

His head snaps towards mine. “Yeah?”

I nod. He turns back to the road, turning on the radio, making the music fill the car, fill the silence between us and make us forget about everything for a moment.

After a while of driving, the car slows down until Grayson pulls it to a stop. I jerk my head up, trying to figure out where we are.

“C’mon,” he says.

I get out of the car and make my way towards him. I look ahead, seeing a row of cars lined up inside this building.

To my right, there are about three or four men standing by, most of them in tank tops. They whistle as I make my way to the door, and I snap my head away from them and look at Grayson instead.

He interlocks his fingers with mine, squeezing to give me some reassurance. He scowls at the men standing in front of the garage. "Show some respect," he spits out. "She's with me."

Those words make my eyes light up as I look at him. He glances down at me and squeezes my hand in his, tugging me away and into the garage. The sound of scraping and rattling of metal surrounds me as Grayson and I walk into the garage. What are we doing here?

"Is Mattie here?" Grayson asks the guy working on a car in the garage. The hood is popped open, and his forehead and tank top are covered in grime. He gestures with his head over to the right, and Grayson thanks him.

His fingers are still clasping mine, even though we're long gone from the men outside, and I don't mind it. I like it. I try to remember that this doesn't mean anything. He's told me this so many times before.

We approach the door that the man gestured to, and Grayson knocks on it. "Hey, Mattie. It's Grayson," he says.

"Come in." A deep voice says on the other side of the door.

Grayson faces me and pulls his hand away from mine. I frown, feeling the loss of his touch. "I'll be right back. Stay here," he tells me.

I nod, and he disappears into the office.

Why did Grayson bring me here? I look behind me, seeing the man Grayson was talking to before staring back at me with a face covered in dirt. He smirks at me, and the sight makes me feel uneasy. I turn around and keep my eyes on the door in front of me.

The door opens quickly after, and Grayson comes out, locking eyes with me. “Come on,” Grayson says, tugging on my hand and walking towards the back of the garage.

I follow him out of the garage from the back exit. He lets go of my hand and climbs onto a motorcycle, fitting a helmet on his head.

“Uh…” Does he want me to get on that?

He smirks, holding out a helmet to me. “Have you ever been on a motorcycle, angel?” he asks.

I shake my head, taking a step back. “I’m not getting on that,” I tell him, looking down at my outfit. “I’m wearing a dress.”

He smirks and takes that as his opportunity to look down my body. I feel the heat of his stare everywhere his eyes roam. “I know,” he says. “And you look gorgeous.”

I blush at the compliment but make no move to get onto the motorcycle.

He sighs. “Come on, Rosie,” he says. “Get on.”

I bite my lip, staring at Grayson on the motorcycle. What if we get in an accident or are arrested? Is the motorcycle even his, or are we stealing it? Oh my god. *We.* I’m an accomplice in this if he is stealing it. I can’t. I’m scared.

“I won’t let anything happen to you,” he says. “Just hold on tight.”

I sigh and say fuck it. I wanted fun, might as well have fun if I’m going to die. I take the helmet from him and place it on my head. He turns around, making sure it’s secure. He turns, facing the road as he grips the handles.

“You’ll be safe, Rosie. I promise,” he says. “Hold on.” I put my arms around his waist, interlocking my fingers together and clutching tight onto him. I squeeze him and let my head fall onto his shoulders.

He starts the bike and speeds off. I gasp when he accelerates, and his deep laugh vibrates through my chest. I snap my eyes closed, gripping tight onto him. It feels so much more dangerous than it did in the car, but I love how I'm experiencing another first with Grayson.

The ground shakes beneath us, and I feel everything. It's like all of my senses are magnified. Maybe that's because my eyes are shut closed, or maybe it's because we're traveling so fast, so recklessly, that I taste, hear and smell everything. I take the plunge and open my eyes, gasping when I see the whole world zooming past us.

"Go faster," I whisper in his ear, clutching tighter onto him.

I feel his laughter deep in the pit of my stomach. "You don't even have to ask, angel," he says before pressing his foot down. Cars on our right, in front, and behind are vast memories by the time we overtake them. It's an indescribable feeling and like nothing I've ever seen or felt before.

My heart is in the back of my throat. I smell the trees and feel the air rushing past us. I can hear the white noise of the wind and the sound of the engine roaring as Grayson speeds up.

All of my emotions are doubled, tripled even. I'm alive. At this moment, I feel more alive than I ever have before. I feel it deep in my bones, and Grayson gave that to me.

I clutch tighter onto him as we speed past the road, letting my eyes explore everything around me. We move so fast against the whole world, making our way into a forest filled with trees, dirt, and grass all around.

When he slows down, I focus on the view in front of us. He climbs off the motorcycle and takes my hand. I clutch my palm in his, and he helps me off the motorcycle. The minute I do, I feel the ground sway beneath my feet. My eyes snap closed, and I grab onto Grayson, gripping his shoulders and waiting for everything to stop spinning.

He clutches my arms, holding me upright. "Whoa. You okay there, Rosie?"

I nod, opening my eyes and looking up at him. His brows are scrunched, and his eyes are dark and full of concern. "Just a little dizzy," I tell him, smiling up at him.

He smirks. "Yeah," he says, nodding. "Happens sometimes when you've been riding so fast and then stop suddenly." He takes off my helmet and straps both of them to the bike. "C'mon," he says, taking my hand in his and guiding us away.

We walk deeper into the forest, getting closer to the water. He sits us down on an old wooden bench that faces out onto a lake. His body turns towards mine and brushes the hair out of my face. "You feeling better?" he asks.

"Yeah."

He smirks, tucking my hair behind my ear, and then his eyes meet mine. He doesn't look away, and neither do I. We continue to stare at each other for a while. But then, he clears his throat and turns back around to face the lake, away from me.

I sigh. "Why didn't you just bring your car?" I ask him. Why did he feel the need to bring the motorcycle instead?

He doesn't turn his head. His eyes stay focused on the water shining underneath the sun, but I can see his Adam's apple bobbing as he swallows. "You didn't like it?" he asks.

I don't even have to think about that for a second. "I loved it."

This time he does turn his head. He's got a slight smirk on his lips. "Yeah?"

I love when he says that. Almost as if he needs the confirmation. "Hell yeah," I assure him, smiling up at him.

He laughs, shaking his head. "You always seem to surprise me, angel."

I feel my cheeks fill with heat, and I avert my gaze from him. "So, is that like your thing?"

"My thing?" he asks.

"Yeah. Motorcycles, cars… fast, reckless driving, I guess."

He laughs, then shrugs. "Yeah," he sighs. "I love feeling the adrenaline of it. There's nothing else like it."

There really isn't. I didn't know it would be this much fun to endanger my life like that, even though I knew I was safe with Grayson. I was alive, feeling every emotion possible from the tip of my toes to the top of my head. I felt it everywhere.

"It's addictive," he says. "The feeling you get. It's hedonistic and exhilarating." His head is turned towards me, but his eyes look past me like he's lost in thought. "I'm always hyper-aware of everything. I'm never relaxed. But the fear makes me feel alive; it makes me feel everything. And I wanted to show you that."

I swallow hard. I felt the exact same way. It was the most thrilling feeling.

"Thank you," I say.

He snaps out of thought, and he focuses on me. "For what?"

"For showing me what it feels like to be alive."

His eyes burn into mine, so dark and intense. I can't look away. He shakes his head. "What do you really want?" he asks.

"What do you mean?"

"I mean, what do *you*, Rosie, want? What do you get out of this?" he asks.

I shrug. "I told you. Everything on the list."

He groans, sliding a hand through his hair. "Don't give me that list bullshit. I want to know what you want, Rosie. Everything that you've ever wanted to do. I want to know."

I open my mouth to speak but then snap it closed again. I'm not sure if I even know what I want exactly. I want to know everything, experience everything, see everything, and live like everyone else.

I shrug. "I want to be a normal teenager, Grayson. I want to do everything people our age do. Smoking, parties, hook-ups, drugs, everything."

He shakes his head. "I can't help you with drugs, Rosie," he says.

I furrow my brows. "But you're a drug dealer, right? I can pay for it. I just want to try some. I want to feel out of control for a bit." I smirk at him. "Part of my college experience."

His jaw clenches. "I thought you didn't believe that crap."

"But I saw you. Today."

He shakes his head. "I can't help you with drugs. I'm not giving you drugs. Don't ask me to."

He looks down, his face pained, so I don't push him on it. "Okay," I say, "but I still want the other things."

He shakes his head. "Don't live for other people. Live for yourself," he says. "Those are things that you think you have to do, what other people want, Rosie. What do *you* want?"

I sigh, letting my head tilt back. "I don't know," I admit.

His thumb brushes my cheek, and I let my eyes flutter closed at the feel of him. "You do know, Rosie. C'mon."

I turn to look at him, staring into his eyes. "I want to go on a date," I tell him. "I want to go skinny dipping. I want a kiss in the rain, like in the movies, you know?" I swallow and turn my head away from him. "I want to have my first kiss."

His thumb drops lower until he cups my chin. He gently tugs my chin and lifts my head until my eyes make contact with his. "You've never been kissed?" he asks, his eyes dropping down to my mouth.

I shake my head, my eyes roaming all over his face, but his gaze remains on my lips. His thumb reaches up and brushes my lower lip. I part my lips for him with a silent gasp. I feel the callouses in his fingers, and they feel so rough against the soft skin of my mouth.

"How is that possible?" he asks; his eyes finally travel up until he meets my eyes. His hands drop from my face, and I let out a breath. I don't know if it's a breath of relief or one that I have been holding in ever since he placed his hands on me.

"I was never allowed out," I tell him. "My mother was… overprotective doesn't even begin to cover it. She was overbearing. I was homeschooled all of my life."

Grayson leans back into the bench, facing the lake as I speak. "I begged her to go to public school for as long as I can remember. I needed something. I hated staying in that house day after day, surrounded by the same people. And in my sophomore year, she allowed me to."

I sighed. "I was shy and a little scared when I first started school, so I didn't really make a memorable impression on a lot of people. Leila became my best friend, and I'm so grateful that I had someone like her. But to answer your question, I've never had an opportunity where I would even be alone with a boy. My first crush was a guy named Tommy." I tell him. "He was in my math class, and he did try to talk to me, but I didn't know what to say, I guess. I was a mess. I couldn't even speak to him."

I turn my body to face him and notice that his eyes are already on me. "So, that's why I'm asking you for this. I don't know why I asked you, really." I admit. "I just thought you'd be the perfect person to help me in any way you could."

I shake my head. "And I know you said we wouldn't ever get involved that way, but," I shrug, "Ben seemed interested. Or maybe if I find someone else —"

"I'll do it."

My eyes widen. "What?"

"I'll do it," he says. "I'll help you. With everything."

Is he saying what I think he is? "You mean…?"

"Yes."

I inhale deeply. "But, what about what you said?"

"That still stands," he says. "We're not dating, and you can't catch feelings. But if you still want to—"

"I want to," I interrupt before he can back out of this.

"Then I'll do it." He leans in closer. "I'll teach you everything; I'll show you everything. Whatever you want, I'll do it."

I hold my breath, unable to form words. "Really?"

His fingers brush my cheek, making me gasp. He cups my face with one hand and leans in until he's right in front of me. "Yes, angel," he whispers. "I'll do it."

16

First kisses

Grayson

I lean in and crash my lips with hers. The moment our lips meet, she lets out a mixture between a gasp and a whimper. It's easily the sexiest sound I've ever heard, and I'll do anything to hear it again. I lift my hand and cup the back of her head, wanting her closer. My other hand strokes her cheek while we kiss.

She tastes so sweet, just like I thought she would. Her lips are nothing like I've ever felt before. They're so soft, like butter, and they taste addictive, like strawberries or candy. I want more, but I need to remember that this is all new to her, and she's inexperienced.

When she admitted that she had never been kissed before, I wanted nothing more than to teach her. To feel her lips on mine, messy and all, and teach her everything. But even though she's never been kissed before, it isn't messy.

It's also not as hot as I would prefer. I want the heat with her, the type of kiss where your brain is muddled up, consumed by lust and need, and you can't think. The feeling so overwhelming that you can't even control yourself.

No, this kiss is soft and delicate, just like my angel. She brushes her lips over mine so softly that we're barely kissing. Her mouth is closed, and I need her closer. I need more. My tongue darts out and licks her bottom lip, beckoning for her to open, but she doesn't. She continues kissing me back, gentle and light. I'm none of those things, and I need to deepen this kiss. I want everything from her. I want it all.

I brush my tongue over her bottom lip again, twice, three times, until she gasps for air, and I take that as my chance. I fit my tongue inside her mouth, and she yelps when she feels it, but she doesn't stop. She meets me halfway, letting me taste her, letting her tongue dance with mine. She moans into my mouth, a sound so sweet I'm debating on how I can give her everything I own.

I want to hear that from her again. Fuck, I *need* to. My teeth gently graze her bottom lip before I soothe it with the lick of my tongue. She moans again. God. I groan, tipping her head back to deepen the kiss.

Jesus, this girl is going to be the death of me. Everything she does, every sound she makes, I need more of. She reaches up, grabs my hair, and pulls it back. I smile against her lips. She's eager for me. And I eat it up.

I leave her mouth, kissing, licking, nibbling down her chin, her jaw until I reach her neck. She tastes like candy everywhere. I never want to stop this. Ever.

"Oh, god," she gasps when I nibble her neck, kissing every inch of her skin. Her breathing is shallow and fast; her chest is rising up and down.

Which makes my eyes drift to her chest. She's wearing a pink corset dress with silk ribbons for straps. Her breasts taunting me in the tight dress, making me drool at the sight of her. She looks down at me, her lips parted in shock, breathing so hard.

I kiss her shoulder, lick it, kiss it again, and then fit the silk straps between my teeth, pulling it down until the bow unravels. I gaze up, and Rosalie closes her eyes, breathing even harder. I can't help but grin when I look at her. God she's so pretty it hurts. Physically hurts me to look at her.

I make my way to her other shoulder, leaving soft kisses in my path. I press an open mouth kissed where the silk ends. My fingers reach up, brushing against her skin and I pull the bow with my hands, unraveling it like she's my very own present. Happy fucking birthday to me.

She releases a deep breath and then a soft, gentle moan, the sound traveling straight to my cock. But I ignore the needy fucker and focus on the beautiful angel in front of me.

I need those lips back on mine badly, and I waste no time, lifting my head and kissing her, deep and hot like I want, like I know she wants, but she's too afraid to take it. Rosalie wraps her arms around my neck, weaving her fingers in my hair and gripping it in her fist, pushing me into her.

My hand is clutching her face, but I drift my hand, tucking her hair behind her ear. I bring my fingers lower to her collarbone and feel the supple skin there marked by my teeth. She whimpers. Christ, I want my mouth all over her, but not here. Not on a bench in the middle of the woods.

When I taste her, I'm going to need my time with her. I want to learn her body, what makes her cry out with pleasure, what makes her whimper and moan out of control until she's shaking underneath me.

I like teasing her, waiting for her to beg me for it. But she doesn't; she just takes whatever I'm willing to give her. Her breathing is erratic, and her eyes are still closed. I don't want her eyes closed. I want to look into those baby blues as she reaches pleasure.

"Oh god," she whimpers again. "Why… what's happening?"

I lift my head, seeing her eyebrows drawn as if she were in pain. "What do you mean?" I grab her chin in my hand, making her head drop to look at me, but her eyes are still closed.

"I don't… I feel… what is this?" She gasps, shaking her head.

"You mean turned on?" I ask her because, by the way she's acting, it's like she's never been horny before.

She nods ecstatically. "Yes. I think…" She squeezes her legs together, making me curse silently. I can only imagine how wet she is. "I'm turned on," she says as if she's just discovered that.

I grip her thigh, lifting the fabric of her dress as I slide my hand up. "Fuck." I groan, leaving a hard, hot peck on her lips.

"Touch me," she breathes out. She places her hand on top of mine on her thigh and lifts it higher. She spreads her legs slightly to make room for me, and I take that as my invitation.

I cup her pussy over her panties, feeling the material drenched. The soft cotton material can't handle how turned on this girl is right now, and I relish the feeling that I made her like this.

She bucks her hips against my hand, and I focus on her face. She's flushed with arousal, and her eyes are still closed like she wants to heighten the feeling. I let my fingers drift up to find her clit over her panties. I press my finger against it, hearing her breathing stop.

I don't rub it or pull the fabric aside. Maybe I just like teasing her, or maybe I'm a secret masochist who likes withholding my own pleasure because all I want to do right now is feel how wet she is under her underwear and make her hum from desire, but I remain still.

"Tell me what you want, Rosie," I husk out. "What do you do when you touch yourself?" I ask, smoothing my finger up and down the wet cotton. I need to know how to bring her there. Since she hasn't been kissed, I can pretty much guess that she hasn't been touched either.

Her eyes snap open, and she clears her throat. "I… I haven't…"

I look up, seeing her face flushed and her eyes brimmed with confusion. My hand stills. Is she saying…? "You've never touched yourself?"

She pulls her bottom lip between her teeth and shakes her head. "No," she says, looking down where my hand disappears under her dress. "Girls don't do that."

I laugh. Maybe it's the wrong time to, but that doesn't stop me. "I hate to break it to you, but yeah, they do."

Her eyes widen. "They do?"

"Most of them, yeah. Girls are just as horny as guys are, if not more." And the thought of Rosalie never experiencing that kind of ecstasy before makes me want to give it to her even more.

"Oh," she breathes out.

As much as I want to touch her, feel her, and see her reach pleasure, I think she needs to do that to herself first. She needs to find out what she likes, and as much as I'd love to give her her first orgasm, I think it needs to be hers.

Instead, I let my hand fall from her thigh and kiss her instead. I need her lips back on mine, and she doesn't object. She opens her mouth for me this time, allowing me to stick my tongue in her mouth and suck on her tongue. I could get drunk off of her lips. She's so sweet, I can't get enough of it.

By some miracle, I'm able to pull away from her. She gasps as she inhales a much-needed breath, and her eyes are hazy and filled with lust. I smooth her hair behind her ear and out of her face.

I pull up the straps of her dress. A slight frown appears on her face as I do, and I restrain the urge to laugh. "How was that for your first kiss?" I ask her, smirking as I remember her squeezing her legs tight from the arousal brewing inside of her. I'm guessing it was a pretty good kiss.

"It was… amazing," she breathes out. Her eyes shine as she grins. "Can we do it again?"

I snort out a laugh. "Fuck yeah," I say before I pull her head close to me and meet her lips halfway for another soft kiss.

Even though I denied her before, even though I told her I would never go there, I couldn't fathom the idea of her asking someone else. For someone else to kiss her and taste how sweet she is, and touch her, and hear her moans and whimpers of pleasure.

I've denied it for too long. I want her, and she wants me for some reason. She trusts me and wants me to touch and kiss her, so I'm doing it.

She doesn't need this. I know that. I've told her that multiple times. A stupid list or losing your virginity isn't going to make her experience anything but pleasure.

She doesn't need to do any of the things on that list to be a normal teenager or have the 'experiences' she thinks she needs. She's perfect just the way she is.

But I can't go back now. She asked me to, begged me to. She wanted me as much as I wanted her at that moment. And nothing, and I mean absolutely nothing, could have stopped me from indulging in her needs.

"Rosie." I sigh, pulling away from her.

"Come on," she begs, her eyes still filled with lust from our kiss. "Don't back out now."

Back out? I couldn't do that if I wanted to. I'm so deep in this that I didn't even think about anything other than tasting her lips.

"I won't," I assure her. "But…"

"Oh great. There's a but coming. I can't wait." She rolls her eyes.

I brush my hand over my lips, trying to hide my snicker. "I need to know that we're on the same page," I tell her. "I want to help you, and I will, but you need to know where we stand."

She frowns a little but then nods. "I know what this is."

I don't know if I believe her. The last thing I want is for her to get unrealistic expectations this arrangement. "If you start to get feelings or blur the lines, we cut it off," I say, shaking my head. "I don't want to hurt you. So, if you don't think you can do it—"

"I can do it," she says.

I raise my eyebrow. "You sure?"

"Yes, Grayson. I can do it." She sits up straight. "I get it. No feelings, just sex, you help me, and I help you," she says with a wiggle of her eyebrows.

Christ, this girl is so fucking adorable.

I laugh. "Okay. Good." I bring my finger to her lips. I can't seem to stop touching her. "And we make our own list from now on. Whatever you want, you tell me, I want this to be about you discovering yourself and everything you think you missed out on, got it?"

She nods, and I let my eyes drift to her mouth. Her hand comes up, touching my arm, and I shut my eyes, running a hand through my hair.

"You can touch me."

I choke out a laugh. She catches on quickly. "I know."

"Then why don't you?" she asks.

I smirk, seeing her staring at my lips. "Because angel, if I start, I won't be able to stop."

She shifts closer to me, wrapping her arms around my neck. "I don't want you to stop."

Fuck. I want to so much. I unwrap her arms from around me and back away from her. "You're trouble," I say, feeling the heat rising through my body. I want to touch her and kiss her, but I also don't want to move too fast.

She shrugs, grinning, clearly pleased with herself. "Only around you."

I laugh. "So, I'm a bad influence? Is that what you're saying?"

"Something like that," she says.

"Why's that?"

"I don't know," she admits. "You make me want to be… different."

I shake my head. "You don't need to be different around me. Just be yourself."

She nods, and her eyes dip to my lips. I lick them instinctively, and she repeats my movement. She rolls her eyes. "You're really not going to touch me?"

I smirk. "Not tonight."

She smiles slightly, and the sight knocks me in the chest. I can't take it anymore. I close the distance and kiss her, hard and branding, making sure she knows where we stand. For as long as she wants to keep doing this, she's mine, and I'm going to have fun with her.

17

Little black bag

Rosalie

I push the doors open and make my way out of the restaurant. It's become one of my go-to spots, especially since it's only five minutes away from my apartment and serves amazing brunch.

I had no idea that brunch was a hard thing to get right. Maybe I'm just spoiled and a picky eater, but most of the time that I had brunch in Pennsylvania, I couldn't finish it.

This little spot served the best omelets and the best avocado toast that I've ever had. Seriously, those high price places in New York that my mother dragged me to don't even top this place.

"Thank you for paying," Madeline says.

"Again." Gabriella finishes for her. "Seriously, Rosie, you don't have to do that for us."

The girls know about my financial situation. I mean, you'd be blind not to. Most of the things that my mother bought to furnish the apartment would be enough to buy a car. But the girls never take advantage of it, or me. In fact, Madeline brings us coffee most mornings when we meet up and never asks for money, so the least I can do is buy them brunch.

"I told you, it's nothing."

"Yeah, for you. That omelet was $30. What kind of eggs are they using?" Gabriella asks.

I laugh, shrugging. "It tastes good, though."

Madeline grimaces. "I hate eggs. I always have to make myself forget I'm eating a chicken's embryo."

"Madi," Gabi scorns. "Why would you say that? I love eggs. You've ruined them for me now."

Madi laughs at Gabi's face of disgust, and I can't help but snicker too. "How can you love eggs?" Madi asks. "They don't taste of anything unless you use salt."

"The same can be said for chicken," Gabi retorts. "And who doesn't like chicken?"

"Leila," both me and Madi reply.

Leila's been a vegetarian for as long as I've known her. I was horrified one day in high school when I offered her a stick of gum, and she gladly stuck a piece in her mouth, only to look at the packet and see that it had gelatin in it. I mean, who knew gum wasn't vegetarian? Definitely not me.

"How is Leila?" Madi asks. "Last I saw her, she seemed stressed out."

"More than usual," Gabi says.

Leila *is* always stressed. She's somehow also the most laid back and carefree of the four of us. She's fun and likes having fun, but when it's to do with work or school, she closes up and becomes a hermit hiding out until she can get whatever it is, done.

But recently, every time I saw Leila, she seemed irritated, and I can pretty much guess why. "It's her roommate, I think," I tell the girls. "Leila walked into her room the other day, and her roommate was on Leila's bed with a guy."

"Oh my god," Gabi says, and then she nudges Madi. "At least I've never done that before."

Madi narrows her eyes at Gabi. "You wouldn't be walking if you had."

Gabi rolls her eyes. "You can stop with the empty threats. I haven't brought anyone back to the dorm after that 'incident.'"

"You mean the incident where I heard you have sex? How nice of you to have the common decency of not hooking up when I'm there."

"Well, you don't have to worry about that. Once we move out next year, we'll have separate bedrooms. I can be as loud as I want." She grins.

Madi stops and holds her hand up. "Um. No, you can't because we'll still share a wall."

Gabi shrugs. "I'll buy you earplugs."

Madi rolls her eyes. "Dear God, help me."

I snicker. "You two are moving out next year?"

"Yep," Gabi says. "I'm sick of dorm rooms. I need a place where I can leave a chocolate wrapper on the floor without Madi here, being passive-aggressive about it."

"Why would you leave a chocolate wrapper on the floor when we have a trash can? Plus, you're my best friend, so I can't be aggressive over it."

"Aw." Gabi coos, looking at me. "She just called us best friends."

Madi tries not to smile but ultimately loses and ends up laughing.

"How was the audition?" I ask Madi.

She groans, her eyes closing for a minute, and she sighs. "I thought it went well, but it's been a week, and they haven't called back yet, so…" she says, shrugging.

"I'm sorry," I tell her. I've seen Madi's audition tapes before, and she's great. I have no doubt that she'll be a famous actress one day.

She smiles weakly. I can see how much she's upset by it, but she still tries to put on a brave face. "It happens."

"Don't worry about it," Gabi says. "You're still in college. I know you'll end up getting the audition that you're perfect for, and that's perfect for you."

Madi squints her eyes, looking at Gabi. "Why are you being nice to me?" she asks. "It's scary."

Gabriella laughs at Madi. "I'm always nice to you."

"Yeah." Madi scoffs. "When you steal all of my snacks and then feel guilty afterwards, so you suck up to me."

"You know about that?" Gabi asks, her eyes widening.

Madi laughs, shaking her head. "Everything in my cupboard is empty. Did you think I just assumed it was a rat?"

"No, I thought you'd think it was a raccoon," Gabi adds with a shrug.

"How would a raccoon break into our dorm room?"

"I don't know," Gabi says. "You never said anything, so I thought you didn't know."

"Because I'm not going to scream at you for eating some snacks."

Gabi grins, throwing her arms over Madi. "Aw. How cute. You love me."

Madi rolls her eyes, stepping back from Gabriella. "I need to get to class. See you later, Rosie. And you too, snack hoarder."

Madi's already walking away when Gabriella yells back at her. "It was the raccoon."

"Weirdo." I hear Madeline mumble as she walks away.

Gabriella and I laugh as we watch Madi walk towards campus.

"Do you have class today?" Gabi asks.

I shake my head. "No, I only had one class. Do you have dance class today?" I ask, knowing she usually has a dance class booked for most days of the week.

She picks up her phone, looking at the time. "Yeah. It's in fifteen. I should probably get going," she says.

"Okay. Have fun." I tell her before giving her a hug, and she smiles back as we separate.

I make my way over to my apartment, dying to get my hands on a sketchbook. I've been doing a lot of sketching recently; I don't know why but my brain is a catalyst for ideas suddenly. Yesterday I came up with five new designs, which were some of my best work.

But that thought evaporates the moment I see a very familiar car. I know that car. I've slept on top of that car. All of a sudden, my brain is consumed with the thoughts of the other night. The bike, the lake, the kiss, the way I all but begged him to touch me.

And now that I see him, everything I felt with him that day is coming back to me. I feel my cheeks warm as I look at him leaning against his car, with a cigarette hanging from his lips. Those lips. I kissed those lips, and it was nothing like I thought it would be.

A girl's first kiss usually happens when she's young, maybe even before puberty, but mine was three days ago, with no other than Grayson Carter. And it was perfect. The way he kissed me was like he couldn't get enough of me like he needed me as close as possible to him. He was demanding and aggressive, and even though I had never kissed anyone before, he didn't seem to mind it.

He took it at my pace and waited for me to get comfortable enough to the point where he could kiss me as he wanted. I thought kisses were meant to be soft and gentle, and that's what I gave him the moment our lips met, but all of that was thrown out of the window the minute Grayson stuck his tongue in my mouth.

The groans and moans, the hair tugging and devouring each other's taste. That was kissing. That was what I wanted, and I didn't even know it. And I want it again.

"Hey," I say, approaching where he is.

His eyes snap to mine, and he lifts himself from the car and smirks. Just a twitch on the side of his lips makes my gaze drop to his mouth, reminiscing on that kiss. "Hey," he says, throwing out the cigarette. "I've been looking for you."

"Really?" Did that sound too desperate?

"Yeah," he says. "I've got a gift for you."

My eyebrows scrunch. "A gift?"

He smirks again and then leans into his car, through the open window, and pulls out a huge bouquet of flowers. Pink roses. They're absolutely gorgeous, and the fact that Grayson bought them for me makes them even better.

"You got me flowers," I say more than ask. I'm in disbelief.

He walks towards me and hands me the flowers. I take them from him and look down at them, unable to stop staring at them. Grayson got me flowers.

"Yeah," he says, sticking his hands in his pockets and shrugging. "When you told me that you buy yourself flowers because you don't have anyone else to buy them for you, I felt bad," he admits, making my breath hitch. "I know I'm not your boyfriend, but… we're friends, right? And well, you have me now, so I'll buy you flowers from now on."

He's waiting for me to reply, but I'm standing here, staring at him dumbfounded. *Grayson got me flowers.*

"I don't even know what to say," I finally speak up. "You didn't have to do that."

He shakes his head, reaching out for my hand. "I want to, Rosie. If anything, then just purely for the look on your face when I give them to you." His hand lifts and strokes my cheek, a smile spreading across his face. "It's priceless."

I smile, too, so wrapped up in this moment. I look down at the flowers in my hand, seeing how big and beautiful they are. I frown a little. They must have cost him a lot, and Grayson needs the money, right? "But… these flowers look expensive," I tell him. "You probably need the money. You don't have to spend it on me."

He grabs my face with both hands, cupping it while staring into my eyes. "Listen to me," he says. "If I'm kissing you and licking your body like it's a fucking feast, then the least I could do is get you some flowers." His thumb strokes back and forth on my cheek, and my breathing becomes heavy. "I don't give a fuck about the money, Rosie."

He leans in, and his lips meet mine in a soft, gentle kiss like I first gave him. But this time, he tastes of smoke, and the taste of cigarettes fills my mouth. I try not to let it affect me because his kiss is still perfect, but he must notice that I grimace because he pulls back.

He searches my face, his brows drawn. "What's wrong?" he asks.

"Nothing," I say way too quickly before leaning in to try and kiss him again, but he stops me.

"What's wrong, Rosalie?" he asks again.

I sigh, giving in. "You taste of smoke," I say. I see him frown a little, and I instantly wish I hadn't said anything. "I'm sorry. I just hate the taste, and the smell, and the way it made me feel," I tell him, honestly. "I don't know how you do it. It seems like every time I see you, you have a cigarette in your mouth. It brings me back to when I smoked on that day when you taught me, remember? Anyway, I didn't mean to hurt you or embarrass you. I just thought I should tell you, but it doesn't—"

He interrupts me with another kiss. This one quick and hard. Just the press of his lips against mine. "I'll quit," he says.

My eyes widen. "What? No. I didn't mean to upset you. I'm sorry, please don't quit this now. I didn't mean it. I love the taste. Do you have one on you now?"

"Angel," he says, laughing. I shouldn't have said anything. Now he wants to quit on me. That's the last thing I want. "Calm down," he says, still laughing. "I meant I'll quit smoking."

"Oh." I breathe out. My shoulders relax a little. "I thought you were quitting on us," I say. "I mean not on us, just this… arrangement. You know what I mean."

"I do."

"But you don't have to quit for me. I'll get used to it. I promise."

Isn't smoking hard to quit? And seeing as Grayson smokes every day, he obviously likes it, and I don't want him to quit just for me.

He shakes his head. "I don't want you to get used to it," he says. "You're right. It's horrible. I hate the taste too."

I squint my eyes at him. "That's not true."

"Yes, it is."

"No, it's not," I say. "You have one every time I see you."

He takes out the pack of cigarettes from his back pocket and crushes it in his palm. I gasp at the sight, but he just smiles. He disposes of it in the trash and walks back over to me.

"As long as I get to taste this," he says, running his thumb over my bottom lip. "I don't give a fuck what I have to give up." I stop breathing. I don't even remember how to breathe in this moment. "I want this more than smokes."

"You do?"

He nods. "I do."

I smile, and I can't help it. I don't care what he tastes like. I crush my lips to his and kiss him.

He pulls back after a minute and looks down at the flowers in my arms. "I didn't know if you had a favorite flower," he says. "So, I just got roses. It seemed fitting, you know… Rosalie."

I grin, knowing he thought of me. The idea of him trying to figure out my favorite flower makes my chest tight. "I don't have a favorite flower," I tell him. "I tend to get a new type every time. Whatever the saleswoman suggests."

He nods. "Okay then, useful information for next time."

"I told you; you don't need to do that."

He rolls his eyes. "I don't care what you say, Rosie. I'm buying you flowers."

I don't really want to argue with him, especially about him buying me flowers, so I smile. "Okay."

He lets out a laugh under his breath. "Okay." He grins. "But that wasn't the only surprise I had."

"There's more?"

He snickers. "You have no idea." He tugs on my hand until we reach his car, and he leans inside again, but this time, he pulls out a small black bag.

He holds it out, and I take it from him. I love surprises. I open the bag and look inside. My cheeks instantly turn red. "Um," I say, not able to make eye contact with him.

He knows I'm flustered because he laughs, and then he leans into me. "I want you to use it," he whispers. "Whenever you feel like you did when we kissed. Whenever you're turned on, use it and explore."

"You want me to use this?" I ask, breathing hard.

"Yes." He tugs my earlobe between his teeth, and I almost moan.

"How?" I ask.

He laughs quietly. "You put it between your legs and move it until it feels good," he says, with another tug of my earlobe.

"Okay." I breathe out.

"Yeah?"

I nod, and he grins. "I've got to go," he says, leaving a quick peck on my lips. "Have fun with your new present," he says, opening his car door and stepping inside. His tone is suggestive, and right now, I wished he would use his gift on me himself.

"Yeah." I swallow. "I will."

He smiles again and then backs out of the driveway and drives off. I'm stuck in that same position for who knows how long, just staring at the road where he drove off.

I eventually move my feet, making my way to my apartment. Once I get in, I dispose of the daisies I bought last week and replace them with the roses Grayson got me. I still can't believe he got me flowers.

I turn around and kick off my shoes and happen to glance at the little black bag standing on the counter in front of me. It's staring back at me, taunting me, daring me. I have never touched myself before. Until Grayson told me, I thought only boys did that.

Another thing that I've been sheltered from. My whole life is rose-tinted glasses, and Grayson is helping me remove them step by step. He's making me see the world how he sees it.

Grayson said it was normal. Girls can experience pleasure just as much as guys. If it's anything how he made me feel the other day, I can't wait to find out for myself.

I keep staring back at the little black bag, sitting there with a toy inside. When I looked at it, it didn't look intimidating. It looked kind of pretty. It's small and pink and honestly cute. I can't believe Grayson got this for me.

I feel heat traveling through my body. My face is hot, my neck is hot, and my whole body is hot all over. I swallow and head towards the counter, pulling the toy out of the bag. I hold it in my hand, running my fingers over it. How does this work?

My heart picks up speed as I stroll toward my bedroom. I feel like I'm doing something wrong, something naughty. I pull my clothes off, wanting some air to hit my skin, and settle in my bed under the sheets. I let myself breathe for a bit, trying to calm my heartbeat down.

I turn the device on, and the sound fills the room. The quiet buzzing of the toy surrounds me, and I press it against my palm, feeling it vibrate against my skin, making it feel numb.

I bring it to my body, pressing it against my chest, bringing it down until it vibrates against my nipples. I gasp, and a moan slips out when the pleasure coils through my body.

I close my eyes, imagining it's Grayson's hands, his mouth over my skin as I drag it down my stomach, feeling the vibrations all over my body until I reach the top of my crotch. I take a deep breath in and drag the toy down and fit it between my legs, allowing the wetness to cover the toy, making it so easy to rub it up and down. I press it harder into me until my back arches uncontrollably.

I press it again in the same spot, feeling my body heat up. I think of the kiss. My first kiss. How demanding and controlling Grayson was in that kiss. How he seemed to know exactly what I wanted when I didn't even know myself. My stomach cramps up, and my breathing becomes deep. A bead of sweat forms on my forehead as I hold the toy between my legs.

I remember Grayson's hand on my thigh, gripping it as he dragged it up higher and higher. I keep the toy pressed against that sweet spot as my hips buck up. My other hand grips the sheets between my clutched fists, unable to contain the pleasure running through my body.

It gets intense. So intense I close my eyes and muffle the noise into the crook of my elbow. I feel the strong feeling deep in my core, sizzling in my body until I find release, making me shake and writhe as the pleasurable feeling crests inside my body.

When I come down from the high, I throw the toy to the side of my bed and lay there, staring up at my ceiling, unable to move, breathing hard for a while. My whole body feels like it went on a rollercoaster. A journey with an unbelievable climax.

So, that was an orgasm.

Fun.

18

Just one taste

Grayson

I've been staring at the TV for who knows how long.

I'm barely paying attention. I keep looking at the screen in front of me, mindlessly watching whatever show is on. I don't even know the name or what is happening, and I can't think of anything other than Rosalie.

The look on her face when I gave her the flowers was the purest thing I have ever witnessed. The pure joy and happiness on her face made my chest tense. I want nothing more than to keep seeing that smile on her face.

I also wouldn't mind seeing her flushed and aroused again. The way she couldn't even look at me when I gave her the vibrator plays in my mind in a loop. Her flushed skin, the twitch of her lips, her eyes widening at the realization that I bought her a sex toy.

She admitted she'd never touched herself before, which probably meant she didn't know how to, so I figured a toy would help. I hope it did. I can think of nothing else but images of Rosie laying on her bed, naked with the small pink toy between her legs as she brings herself to orgasm.

Fuck. I groan, tipping my head back and closing my eyes. I want to see her so badly. I saw her just yesterday; I shouldn't be feeling like this. And these visits shouldn't be a common thing. No more than three times a week. That was the deal I made with myself.

Especially with someone like Rosie, who's new to this whole thing. Sex and intimacy, it could be so easy for her to mix the lines.

My phone rings on the nightstand, and I widen my eyes. Is she calling me? Does she want me to come over? I grab my phone, and my shoulders slump when I see the name on the screen.

I've been avoiding her for weeks. If I don't pick up, who knows what will happen to the money I need? She could withhold it from me and back out of our deal. I need to answer her.

I press the green button and silently curse at myself for answering, but I need to get it over with. "Hey, Mom."

"Grayson," she breathes out. "My goodness. I thought you were dead."

I snicker. "Not yet."

She gasps on the other side. "Don't joke about that."

"Who's joking?"

"Grayson. I'm serious. You haven't answered my calls in weeks. Weeks. Do you know how worried I was wondering if you were lying in a ditch somewhere with a needle in your arm?"

My jaw clenches. "I told you a million times before, I don't do that."

She sighs on the other end. I know she doesn't believe me. No matter how many times I tell her, she will never believe me, and they will never trust me again. "Grayson, why didn't you answer? Where have you been?"

"I've been right here in college, where you and dad forced me to attend, remember?"

"It's for your own good," she says after a minute. "You didn't want to go, and school is good for you. You need to be disciplined and reformed. We obviously did something wrong."

I groan. I don't need to be reformed because I'm not a fucking drug addict, but she never listens. I think the sight from that day will always haunt her, but it haunts me even more. I can never get the image out of my head as hard as I try.

The only time it seems to settle is around Rosie, and I don't even want to think about why that is. Maybe because the whole time I'm with her, we're trying to get through her issues, making me forget about mine, at least for a while.

"We want to see you," she says. "I'll pay for the flight, just… Please, son, come see us."

"What about dad? Does he want to see me?" I ask, already knowing the answer.

She sighs. "You know how he is, Grayson."

I laugh bitterly. Yeah, I know how he is. He's a pain in the ass who wishes I was never born. He hates me. I have no idea why, but the old man and I have never bonded before.

"Why should I come home when he can't stand to look at me?" I ask.

"Because he loves you, Grayson. We both do."

I roll my eyes. "No, he doesn't, mom."

"Your father… it's complicated, Grayson. Especially after what happened—" she says, making me flinch a little.

"So, you're saying it's my own fault that my father doesn't love me?" I ask in disbelief. I don't know why she's defending him so much. If only she knew that her sweet husband screws his assistants every day. If she only knew how many times the son of a bitch has cheated on her, then maybe she'd be on my side and see what a prick he really is.

"That's not what I said," she says, trying to backtrack on the fact she just told me I'm unworthy of my parents' love because of a mistake.

"That's exactly what you said."

"Grayson—" she starts, but I cut her off.

"What more do you want from me?" I ask. "I'm going to college, I'm keeping my grades up, and I'm staying out of trouble, just like you wanted."

She doesn't speak and doesn't make a sound. We just sit in silence. My words flowing between us. I know no matter what I do, they will never trust me and will always see me as a screw-up. Maybe I am. However, one mistake shouldn't dictate whether I need to earn my parent's love or admiration

"Come home," she finally says.

I scoff. "New York is the last place I want to go."

"Grayson, please." Her voice is low and pleading. I can imagine her frowning on the other end. "I want to see my son. We'll talk more about this when you come home. Just one weekend. We'll have a family dinner."

I can't even remember a time when we had a family dinner. Family dinner in my house consisted of my father staying long nights in his office and my mother eating alone. I'd grab some fast food and eat in my car.

And now she wants a family dinner. Spare me the theatrics of pretending we're a happy family. It's nothing but lies. "Fine," I agree.

"I love you, Grayson," she says. "You know that."

I sigh. "Yeah. I guess." I hang up the phone and tip my head back onto the headboard.

I love her too. I think. In the unconditional way, as in she's family. As in, if anything happened to her, I'd be heartbroken. She's my mother, so of course, I love her. But that doesn't compare to romantic love, which I know is bullshit.

There is no way you can love someone with everything you have and have it be the same unconditional love you would have for family. You can't love someone and then sleep with the first girl you see on the street. That isn't possible.

I just agreed to spend a weekend with my parents. I have no idea what I'll be walking into or what this dinner even consists of. Will it be just my parents grilling me again? Looking at me like I'm a crazy, deranged person for the worst mistake I've ever made in my life? I can't deal with that again.

Fuck, I need a smoke. I reach for my nightstand for the pack of cigarettes… which isn't there. Jesus Christ, I don't have any cigarettes. Because I quit smoking. Who am I?

I can't believe I quit smoking. At the moment, it was the only option. The only answer, the right answer. But now, I have no idea what I was thinking. I need the chemicals to do their job and calm me the fuck down.

I really need a smoke, but I guess that's out of the question now. The way she looked when she kissed me hit me in the stomach like a ton of bricks. I want to kiss the living daylights out of her every time I see her, and that won't be possible if I taste of smoke. I don't ever want to see that look of disgust on her face again.

And right now, I need to see her. I need to kiss her again. I need to be with her. I can't take my parents' bullshit anymore. At this moment, the only thing that I want is to be around her.

I lift off my bed and grab the keys from the top of my dresser and head out of the door.

Ten minutes later, I'm standing outside her door. I should have called first. What if she's not home, what if she's out, or what if she's sleeping? It's only nine, but what if she's the type of girl who sleeps really early?

I can't go back now. I'm here, and I want to see her. I lift my hand and knock on her door, staring back at the grey door, and a minute later, she opens it.

My eyes drift down her body, seeing her pajamas plastered to her body, making me groan. Little blue silk shorts hang from her hips, and a sliver of her stomach pokes out between the shorts and the matching silk tank top. Her nipples are visible beneath the fabric, and I have to swallow. My mouth is so dry at the sight of her.

Her blonde hair is pinned up in a bun, and her face is fresh, without an ounce of makeup. She doesn't normally wear that much makeup, anyway. Just the subtle pink cheeks and rosy lips. But without any makeup, I can see the little mole on her upper lip.

I want to kiss that mole. It's so beautiful. She's so beautiful. Christ.

If she's wearing pajamas, she must have been getting ready for bed. "Were you sleeping?" I ask.

She shakes her head, opening the door for me to come in. "No, I was watching a movie." I nod and step into the apartment. I didn't really pay attention to her apartment last time I was here. I was more focused on trying to get the drunk girl in my arms tucked into bed.

Jesus, this girl is loaded. I mean, who am I to talk, but seriously? Her couch is expensive as fuck. My mother has that same couch sitting in our living room, and this chick happens to have a ten-thousand-dollar couch in her off-campus apartment.

I snicker at the sight, scanning around the place. It's a one-bedroom, so not as big as my and Aiden's place. But she has a big ass kitchen, no island but a shit ton of counters. White, of course. Everything about her screams neat and clean.

I see the flowers I gave her in a crystal vase that must have cost a shit ton of money. A smile creeps up on my face. I can't help but think of the look on her face when I gave her the flowers. I love being the cause of those smiles and the way her cheeks get red. I love it all.

"You want to eat?" she asks behind me.

Yes. I want to eat you.

I turn to face her, and she's leaning against the back of the couch, watching me. "I just made some pasta, and there's a ton left over that I was going to eat tomorrow, but you can have it if you want."

I smirk. "You cook?" I can't think of this girl in the kitchen. She's rich. I know she comes from the type of family that hires maids to do everything. She wouldn't need to get her pretty little hands dirty.

She nods. "Martin, our cook, taught me. I'm not a Michelin star chef or anything, but I know the basics."

I do nothing but grin as I stare at her. I want to hear more about her life. I want to hear everything that this girl is willing to tell me. But I also want to shut her up with a hot kiss.

I stalk towards her, taking small step after small step to reach her. I'm so close to her, I tower over her, looking down at that angelic face.

"So, are you hungr—"

A yelp escapes her pouty pink lips when I interrupt her with a hard kiss. I press my mouth against hers, grabbing her face to keep her connected to me. The minute our lips meet, it's like a relief. My shoulders relax, and I melt into her. She wraps her arms around my neck and opens her mouth, inviting me in.

I suck on her tongue, and she moans into the kiss, and then, she copies my moves, sucking on my tongue until I groan. She's a quick learner.

"I'll take that as a no," she says, as she takes a minute to breathe, and she grins at me.

I shake my head. "I'm starving, angel," I tell her. "But for something other than pasta."

I see her grin for a second before I press our lips together again. I kiss her as we walk toward her bedroom. We're a mess of limbs and clothes as we step toward her bed. She reaches up and unravels her hair, letting it flow behind her back. She stumbles backward until she's sitting on the bed, and I'm standing above her, bending so that our lips remain connected.

I leave one soft kiss on that sexy mole on her upper lip and then pull back to push her onto the bed until she's on her back. I'm stretched out on top of her seconds later, and I hover on my elbows so that I don't crush her with my weight. My tongue is in her mouth again, sucking and licking and tasting her sweetness.

I grind my hips against hers. Between the roughness of my jeans and the thin silk of her shorts, she feels my erection pressing into her, providing the friction she needs right now. I thrust my hips again, and she gasps into my mouth when I press against her. She bucks her hips up, and her hands detach from my neck and make their way down to my belt.

My eyes snap open, and I pull back. “I’m not going to fuck you,” I tell her.

She frowns. “You’re not?”

I shake my head. “No, Rosie. Not tonight.” I drag my finger from her chin down the center of her breasts. “I just want to play with you for a bit.”

She’ll take any pleasure I’m willing to give her, I’ve gathered. Her breathing becomes fast and shallow as her eyes fill with lust and desire. “Okay,” she breathes out.

My mouth latches on to her nipples, sucking them through the fabric until the soft blue silk becomes wet, and I can see the print of her hardened tight nipples. I need it off. I pull the tank up and away from her body.

Jesus, those tits. She’s on the smaller side but still a handful. I do nothing. I don’t touch or lick. I just stare. Her nipples are so pink and small. They're so cute, just like she is.

She tries to cover herself up with her arm, and I pull it away from her body. “Don’t be shy in front of me, angel,” I tell her. “You’re perfect.” Pink tints her supple cheeks as she lets me feast on her with my eyes.

The last time at the lake, it was so quick, so rushed, I didn’t have time to appreciate her fully. But this time, I’m taking my fill.

My hands reach for her shorts, and her breath hitches. I watch her for a minute to see if she’s okay with this, and she lets out a breath. I pull them down her legs and almost choke at the sight of her pussy.

She must see the shocked reaction I have because she tentatively presses her legs together. "It's bad to sleep in underwear," she says.

I grin. "I second that." I wouldn't mind sleeping next to her, knowing she's bare under her shorts.

I look at the spot between her legs. I can see her soft blonde hair poking out through her legs that are clamped closed. I'm dying to see what she looks like.

"Did you touch yourself?" I ask her, wanting to know if she used my little gift to get herself off.

She nods.

I grin, loving the idea of her using something I bought to pleasure herself.

"What did you think of?" I whisper.

She swallows. I see her throat bob up and down before she answers. "You," she rasps out.

Fuck. I can't contain the groan that I let out, knowing I was in her dirty fantasy. I have all kinds of images running in my mind, but I want to see for myself.

I pick myself off the bed and head towards the nightstand. She lifts herself onto her elbows, watching me as I move around in her bedroom. I open her nightstand and smirk when I find the little pink toy sitting inside.

I head to the foot of the bed, where she's lying naked and waiting for me, and I stretch my arm out to hand her the toy. "Show me," I say.

Her eyes widen. "What?"

"Let me see you, Rosie. I want you to show me how you got yourself off."

She swallows again, and then her tongue darts out to lick her lips. "In front of you?" she asks.

"Yes."

"But." She falters, covering up her chest again with her arms. "That's private."

Jesus, this girl. I smile. "I had my hand on your pussy and my mouth on your tits, angel. You have nothing to be embarrassed about. I want to see it. I want to see you." I say, holding out the toy for her to grab it.

She reaches out and clutches the toy in her small hand, and I grin. I take a seat on the small, pink couch that she has in her bedroom, which just so happens to face the bed. I stretch my arms over the back of it as I lean back and get ready for the show.

She licks her lips again, still covering her body. I want to see all of her.

"Spread your legs, angel. I want to see." My voice is like gravel, consumed by lust. I'm dying over here, waiting for her to show me all of her.

She leans back on her elbows, making her tits the center of attention. She stares at me for a while, breathing in and out, before she parts her legs.

Oh, sweet Jesus. She spreads her legs apart, making her pussy completely visible to me. She's so pretty, pink, and glistening wet. She's drenched with her arousal, and she hasn't even started touching herself yet. The soft blonde curls cover her pussy, but when her legs are spread like this, I can see her wet, pink center.

I clear my throat, feeling my cock harden in my jeans even more than it was before. It hurts. It aches so badly, and I'm the only one to blame for my slow torture. But the sight of her naked and spread out for me has me wanting to forget about me and focus on her.

She brings the toy to her center, pressing it against her clit. She must have figured it out yesterday because, from where I'm sitting, she has no problem finding the sweet spot that makes her whimper. A sound so heavenly. I've become jealous of a toy for bringing those sounds out of her when it could be me.

"Jesus, that pussy is pretty." I husk out, earning a soft moan from her. I place my hand on my crotch, feeling my dick threatening to rip through my jeans. I give it a slow stroke, trying to ease the ache. "You're doing so good, Rosie."

She closes her eyes and continues pleasuring herself. The sound of the vibrator and her quiet moans fill the room. I'm breathless and painfully hard. This was a bad idea, sitting here torturing myself while I watch her. I need to touch her, to taste her, to be consumed by her.

I can't sit here and watch this any longer. The more I watch her arch her back and use her finger to toy with her nipples, the harder I get and the more desperate for her I get.

I fall to my knees. She literally has me on my knees, crawling to where she's dangling off the foot of the bed.

I run my hand up her thigh, gripping her supple skin, staring at the glorious sight in front of me. "Can I taste?" I whisper, almost like I don't want to break this moment. I'm right in front of her sweet pussy, so pretty and wet for me. "Just one taste," I whisper again and then look up to gauge Rosalie's reaction.

She keeps the vibrator on her clit, but her eyes are now open and hazy. "Yes." She nods. "Please."

That's all that I need. I dip my head, leaving a soft kiss on her thigh. Her hand is still between her legs, so instead, I tease her, licking and biting the soft skin of her thigh, dragging my tongue up until I reach her pussy. I dive in, flattening my tongue against her. My mouth is covered in her. She's so fucking wet that I could drown in her. She stops the vibrator and falls onto her back, giving in to the pleasure I'm giving her.

She tastes delicious. If I died right now, I'd die a happy man. I feast on her, licking and sucking and feeling her shiver under me. She's panting and crying out, her moans so sweet and gentle even when she's on the brink of an orgasm.

I lick her up, drinking up all of her wetness. Her thighs are coated in it, my mouth and face are coated in it, and I still want more. I don't want this to end, but she's close. I can feel it in the way she bucks her hips and twists her head from side to side as her moans get louder and louder.

Unfortunately for me, she's right there. Her back arches, and she stills, shaking as she comes all over my tongue. Fuck, I might actually die tonight.

When she finally comes down from her orgasm, and her breathing slows down, she jumps up onto her knees and wraps her arms around my neck. "Oh my god," she gasps. "You're so good at that!"

Fuck, if that doesn't make my dick press even harder into my jeans. "Yeah?"

Instead of replying, she kisses me, sticking her tongue in my mouth and kissing me hard and fast. When she pulls back, she's grinning from ear to ear. "Can we do it again?" she asks.

I laugh. She has no idea how much I want to do that again. And again and again, until she's a panting mess, unable to speak, begging me to stop. "Anytime," I say.

19

What are friends for?

Rosalie

I take the pin out of my mouth and attach it to the fabric, making it snug to Leila's body. She's used to this, so I have no issues with asking her to stand still or move when I need her to. She seems to sense it, which makes my job a hell of a lot easier.

Leila hasn't been the only person to be my human mannequin when I needed to visualize a design on a body. I've hired models before, especially when I was designing clothes back home, but it was a hassle trying to figure out the way they worked, the way their bodies moved and formed to the clothes. Having Leila here makes it so much easier to figure it out on one person first.

While I'd prefer for my concentration to be focused on the dress right now, especially since I'm afraid I might accidentally poke Leila, my head is somewhere else completely.

"I know, mom. I'm sorry, again."

After I ditched her plane ticket to go to New York, she hasn't called me back or even texted. I thought she'd be mad, furious even, and that she'd fly here and drag me to New York with her. She threatened to do exactly that. I didn't expect her to not react at all. That is, until now

I've been on the phone for nearly half an hour, trying to placate her for my not attending the charity gala. I didn't even want to go. I hate those events. They're nothing but tax write-offs.

She's been ignoring me for weeks. She didn't call or text or even answer my calls. She's been giving me the silent treatment. Either that, or she just forgot about me, which wouldn't be the first time.

I seem to be forgettable and invisible in this family. Nothing I do is ever good enough for my parents. Well, my mother. My father could care less. I wonder if he was like this with my brother, Travis, or if he was actually a caring, loving father to him. If so, I'm jealous I never got that.

I'm smart and educated. I get good grades, and I'm polite. I've never been in trouble, but it still isn't good enough for them. I tried so hard to make them appreciate me. I followed orders and did exactly as they wanted me to do. I never rebelled or tried to disobey them, but nothing worked. I think I'm at a point where I need to stop trying to get their validation, no matter how much I want it.

"Do you know how humiliating that was?" she asks.

I sigh, sitting back on my heels. "The cab was late, mom. I lost my flight, I couldn't go."

The lie rolls off my tongue with no effort at all. It was getting easier to lie. I am an expert at it now. I'm lying to everyone I know. My friends, my family, everyone.

Grayson is this huge secret in my life, and I'm not sure what exactly I'm hiding. He taught me about sex, how to feel good, how to experience things I've always wanted. Like my first kiss and my first orgasm. And my first hook-up, which were all perfect. But that doesn't mean I want to air out my dirty laundry for everyone to know.

No one needs to know about Grayson or what we're doing. I love how he makes me feel. Being around him is like being in my own bubble away from the real world. I can escape for a few hours with him and then return to my normal life like it never even happened.

"You could have bought another flight, Rosalie. You have enough money in your trust fund for that," she spits. "Or have you already spent it all on tattoos and drugs?"

Above me, Leila snorts and then covers her mouth. Yeah, Leila knew none of that even sounded remotely like me.

I clamp my mouth shut. She always finds a way to throw that money back in my face. It didn't matter that they left it for me to access when I turned eighteen or that it was rightfully mine. In her head, I owed her for it. I owed her for finally becoming my own person and living my life.

I don't think my mother wanted a daughter. What she wanted was another version of her that she could control and mold into who she was. She never earned a dime in her life. I don't think she even knows what working entails.

"No," I sigh. "I just didn't think. I'll be there next time."

"Good," she replies. "Then you'll be here next Friday for the cocktail party."

"Mom, I can't Friday, I have class."

"Really? Because Lizzie told me that you skipped class last Friday."

I still, looking up at Leila, and she arches her brow in humor. Yeah, I didn't tell her about that either. "Who's Lizzie?"

"The dean, Rosalie." I almost roll my eyes. Of course, my mother would be on a nickname basis with the dean of the school. "If you didn't go to class, then where did you go?" she asks.

A smile appears on Leila's face, no doubt wondering the same thing. What would I even say? *Oh, you know, I skipped class to ride a motorcycle with a drug dealer who then gave me my first kiss and nearly made me orgasm.* Yeah, no.

I hesitate. Not knowing what to say.

"Well?" My mom asks.

"Uh… I was sick," I tell her.

"Sick?"

I clear my throat, trying to cover up Leila's laughing. "Yes, mom. I got a cold and couldn't go."

"A cold? Did you go to the hospital? You know I have Dr. Derin's number. I'm sure he could make a house call to your apartment if you're not feeling well."

"Mom." I interrupt her. "I'm fine. It was just a cold, and I'm better now."

"Are you sure? I could call Dr. Derin."

"He lives in New York." I doubt our family doctor would be making out-of-state house calls.

"He could get a flight. Lord knows we pay him enough."

I sigh, shaking my head. "I'll be there next week, mom," I tell her.

"Good," she says. "Beth's son was so disappointed that you weren't there. He's looking forward to meeting you. And preferably in an appropriate dress. I don't know what you've been doing while in college, Rosalie, but you need to come with the attitude of the girl I raised."

"Dress appropriately, got it," I tell her.

"Tilly is coming soon to plan the party. I've got to go."

"Okay, mom. Love you."

"Love you too, Rosalie."

I hang up the phone and let out a deep breath. I thought I got out of attending the charity gala to virtually sell me off. But instead, I got myself invited to another one.

"Sorry about that," I tell Leila, pinning the hem of the dress a little higher.

"No worries," she says. I fix the dress to mold her body, and after a while, she clears her throat. "So, where did you go last Friday?"

I groan. "Not you too."

She laughs. "I know you weren't sick, which means it must be good if you'd lie to your mother about it."

"Why? Because I'm a goody two shoes."

"Yes," she says. I narrow my eyes at her, and she shrugs. "It's not a bad thing. That's just who you are."

I shake my head. "Yeah, well, I'm trying to change that."

"By doing…"

"Not answering that."

She laughs again, and I get up off the floor, spinning her around to view the dress from the front. It's a long satin green dress that hugs her curves and flows out at the bottom.

"It looks great." I smile at her. "Thank you again for agreeing to model for me again."

She's the best to work with. And obviously, seeing as we're best friends, it was the best choice. But no matter how much I try to force the money on her, she always denies it.

I get it. We're friends, and she feels bad taking money from me. At the same time, it's a stupid thing to decline. If I were to hire another model, I would have to pay them either way. The only reason I ask Leila to model for me is that she's around me often, and I already know her body, her measurements, and the way clothes fit on her. It makes it so much easier to get a design done.

"You don't need to thank me. It's not a big deal," she says, turning around to face the mirror. "I should thank you," she says, her eyes widening as she smooths her hand over the dress. "My butt looks good."

I let out a laugh. "That's your body, not the dress," I tell her. Her curves are perfect for the fit of this dress and make the fabric cling to her body while highlighting every dip and curve in her body.

"Trust me, it's the dress," she says. "You know, I'm going to an event this week. If you want, I can wear it to the party and promote it."

My brows snap up. "You'd do that?"

She shrugs, looking at me in the mirror. "Of course. Your designs are great, Rosie. They'll get the traction they deserve, and I want to be a part of that." She smiles. "Especially because I think it's amazing that you're designing a luxury fashion brand that's inclusive."

My eyes soften. "That was a given. I want everyone to be able to wear my designs." The thought of having a plus-size best friend and ending up designing a line that would be for straight sizes only would be like a slap in the face to her.

I wasn't even aware that there weren't many designer brands that offered plus sizes until Leila told me. It's the dumbest thing I've heard. People of all sizes love designer clothes, and they're missing out on a market with a lot of potential customers.

She laughs. "Yeah, speaking of, I'm keeping this."

I snicker. "It's all yours," I tell her. "After I make the changes." I snap my fingers. "Strip."

"Bossy," she says as she pulls the zip down and steps out of the dress.

"I'm practicing for when I'm a ruthless famous designer." I joke.

She places the dress on the couch and heads towards my bed, where her clothes are sprawled out. She starts putting her clothes back on, and I take a seat on the couch, folding up the dress so I can fix it later.

"Do you know where I can get drugs?" I blurt out.

She stills, her head stuck through her shirt as she stands there, frozen in place, gaping at me. "What?"

I pull my lip between my teeth. "I was thinking." I start. "I wanted to have the college experience that other people have, and that includes experimenting with new things."

"And you want to do drugs?" she asks.

I nod. "Yeah. Have you done it before?"

She sits on my bed, sighing. "Yeah," she admits. "Once or twice."

"In college?"

She shakes her head. "In high school. Jake was always smoking, and he gave me some to try." Her face falls a little at the mention of her ex-boyfriend.

"Did you like it?"

She scrunches her brows. "I don't know. It just made me a little drowsy and hungry, I guess." She shakes her head and pins me with a concerned stare. "What's this about?"

I haven't told her how humiliated I felt at the party when everyone practically gaped at me for not drinking to anything. I felt like an outsider, like I didn't belong all over again.

"I never got to do anything like that," I tell her. "You know how my mom was. I missed out on a lot."

"I get it, Rosie, but drugs, really?"

I shrugged. "Nothing too dangerous," I say. "Just a little weed or something."

"Do you want to talk about it?" she says.

I tilt my head. "Talk about what?"

"About whatever it is you're trying to escape from."

I let out a scoff. She just heard what I'm trying to escape from. I want some excitement in my life before I'm subjected to a life where I'm planning cocktail parties with my country club buddies. "I'm not trying to escape," I tell her. I don't want to go into the details of my impending doom.

"Really?" she asks. "Because I never see you anymore, and you've been skipping class, and now you're asking for drugs." She exhales. "Is there anything going on?"

"I promise, nothing's going on." I bite my tongue. I feel bad for lying to her, not letting her in on what I've been doing and who I've been seeing. But we said this would be a secret, so I don't want to break the spell of whatever it is we have. If I start to tell people, it'll become real. They'll ask questions about what we're doing and what this means, and I don't have the answers to that.

What even is my and Grayson's relationship? Fuck buddies? We haven't even had sex yet. Last night, he gave me two of the best orgasms of my life. But he left right after. He was hard; I could see it poking against the fabric of his jeans, and even though I didn't know how to please him, I wanted to learn, I wanted to try. But instead, he helped me into the shower, gave me a kiss, and left. By the time I stepped out of my bathroom, he was gone, and the apartment was painfully silent.

I wanted him to stay a little longer, and maybe even stay the night, but he obviously didn't want the same thing. I know he doesn't want me to catch feelings, but I don't think that will happen. I just like spending time with him.

"Yeah," Leila says. "I think I can get some for you."

I smile at my best friend. Grayson turned me down when I asked him for drugs. I'm not exactly sure why, but Leila was my next best option, and she's willing to deliver.

20

A bad high

Rosalie

I've never been happier to see my apartment building.

I'm drained. I can't think of anything better than going home after a long day of classes.

I push open the revolving doors and walk inside the lobby, seeing my favorite concierge ever. My smile grows. "Hey, Andrew."

His pale face heats with warmth, and he smiles back at me. "Rosie, darling. How are you?"

I sigh. "A bunch of homework and not enough time."

He laughs, and the sound makes me feel warm. Andrew told me he's been working at this apartment building for twenty years and has seen all of the changes the building's been through.

When I first moved in, I used to talk to him a lot. I find it endearing that he says I remind him of his granddaughter. I always wondered what my grandparents were like. My father's grandparents were loaded and bought him his first house, but I never got to know them because they died when I was still young.

I never really heard about my mother's parents. My mother once told me that she didn't have the life I had and wasn't given everything like I was. Other than that, I know nothing about them.

"Well, I won't keep you," he says. "I'll just give you your mail and let you go on your way."

He hands me a bouquet of flowers and a small cardboard box. I can't stop the grin that blooms over my face at the sight of those flowers.

"Got yourself a boyfriend?" he asks.

"No, just a friend," I say.

He shakes his head as I take the flowers and box from him. "Friends don't give other friends flowers, Rosie."

I smile sweetly at Andrew. "It's not like that. We really are just friends." *Friends who've seen each other naked.* But I don't mention that to him.

"See you later, Andrew," I call out as I make my way to the elevator.

I head towards my apartment door, unlock it, and step inside. I look down at the flowers grinning at the fact Grayson bought me flowers again. I replace the roses with these new ones. They're different this time but equally as beautiful. Blue. The most beautiful blue I've seen.

I notice a card stuck to the white paper the flowers are wrapped in. I pick up the card and open it up.

The woman said these were called tulips.

They reminded me of what you were wearing last time I saw you.

And now I'm thinking of your lips.

I can't contain the smile I let out. I love that he thought of me when buying me flowers. I love that he asked the woman what to buy. I love that he's thinking of kissing me again because that's all I can think of.

I'm thinking of that night all over again. Loving what and how it happened but hating how it ended. I haven't seen him since. We don't really talk outside of the 'lessons.' He texts me whenever he wants to see me, and I reply, but other than that, we don't really communicate. I never text him, and he's always the first one to reach out.

I don't want to be the kind of girl who blows up his phone. We see each other a few times a week, sometimes less, which is fine. I guess it's what Grayson wants, but if it were up to me, I'd be seeing him a lot more.

I pick up the cardboard box, opening it up to reveal two brownies. He got me brownies, too?

I reach for my phone to text him. I never do that, but this deserves at least a text. Maybe I'll even ask him to come over so I can thank him properly. I tap my phone, and it's black. I tap it again, but the screen isn't turning on.

I groan. It must be dead. I had it on the whole time in class. I usually turn it off so it won't accidentally go off in the middle of the lecture hall, but this time I forgot, and now it was dead.

I head to my bedroom and throw it on the nightstand, grab my charger, and plug it in.

My eyes catch Leila's dress still folded up and lying on the couch in front of me. Might as well get started on it now if I want it to be finished anytime soon. I lift myself off the bed and grab the dress, heading to the kitchen.

I place it on the table and bring my sewing equipment with me. The sunlight blares into the apartment from the huge windows, making it light up. The brightness of the apartment is what I love most about this place.

As soon as I start to unpin the dress, my stomach rumbles, making me groan. I forgot to eat all day, and I don't have time to cook, not when I need to finish this dress.

I eye the brownies on the counter and bring one with me. I look back at the cardboard box that's sitting on the counter. I don't know how long I'll be working on this, so I might as well have the other brownie now to tide me over until dinner. I grab both of them and head back to the table. Brownies for lunch aren't ideal, but they will do until I'm done with the dress. I ravish the brownies, dying to get back to finishing this design.

After about twenty minutes of trying to work on this dress, my skin feels cold. I shiver, feeling chills on the surface of my skin. I rub my arms, trying to warm them up.

I try to focus on the task at hand, but my mouth feels dry. I need a drink. I get up and fill a cup with water, downing the whole thing.

My head jerks when I hear a tapping noise. What the hell is that? I look out of my window, thinking it's rain, but it's pure sunshine out there. The tapping noise won't stop.

Tap. Tap. Tap.

I check the faucet to make sure it's closed. It is. I head to my bathroom to check the faucet in there. It's closed.

Tap. Tap. Tap.

My heartbeat starts to pick up. I feel it race against my chest. My breathing starts getting heavier and heavier. What the hell is that noise?

Something's wrong. I can feel it. I need to call someone. I rush to my bedroom, grabbing my phone from the nightstand and cursing when the screen doesn't turn on. I look behind the nightstand seeing the charger isn't plugged in.

I can't take it anymore. It won't stop. The noise is everywhere, and it's getting faster, louder, and closer. I drag my body down the wall, sitting in a ball with my knees tucked under my chin. It's everywhere.

The tapping noise doesn't stop. It will never stop. I press my hands to my ears, begging it to stop. But it doesn't.

In the distance, I hear a voice, and I burst out crying.

I feel a hand wrap around my wrist, and I try to crawl away, but the hand grips me tighter. I rip my eyes open and see Grayson crouched down in front of me.

Grayson is here. He'll save me, everything is going to be okay.

"Rosie, what's going on? What's wrong?" he asks in a panicked voice.

"It's everywhere," I croak out.

"What is?"

"I don't know. It won't stop, Grayson. Make it stop, please."

He tries to make me look at him, but I can't. I bury my face in my knees. "Make what stop?"

"The tapping noises. It won't stop. Tap, tap, tap."

He stays silent for a while. Grayson is here, and everything will be fine. At least that's what I tell myself as my heartbeat is faster than ever.

"Rosie," he says. "I don't hear anything. There's no noise."

But I hear it. It's everywhere, and I can't escape it. Tears stream down my face when I realize he can't help me.

I feel his hands on my face, cupping it and making me look at him. "Rosie," he says, his face looking pained. His Adam's apple bobs as he looks at my face. "What the hell did you take?"

"What do you mean?" I ask him.

"Your eyes. They're bloodshot. What the fuck did you take?" he growls, staring into my eyes.

"Nothing," I cry out, hearing the tapping noise get louder.

"Please, angel. Just tell me. What did you take?" he asks again.

I didn't take anything. I didn't do anything. I shake my head. "Grayson," I choke out. "Make it stop."

"Fuck, Rosie. Don't do this to me, please," he rasps, his voice breaking. "Not again."

I rip my head from his hands and press it into my hands. "I can't take it anymore," I mumble.

"Did you eat or drink anything?"

"I had the brownies you gave me," I tell him, the sound muffled from my head being buried in my hands.

"What brownies?" he asks. "I didn't give you any brownies."

I force myself to look at him, seeing his face pained and hurt and angry. His brows are furrowed, and the vein in his neck threatens to break through his skin. "You didn't?" I ask.

"No." Then, who gave me the brownies? "Were they edibles?" he asks me when I don't reply.

I shrug, tears still falling down my face. "I don't know. They didn't taste weird."

"How many did you have?"

I hold up two fingers, and his face turns red. He runs a hand through his hair and curses. "Fuck."

I cry out again, the tapping noise surrounds me.

"Rosie," he says. "Angel, look at me." He pulls my chin up until I'm looking at him. "I think you had too much. It's just a hallucination, okay?" he says, brushing my hair out of my face. "I need you to breathe for me. Can you do that?"

I shake my head. I can't catch my breath, and my heart is beating a hundred miles per hour.

"Breathe," he orders me. I try to take a deep inhale and feel my heartbeat slow down a little. "Good girl," he soothes, running his thumbs on my face. "Nothing's going to happen to you, okay? You're just having a bad high."

I exhale and nod.

He stands and holds his hand out. "Come here."

"What are you doing?" I ask.

"I'm going to help you through this."

21

Teach me

Grayson

I can’t believe she did drugs. What was she thinking?

When she asked me for them back at the lake, I didn’t think that if I denied her, she would find them from someone else. Who gave her edibles anyway? Is it some other guy that she's seeing? Ben Reed? He'd be the type. The thought repulses me. The idea of her going to somebody else to help her with something that I wouldn't makes me sick.

Jesus, the sight of her crying and bloodshot eyes almost killed me. I felt like I was back there, seeing him convulse on the ground while I watched it happen, feeling completely useless.

I wasn’t going to let this happen again. Last time I didn’t do anything, but this time it’s different. I’m going to do everything I can to help her. I’m going to get her through this, and I won’t let anything happen to her.

I pick up her small hand and grasp it in mine, feeling it shake as I drag her to the bathroom. The last time I was here, I left her in the shower and left her apartment. But not this time. This time, I’m staying with her for as long as she needs me to.

I turn on the faucet and fill the bath up. I sit her on the toilet lid and start to strip off her clothes. Her breathing seems to have calmed down a lot more, so maybe she's feeling better now, knowing she was just hallucinating.

I can't help but think of her here alone with no one to help her while she was experiencing a bad high the first time that she tried drugs. When I called her, and it went straight to voicemail, I knew something was wrong. I just didn't expect it to be this. Thank God that asshole concierge from last time wasn't here.

The bath fills up, and I dip my hand, making sure the temperature is right.

I hold her hand, guiding her inside the bath. When she's in and covered by the soapy water, I exhale. Letting out a breath from deep inside my lungs. She relaxes into the bath and closes her eyes, letting her head fall back.

We don't talk. I let her sit there, making her body relax and trying to calm her down. She had a huge panic attack from the hallucination. I hate the fact that she was going through that alone.

When she's done with the bath, I wrap her up in her towel, dry her off, and help her to her bed. I close all of the blinds, making the room as dark as possible, and get her underneath her sheets.

She drifts off to sleep almost instantly, probably not even aware of my presence. She seems fine. She doesn't look like she's panicking anymore, but I can't leave her. I won't leave her. Not again.

I sit on her bed, looking down at her face, feeling a knot the size of a rock stuck in my throat. It scared the fuck out of me to see her like that.

I don't know how much time has passed, exactly. I know it's been hours, but to me, it felt like minutes. I spent the whole time staring down at her with only the dim lamp to light up the room, making sure she was breathing and alive and that she was okay.

But when her eyes open and she stretches her arms over her head, with a cute little sound, I exhale so hard. She's fine. She's okay.

She turns and squints when she sees me lying next to her. "Good morning."

My chest hurts. I smile at her, tucking her hair behind her ear. "It's two am, angel."

"Oh," she says. "Good night, then."

I choke out a laugh and lean in to kiss her forehead. "Good night." I pull back and scan her face, worry settling in. "How are you feeling?" I ask.

She lets out a breath. "Good." Her face falls, a frown replacing her smile from before. "It was so scary," she tells me, making my chest tense. "I felt like I was going crazy."

I cradle her against me, hugging her tight to me. "It was just a hallucination. You're okay, Rosie."

She nods against my chest, and I pull her chin up to look at me. "Promise me, you won't ever do that again," I tell her. "Please, Rosie. I can't take it."

She nods again, her eyes shining in the dim room. "I promise."

I let out a breath of relief and kiss her forehead again and again. She lifts her head and places her soft lips against mine. Fuck, it feels so good. Just kissing her feels amazing. Having her lips on mine, feeling her breath mix with mine as she wraps her hand around my neck and pulls me closer to her.

I slide my tongue in her mouth, tasting her, licking her up like she's dessert. Her hips bump up and scrape against my dick. That brings me back to reality, and I hum into her mouth as I pull back.

I'm already shaking my head. "No, Rosie. We can't."

"Why not?"

I'm asking myself the same question as I run a hand down my face. "You've just been through something traumatic. You need to take it easy."

She closes her eyes and tips her head back into the pillow as she sighs. "I'm getting sick of being rejected," she says. With that, she opens her eyes and turns to face me. "I'm fine, Grayson, you helped me, and I'm so grateful for that. But now, I want you."

The words travel straight to my cock. Hearing her tell me she wants me is better than anything. "Are you sure?" I ask.

She nods, her tongue drifting out to wet her lips. "More than anything."

My mouth is on hers again, kissing her as she gasps and moans into my mouth, and I swallow up every sexy noise she lets out.

She rips her mouth away from mine, and her eyes are hooded and hazy. "I'm ready," she says, her eyes shining, making her intentions crystal clear.

Oh, Christ. “Not yet,” I tell her.

“Please?” she begs.

I let out a laugh. The way she begs me has me wanting to bow down at her feet and give her everything she wants, but I know that the first time I have her, it won’t be after something horrible just happened. Patience is hard, but she’s going to have to get used to it.

I shake my head again, leaning down to leave a soft, gentle kiss on her lips. “Let me play with you some more,” I tell her instead because ever since I left her apartment the other night, I can think of nothing else but images of Rosie coming all over my tongue, her moans and whimpers, and the way her body shakes when her orgasm hits.

I want it all again. I don’t even care that I went home with the mother of all boners. I didn’t want her to feel like she needed to return the favor. I just wanted her to feel it all. I mean, this whole thing was to help her, after all.

She nods, her lips parted as she stares back at me, and I grin. Fuck yeah. I dive back in, catching her bottom lip between my teeth as my fingers drift down to her breasts.

I let the tip of my finger tease her nipple, rubbing it and pinching it between my fingers until she’s rocking her hips, looking for my cock. I rip the sheets off her, and her hands grasp at my t-shirt, pulling it up.

I help her out and rip it over my head. She looks at me like she’s never seen a man’s chest before, and she probably hasn’t.

“You need to stop looking at me like that,” I tell her.

She frowns. “Why?”

“Because otherwise, this will be over before it even starts,” I rasp out. The feel of her eyes on my bare chest has me breathless. I get off the bed and pull my jeans down my body, standing in nothing but a pair of boxers.

I want to rip these off so badly. I want nothing more than to slide inside of her so deep, but I know how to control myself. And control myself, I will. Which means my boxers stay on.

Two seconds later, I'm back on that bed, hovering over her, tasting her body like I crave every night. I lick and suck on her neck, flattening my tongue against her skin and dragging it down her body. I flick her nipples with my tongue, feeling them so tight and hard in my mouth.

She arches her back, pressing her breasts into my mouth, and lets out a sexy little moan. Those sounds. "That feels so good," she says breathlessly. "I wish this feeling could last forever."

I grin. "I can make that happen."

I crawl down her body until my face is between her legs. I leave a soft kiss on her pussy, feeling the skin bare. I look down, and my brows furrow.

"You waxed?" I ask her.

"Yeah," she says, tucking her hair behind her ears. She's gone shy, and I don't like that at all. "Last time, I didn't come prepared, so I figured I'd wax if it happened again."

I look up at her face. "You're a woman. I expect hair, Rosie. I don't want you to think you need to prepare yourself for me. Whether you're waxed or not, I'll still eat your pussy like it's a fucking meal. You got that?"

She bites her lip and nods, looking down at me.

I lean down, leaving soft kisses on her soft, bare lips. Her breathing gets heavy, and I know I'm teasing her. Good, because this is going to last a long time.

I lick and suck until she's panting and bucking her hips to meet me halfway. Her breathing gets louder and heavier, and I know she's close. I suck her clit into my mouth hard, and when she starts to moan louder, I stop.

I pull back completely and stand up from the bed, looking down at her lying there, naked and wet.

"What…" she asks breathlessly. She's a cloud of confusion and lost orgasm as she props herself on her elbows to look at me. "Why did you stop?" she asks.

My lips twitch in amusement. "It's called edging, angel," I tell her.

"Edging?" she asks.

I nod, bringing my hand to run it up her thigh. "I'm going to make you feel so good," I tell her. "I'm going to lick you and suck you until you reach your peak." I bring my hand to rub slow circles over her clit. She starts breathing heavily again, and I pull my hand away. "And right before you come, I'll stop."

She looks pained. Her brows are in a knot as she lets out a frustrated sigh. "Why?"

I walk over to her nightstand and pull out her little pink toy. "Because," I tell her. "You said you wanted this to last forever." I press the button, making the toy roar to life. "And I'm going to make that happen."

She lets her head fall back and melts into the mattress when I press the toy to her clit, on the lowest setting. My dick is so fucking hard, I can feel the tip leaking pre-come. I rest my hand over my boxers, squeezing my dick slightly to ease the ache, but it does nothing for me. So, I let my hand drop and bring it to Rosalie's pussy instead.

I circle my middle finger against her opening as the toy continues to torture her clit. She lets out a breathy moan, making my dick twitch. She's so wet the tip of my finger slips in. Not too far, but far enough that she stills.

"You okay?" I ask.

"Yeah." She gulps. "Keep going."

I push forward, letting my finger slip until the first knuckle. Fuck. I groan, feeling how tight she is around my finger. I push in again, bottoming out, and she arches her back. She's way too close. I pull the toy away from her clit, but my finger stays inside of her.

She cries out, no doubt frustrated that I stopped her from coming again. But I want this to last forever, and having her edged and crying for release is sexier than ever.

"I was so close," she growls at me. I choke out a laugh, hearing how frustrated she is.

I pull my finger nearly all the way out and then slide it back in, crooking it to hit her g-spot. I know when she feels it because she lets out a high-pitched cry, clamping her legs shut around my finger.

"Open," I tell her. She does, and I rub up and down her thigh. "Good girl."

She lets out a whimper, and I groan. I fucking love those noises. "Jesus, angel," I breathe out, bringing the toy to her clit again. "You take my finger so well." She moans again, and I reward her with a higher speed of the vibrator.

The toy keeps her on edge. Every time she's close, I pull it away, but my finger never leaves her. I keep it lodged in there, hitting her sweet spot when she's been good.

I keep her close to climaxing for over half an hour until she's crying out, moaning relentlessly, and bucking her hips with abandon. She's so cute when she's a wreck like this.

"You're dripping, Rosie," I tell her when I pull the vibrator away from her again. She cries out again, and I grin. "It would be so easy to slide my cock inside of you," I tell her, letting my finger get covered and drenched in her juices.

"Please," she cries, tears streaming down her face. "Please, Grayson. Please."

"Please, what?"

"Make me come," she begs. "Fuck me, do whatever you want, just make me come, please." She bucks her hips again. "Please."

I take pity on her, seeing her cry and writhe, a mess underneath me, and I give her what she wants.

I brush her hair away from her face, her forehead covered in sweat. "You've been such a good girl," I tell her, loving how her eyes light up. "You want to come, angel?" I ask.

She nods vigorously.

I laugh and crawl at her feet. I want to feel her come all over my face again. I let my tongue circle her hard, wet clit, and at the same time, I push my finger inside of her. Two this time, and she's so wet, she takes me in without any restraints. I finger her while torturing her clit. She reaches up and grabs my hair through her fingers and pushes me down onto her until she moans so sweetly and finally finds release, coming so hard and shaking so violently under me.

I groan, sucking her into my mouth. I can't breathe. I'm deep in her pussy, covered in her wetness, and I fucking love it.

She cries out so loudly while she comes and comes all over my tongue. When she finally comes down from her orgasm, she falls back onto the bed, but I don't stop. I keep licking her until she whimpers, letting me know she's sensitive as hell right now. I indulge in one more lick, seeing her twitch, and then come up for air.

I lie next to her, seeing her so relaxed and satiated. God damn, she's fucking gorgeous.

She turns her head to look at me, her chest rising and falling as her breathing calms, and then, she shocks me by climbing on top of me until she's straddling me.

"Rosie," I warn.

"I know," she says, starting to rock her hips over me. "I just want to feel you," she says and presses herself down onto me. I sigh, my eyes drifting closed. She feels so good on top of me, rubbing herself all over my aching cock.

"I want you in my mouth," she says, continuing the slow roll of her hips over me.

I snap my eyes open, nearly bucking over when I see the sight of her naked, riding my cock over my boxers. "You sure?" I ask her.

She nods and shifts back to grab my dick inside my boxers. My hips shift off the bed at the feel of her soft hand tightening around my shaft.

"Fuck," I groan.

Her eyes lock with mine, and she swallows. "Teach me," she tells me.

Oh fuck yeah. "Spit on it." I tell her. "Get it wet for me."

Her eyes widen for a second, before she leans down and a drop of spit hits my shaft. She uses it as lube to stroke my dick. The feel of her hands around me is so good. Damn. I almost lose focus for a second, almost let myself fall into the pleasure before I remember this is new to her. She wants to learn.

"Tighter," I growl, eager to teach her.

Her hold tightens on my dick, stroking it up and down. "Doesn't it hurt?" she asks.

I shake my head. "It feels good, angel." She gives my shaft a squeeze, and I groan. "Oh shit." I'm way too close.

I sit up and take her with me until we're both standing. "On your knees," I tell her. I want to look down at that angelic face when she swallows me down her tight throat.

She obeys and gets on her knees in front of me, pulling down my boxers and throwing them to the side.

I fix her hair, collecting all of it in my palm and out of her face. "You look good on your knees, angel."

She smiles, her eyes glistening with need. "Do you remember when you tried smoking?" I ask her, and she nods. "Open," I instruct her, just like I did back then.

She grabs my dick in her hand and opens her mouth, her eyes locked on me. The sight almost makes me shoot, but I hold it.

I cover her hand with mine, and bring it to her open mouth. "Suck," I tell her.

She brings her mouth to the tip of my dick and gives it a slow suck, making my hand drop and my butt clench. "Fuck, that feels good." She continues her torturous, slow licks while she sucks the tip.

"Take more," I tell her. She fits more and more of me in her mouth until I'm nearly stuffed in her throat. She sucks and licks and bobs her head up and down, slowly sliding me in and out.

"Faster," I breathe out, and she obeys. She sucks me faster, taking me deeper into her mouth, and I can feel my release sizzle in my balls, ready to shoot at any minute. I pull out of her mouth completely and hold her head back, beckoning her to keep her mouth open.

I spit into her mouth, loving how some of it drools down her chin. She gasps, and I grin, bringing my dick back into it, feeling mine and her spit cover my wet dick. She grips my dick with her hand as she sucks me deeper into her mouth.

How the fuck has she never done this before? Christ. I give her hair a tight pull, hearing her gasp, which makes her teeth scrape my dick.

I groan, the tiny bit of pain somehow making this even hotter. My hips buck, thrusting my cock down her mouth. She gags, but she doesn't stop. Tears are streaming down her face as she keeps sucking my dick deeper into her mouth. I wipe away the tears and keep my grip on her hair.

"Shit. I'm coming." I warn her, expecting her to pull me out and stroke me through release, but she doesn't stop. She sucks and licks until I'm shooting down her throat, coming on a groan.

I pull back when I'm completely spent, and she licks her lips and grins up at me. Fuck, if that doesn't make me start hardening again. "How was that?" she asks me.

I lift her off the floor and kiss the shit out of her. That was the hottest fucking thing I've ever experienced.

22

Busted

Rosalie

"And that's how it's done." Gabriella takes a seat at our table, throwing down a piece of paper with a number scrawled on it.

She bet Madeline she could get a guy's number in less than a minute, and even though she seemed confident, I didn't think she'd be able to pull it off. I mean, sixty seconds is nothing, but she managed to do it.

Madeline's jaw drops. "Unbelievable. That took less than thirty seconds."

She shrugs, bringing her glass to her mouth and taking a sip of her drink. "I'm just that good."

Leila snorts. "No, he's just that horny."

"True," Gabriella replies.

Madeline studies the piece of paper. "You cheated."

Gabi raises her brows, looking offended. "What do you mean I cheated?"

"You probably told him about the bet," Madi says. "I'm not paying you."

Gabi shakes her head. "No, I won that fair and square. Now give me my $20."

Madi scoffs and takes out a twenty from her purse, handing it to Gabi, who takes it from her with a grin as she tucks it into her bra.

The door opens, and in come a group of guys, the laughter and deep voices filling the room. My eyes instantly snap up, trying to find Grayson.

I need to relax. It's been two days. It's not like I need to be around him every second of every day, no matter how much I want to. I can't stop picturing his face when he found me high and out of my mind.

The way he almost broke down, his voice cracking. I don't know what I would have done without him there. And once he left, I felt empty again. I need to not think about him.

But it isn't working. Every time the door opens, my head snaps up, trying to see if Grayson walks in. I don't know why my mind is consumed with him. He's not my boyfriend; that's clear. He's just a friend that gives me orgasms sometimes and takes me on adventures, which is totally normal, right?

I don't know how Leila and Gabi do it. How they hook up with different people so often and never catch feelings. I don't understand how they're so comfortable in sharing such a vulnerable part of themselves with just anyone.

I know I went to Grayson's house, willingly looking for him to take my virginity without even knowing the guy, but I'm so glad he denied me. The first time we ever hooked up was so much more fun and easier to let go because I knew him, and I trusted him.

"You looking for anyone in specific?" Leila asks.

I cock my head towards her. "No." I furrow my brows, wondering if she can see through my lies.

Her eyes narrow a bit, and I swallow. "Really?"

She seems suspicious. What would she be suspicious about? I haven't told them about Grayson, and it's not like we hang out together around campus. We're always alone.

The one time we went to a bar together, the only people who had seen us were the football team. She had nothing to be suspicious about.

I keep telling that to myself as I swallow the rest of my drink. “Yes,” I say, looking at the bottom of the empty glass.

“Okay,” she says, sipping her drink. Her tone sounds like she doesn’t believe me, which I don’t know what to do with. Do I sit here and try to convince her of the fact, or do I leave?

I choose the latter, standing up from the table. “I’m going to get a refill. You want another drink?” I ask Leila.

Her glass is still half full, so she shakes her head. “No, I’m fine.”

I nod, turning to Madeline and Gabi. “Do you guys want anything?”

They both shake their heads, and I turn, heading for the bar.

I recognize the bartender. He’s got a grin on his face as he hands a drink to a gorgeous brunette at the end of the bar. Jesus, he's a flirt. I mean, you would have to be with the kind of attention that he gets. He's handsome, tall as hell, and a basketball player. I can only imagine how many girls claw at his feet. And now has the ability to get me drunk, which makes him even more enticing.

He sees me approaching, and his eyes lock with mine. He gives me a warm smile, and I return it. This guy's smile could bring anyone to their knees. “Rosalie, right?” he asks.

“Yep, Aiden, right?”

He laughs. “Yes, that’s me.”

“So,” I say, taking a seat on the barstool. “You moonlight as a bartender?” I ask him.

He shrugs, leaning on the bar. “When I need to.”

"Great, then I'd like a margarita, please." I slide my fake ID towards him that the girls had gotten me. It looks real, and hopefully, Aiden won't suspect anything. He raises an eyebrow at me. I think he knows I'm not twenty-two, as the ID suggests, but he doesn't seem to care.

He nods, stepping back. "Coming right up."

He makes the drink in a flash. One minute I'm looking behind my shoulder at that damn door again, and the next, I turn my head, seeing the drink in front of me.

I hand him the cash, and he shakes his head. "No need," he says. "It's already been paid for."

My brows furrow. "By who?" If he's about to tell me he paid for my drink, it's about to get awkward as hell. He's attractive, sure, but I'm hooking up with his roommate, who I'd rather be with right now.

He smirks and gestures to my left with his head.

I turn and see a guy sitting next to me. "By me," the guy says. His striking green eyes wink at me as he flashes a grin. "Hi."

His hair is tousled with dark blonde strands. He looks like a model or a surfer. He's attractive, sure, but I feel nothing when I look at him.

"And your name is?" I ask him.

"Mark," he says, scooting closer to me. "What's your name?"

I bite my tongue, holding out the $10 in front of me. "Not interested," I say. I don't want to be rude. I don't want him to get the wrong idea.

He chuckles, not taking the money from me. "How weird. My last girlfriend's name was the same, and we ended up dating for two years."

I lift my brows at him. "Really? You're asking me out by talking about your ex?"

I can see why Gabriella got that number so quickly. If this is what guys think are good pick-up lines, I'm suddenly not so surprised they gave in so easily to Gabi.

He shrugs. "I thought a joke would help break the ice."

"Consider it very much intact still."

I slide the money over to him, but he makes no move to retrieve it. "Playing hard to get, huh?"

I resist the urge to roll my eyes. Seriously? "Nope," I tell him. "Just not interested, so take the money, I wouldn't want you getting the wrong idea."

"Not interested," he muses, scanning my face. "And why's that?"

"Because I have a boyfriend," I blurt out. I bite my tongue, not wanting to say anymore. The idea of having a boyfriend doesn't scare me. What does is that Grayson's face popped into my mind when I muttered those words. He isn't my boyfriend, he's nothing. I need to keep reminding myself of that.

Mark finally gives up. He slides the money back to me. "Keep it," he says, taking a sip of his drink and then sighs. "He's a lucky guy."

I smile, trying to make him feel a little worse about being rejected. "Thanks."

With that, I stand up and make my way back to the table, where Leila is already looking back at me with that same suspicious look on her face.

"Who was that?" she asks when I sit beside her.

I shrug. "I don't know. He bought me a drink and tried to ask me out."

“And you said no?”

I take a sip of my drink. “I said no to him, I said yes to the drink.”

“Why did you say no?” Gabriella asks. “He’s cute.”

“Not interested.”

“Hmm,” Leila murmurs.

I sigh, turning to face her. “What is it? I know you have something you want to ask me, so do it already.”

“Does the fact that you’re not interested have anything to do with Grayson Carter?” she asks, making my face drain of its color. How the hell does she know about Grayson?

“What?” Gabriella shrieks. “Grayson Carter?”

“What’s going on with you and Grayson Carter?” Madeline asks, sounding as shocked as Gabi did.

“Nothing,” I lie. “Nothing’s going on with Grayson.”

The girls don't take my bullshit. They give me a look of disbelief and then turn to Leila, who seems to know something since she's smiling.

“He called me yesterday,” she says. “And ended up giving me what could only be described as a lecture about the danger of drugs.” She smiles at me. “I didn’t know whether to be pissed at him or grateful. He seemed like he was really worried about you.”

I swallow. “He told you about that?”

She nods, her eyes softening as a slight frown forms on her face. “He told me you freaked out and ended up having a hallucination, and he found you having a panic attack.”

“What?” Gabriella shrieks again.

“Is this true?” Madi asks.

“Yeah,” I admit with a nod.

Madi's face turns pained. "You gave her drugs?" she asks Leila.

"She asked me for it," Leila says. "I didn't think she'd be able to smoke a joint, so I got her some edibles. I thought they'd be better."

"How did you even get it?" Madi asks.

"I asked this kid in my business class who always comes in high. He cooked up a batch of brownies and gave me a few."

"Are you okay?" Gabi asks me.

"Yeah," I reassure them. "I'm fine. It was just scary."

"I texted you," Leila says with a frown. "I went over to your apartment, but the concierge said you weren't inside, so I left the package with them and texted you to let you know." She shakes her head, her brows pulled together. "I'm so sorry. I should have been there with you."

"My phone was dead," I tell her. "I didn't see the text." The next morning, I woke up with Grayson lying beside me, sleeping next to me. I thought he would have left after we hooked up, but he stayed. And when I checked my phone, Leila's text was there, telling me she got me pot brownies and to wait for her. I told Grayson about it, but I would never have thought he'd call Leila.

"It's all my fault," she says. "I should have been there. I didn't know you'd react like that."

I don't blame Leila. It wasn't her fault. It was just bad timing. The text was enough, it was just bad luck that my phone was dead, and I didn't end up seeing it.

"Me neither. I didn't know they were edibles, and I was starving, so I had two."

Leila closes her eyes, a pained expression painted on her face as she mutters 'Mierda' under her breath.

"This makes me want to do drugs even less than before," Madeline says.

"Not everyone has a bad reaction like Rosie did," Gabi says, leaning back on her chair. "When I smoked weed, It was great."

"Yeah." Leila agrees. "I just felt relaxed."

I exhale. "What I felt was the furthest from relaxed." It sucks that I had a bad reaction to it the first time I tried it.

"Why did you ask Leila for drugs?" Madi asks.

I shrug. "I don't know. I just wanted to try it, I guess."

"And Grayson Carter?" Gabi asks. "What's that about?"

"Nothing," I say, sipping my drink. When I look up, all of them are staring back at me, waiting for me to explain. I sigh. "He just happened to be there. He's helping me with something."

"With what?" Leila asks.

"Something," I say with a shrug.

"Are you hooking up with Grayson?" Gabi asks.

I don't reply. Instead, I take a long sip of my drink, wanting to avoid answering.

She gasps. "Oh my god, you totally are."

Leila laughs. "Who are you, and what have you done with Rosalie Whitton?"

"I want to reinvent myself," I tell them. "I'm becoming a different version than the Rosalie Whitton you know."

"But I love her," Leila says. "She's my best friend."

I shake my head. "She's boring."

"Rosie. You couldn't be boring if you tried." Leila says, repeating her words from the party.

Madi nods. "I second that."

"I third that," Gabi mumbles, holding up her hand in the air.

"That doesn't make sense," Madi says to Gabi.

She rolls her eyes. "You know what I mean."

"I never know what you mean," Madi says, making us all laugh.

"Do you have plans tomorrow?" Leila asks. "I was thinking of going to the party the football team is hosting."

I groan. "I can't. I have to go to New York." I close my eyes, regretting my decision to say yes to attending the event.

"I've always wanted to go to New York," Madi says. "Fashion capital. It sounds amazing."

I nod. "It is when I don't have to be around my mother. She drains me."

"Then don't go," Gabi says. "She can't exactly ground you."

I nod. "True, but she's relentless. She'll never stop. It's better if I get it over with than have her yelling in my ear for hours."

Gabi glances at Madi's phone that's sitting on the table. "What time is it?" she asks.

Madi checks her phone, then turns to Gabi. "Then-thirty, why?"

Gabriella stands from the table, picking up her drink and downing it before placing it back on the table. "Because I've got to go."

"Where are you going?" I ask.

"Nowhere. I'm just tired." She opens her mouth to imitate a yawn that's obviously fake. "Good night," she says before turning around and heading out of the door.

We stare at the door that closed behind her, wondering what the hell just happened. Leila and I look at Madi, waiting for her to explain.

She shakes her head. "Don't ask me," Madi says. "I can't keep up with her."

We all laugh at Gabi's theatrics, but in the back of my mind, I keep thinking about tomorrow, dreading going to New York, dealing with everything I'm trying to run from.

23

Mother of pearls

Rosalie

My tongue runs over my lips as I take a sip of my mojito.

I look over my shoulder seeing my mother in the corner, surrounded by three other women, all carrying pearls around their necks. They probably cost more than the tuition I paid to Redfield.

She's distracted. That's perfect. I turn back around and down the drink. If my mother sees me drinking, I'll no doubt get an earful, but I need something to take the edge off.

She's been after me all evening. I got on the flight less than five hours ago, and now I'm surrounded by people I've been trying to escape for the past five months.

I don't belong here. I might have once upon a time, but I know this isn't the place for me. I don't want this to be my life, and I don't want to become my mother.

I let out a breath as I swirl the now-empty glass in my hand. I've been trying to hide in the corner of the room ever since I got here.

"Rosalie." My mother calls from the other end of the room. I turn and am met with eyes all looking at me as she hauls me over. "Come here," she calls out.

I sigh and make my way over to my mother and her friends. I smile and greet the other women. They barely register a 'hmm' my way, but I don't take it personally.

"Rosalie, you've grown up so much," my sister-in-law, Sarah, says. My eyes drift to her round belly. She's almost six months pregnant. I didn't even know they were having a baby until tonight. That's how much my brother and I talk. I can count the number of times on one hand that I've talked to him since he moved out. My brother and I grew up in the same house, but with a seven-year age gap, we were practically strangers living together.

"Yes," my mother says. "She's old enough to start her own family." She smiles down at me, and I resist the urge to grimace. I can't imagine having a baby this early. My mother got married and pregnant straight after high school, but that isn't me. I don't want a family for a long, long time.

My mother points to the woman closest to her. She looks just like my mother, blonde hair, blue eyes, and high cheekbones. Ears and chest covered in jewels. The only difference is my mother doesn't have a botched Botox.

"This is Beth." My mother says. "Remember I was telling you about her son?" I barely nod at the woman in front of me as she looks me up and down, no doubt trying to figure out if she thinks I'm good enough for her son. Well, there's nothing to worry about. I'm not interested.

"Jackson, come here," Beth calls out to her left, and I turn to see a tall man with bright blue eyes smile as he walks into the huddle of my mother's friends. He flashes a smile, and I smile back. He's definitely attractive and young, as opposed to the other men my mother's been trying to set me up with tonight. Though, I'm still not interested.

He grins. "You must be Rosalie."

I nod. "Yeah, that's me."

Rosalie:

Can't. I'm in New York, meeting my new husband.

Grayson:

Yeah? Any luck?

I'm coming back as an engaged woman.

Rosalie:

I snicker as I press send. Three little dots appear and disappear on the screen, I stare at my screen, waiting for him to reply, but he doesn't.

Rosalie:

Kidding.

I reply when he doesn't answer me. After a minute, another text pops up.

Grayson:

Don't play with me like that, angel.

I smile at my screen, that nickname will never get old.

Grayson:

When do you get back?

Rosalie:

Not until Sunday morning.

Grayson:

Are you trying to run from me? Because let me tell you, Rosie, no matter where you go, I will scour the earth to find you.

I feel a twinge in my chest reading those words from him. I would never want to run from him. The only thing I'm thinking about is how much longer until I go home to him.

Rosalie:

I never want to run from you.

Grayson:

Thank fuck for that.

Send pics of your outfit.

My brows draw together.

Rosalie:

You want to see my outfit?

Grayson:

Rosie. Every time I see you, I don't know whether I want to take you out of your clothes or fuck you in them. They drive me crazy. Everything you wear looks amazing on you.

I press my thighs together, looking around to check if anyone can tell I'm having dirty thoughts right now. The nights between Grayson and me flash through my mind, wanting to book a plane ticket back home this instant.

Rosalie:

Ok. I will.

I take a deep breath, trying to compose myself, and press send.

One more day. And then I can go home. I can see Grayson again. The thought makes the rest of this night tolerable.

24

Au revoir to my dreams

Rosalie

I feel like a stranger in my own room.

I haven't been here in so long. Realistically, it's only been five months since I last woke up in my childhood bedroom, but the past five months have felt like an eternity. I don't feel like I can relate to the girl I was five months ago. I've changed.

My room is exactly how I left it. And being back here makes me realize how empty it feels. The beige comforter, beige curtains, beige rug. The room of a New York princess.

I remember the first time I ever saw Leila's house. It was chaos. Color, smells, flavors, mess. It was a home. It was a home with a loving family. And when I went back to my house, I saw everything differently. This wasn't a home. It was a museum. A gallery of the perfect family. But we were anything but.

I step out of my room, making my way to the terrace. I step outside, seeing my father standing by the table, talking to someone on the phone. He doesn't even look my way, he just walks back and forth around the terrace. My mother's sitting at the table, texting away on her phone.

"Good morning," I say, taking a seat at the table.

My father glances at me and then turns back around. "Hold on, there's too much noise out here," he says to whoever he's talking to and then leaves. What a big happy family.

My shoulders slump, feeling a little deflated that my dad just ignored me. I try to stuff those emotions down and take a bite of toast instead.

"Rosalie. Good," my mother says, looking up as if she only now realized I was here. "I was thinking, do you want to go shopping tomorrow? You know, like old times?" She smiles at me.

I squint at her, taking a sip of my orange juice. "Mom, we've never been shopping together."

She rolls her eyes. "Well, we can make up for that now, can't we?" she says before looking back down at her phone, texting away.

I shake my head. "No, mom, I've got to go back to Redfield tomorrow."

She lets out a breath, places her phone down on the table, and interlocks her hands in front of her. "Rosalie, sweetheart. What is it about this college? Is this about a boy? Is that why you're so hellbent on ruining everything we gave you?"

I frown at her. "Ruining? Mom, I'm going to college because I want to. I want to become my own person. I want to design clothes. I want to start my own clothing line. Why don't you understand that?"

She sighs, shaking her head at me like she's disappointed. I've seen that look plenty of times. She's always disappointed in me. "I just don't understand why you feel the need to throw away all the resources you could have," she says.

"Mom. I don't need your resources."

Her brows raise. “You wouldn’t have gotten an interview with Emily Livingston if it wasn’t for the Whitton name.”

I realize that’s true. Only the elite with connections can get a hold of whatever they want and need. But it doesn’t mean I want to be a part of this world.

“Why are you so against me attending college? Travis went to college. He graduated as a business major. You didn’t try to stop him. You encouraged him. Why did you accept my brother’s dream but not mine?”

Her mouth drops open a little in disbelief. “Rosalie. I want everything for you,” she says, placing a hand on her chest.

I let out a laugh. “Sure seems like it,” I mutter, taking another sip of the orange juice.

My mother doesn’t say anything. She’s quiet, silent. Looking at me with an expression I can’t decipher.

She lets out a breath. “I wasn’t always like this, you know.”

My eyes snap towards her, brows furrowed. “What do you mean?”

“I mean, I didn’t come from this life. I didn’t have what you had,” she tells me. I see a little sadness in her eyes as she talks about it. “I didn’t have food for a month.”

“What?” I ask her in disbelief.

She nods. “If it wasn’t for one godsend of a neighbor, me and my sister wouldn’t have survived.”

I’m more confused than ever. I wasn’t aware that my mother had any family, let alone a sister. “Your sister?”

She nods. “I’m sorry I never talked about her before,” she says. “She died before you were born. It was hard to talk about it.” Her eyes drift closed for a second. “Her name was Kelly. She was my little sister. She reminded me a lot of you,

you know," she says, the corner of her mouth lifting in a small smile. "We were very close. And I was supposed to protect her."

"What happened?" I ask.

"My parents were neglectful. They would leave for days at a time. We never knew when they would be back, but they always came back. Until they didn't."

"Mom."

"I tried to make it work. But I was only ten at the time," she tells me. "I couldn't do anything. The neighbor noticed that my parents hadn't come home, and she saved us."

"Mom," I say again because I don't know what else to say. I had no idea that my mother had gone through that.

She shakes her head a little. "The point is, I didn't have what you have. That neighbor saved us. She took us in and raised us as her own. We had food on the table, a good home, and I went to a good school, where I met your father. And as soon as I stepped into his world, I never wanted to look back. It was a complete 180 from how I grew up, and I knew I wouldn't give it up."

She gives me a weak smile, and I think I get it now. Why she's so adamant about me taking advantage of everything we have.

"Kelly was the opposite," she says. "She was kind of like you in a way. She didn't want the money or the life that I did. She got in with the wrong crowd, and she, um…" my mother breaks, tears falling down her face. I don't think I've ever seen my mother cry. "She was in the car with her friends who were drunk and…" She says, shaking her head. "I couldn't protect her, but I don't want to repeat the same mistakes again. I want to protect you. I need to. I want you to have the best life possible, Rosalie. I felt abandoned. Neglected, like I wasn't wanted. I never want that for you, Rosie."

I swallow. "Mom. I felt like that all the time growing up. I still do." I tell her.

She flinches like I slapped her. "What are you talking about?"

Does she really not see it? "Dad doesn't acknowledge me. You never seem to be happy with what I do, no matter how hard I try. I try so hard." I say, my voice breaking a little.

She reaches out, placing her hand on top of mine. "Rosie. I'm so sorry, sweetheart. I never meant for you to feel that way. Your brother followed the rules and did everything we wanted him to do. But you, you were so different. Dear god, you wanted to go to public school," she says with an eye roll, making me laugh through the tears. "I just didn't feel like I could relate to you anymore."

I guess I get where she's coming from, dealing with all of that when she was younger. But I am not her.

"Mom. I'm different. The things I want are different than what you wanted."

She nods. "I know that, Rosie. I think… I think I'm starting to see that you won't be like me. And that's okay."

She squeezes my hand, and I sigh. "Why does dad avoid me?"

She lets out a breath. "I don't think he knows how to be a father. He never took care of your brother. He wasn't an active dad, you know. We had people for that. I never had to get my hands dirty with the baby stuff."

I look up at her. I feel like I'm seeing my mother completely differently. She needs this life. She needs the money and country club because she didn't grow up with it.

I did, and it's the farthest thing from what I want for my life. "I want to go to college, mom," I tell her. "I want to find myself and follow my dreams. And you have to accept that."

She lets out a breath and then nods, giving me a smile. "I think I spent so long trying to fix the mistake I made with Kelly and trying to deter you from becoming her. But you're not her. And you're not me. I'm starting to see that it's okay. If this is what you want to do, then I will support you, Rosie. I just... are you not going to attend the meeting today? Because Emily Livingston is a powerful woman, and if you stand her up, it will look very bad on the Whitton name."

I let out a laugh. "Yes, I'm still going to go. I can't waste an opportunity like that."

She gives my hand a squeeze. "I love you, Rosie. You know that, right?"

"I know, mom. I love you too, mom."

She smiles at me, taking a sip of her orange juice. "So, about Jackson. Are you completely sure you don't want to give it another go?"

"Mom."

"I was only asking, sweetheart." She smiles when I roll my eyes. "Was worth a try."

"Thank you for waiting," Emily says as she sits down at the table in front of me. She's right in front of me. The woman is a legend. One of the first designers I admired. And here I am, having lunch with her.

"It's not a problem," I tell her. I've been waiting for over twenty minutes, but Emily Livingston is a busy woman, I'm sure. I'd wait an hour for a meeting with her. "I'm happy you wanted to meet," I tell her.

"Of course," she says. "Your mother is a wise woman. She vouched for you and said that you'd be the next, well...me," she says, laughing.

"She said that?" I have to admit, it's a little crazy to believe that my mother would say that about me. But I guess I don't know my mother as well as I thought.

"She did," Emily says, interlocking her hands in front of her. "She also said you started very early. That's good, as you're so young."

"I guess I did. I love clothes. My mother used to sneak me in to see the runway shows ever since I was twelve. I fell in love with the designs. The way clothes could tell a story, invoke emotions, it was art."

She nods, smiling. "That's a good response," she says, taking a sip of her coffee. "Do you have your portfolio with you?"

I nod, taking out my binder from my purse. "Yes, I brought it with me." I hand over the binder to her as she opens it up and studies the years of designs I have done.

I started designing my own clothes when I was around thirteen, but ultimately started making my designs into reality when I was fifteen, so I have years of trial and error, with only the best of designs in that portfolio.

I know I'm good and that my designs are innovative, but does that stop me from psychoanalyzing every expression on Emily's face? No. Any time she hums, I start to panic, and when her eyes widen, my heartbeat picks up. I know I'm good enough, but I've had years of the opposite being engrained into me, and despite never being enough for my parents, I know my designs tell a different story. This is what I'm meant to do.

She continues scanning through my designs, and when she closes the binder, she has a warm smile on her face. "I love them," she says. I let out a breath of relief. "I think you'd be a great fit for our line. The designs are new, fun, and absolutely gorgeous."

"Thank you, I really appreciate that," I tell her.

She nods. "Good talent needs to be recognized, and you," she says, pointing at me, "have talent."

I grin. Hearing it sounds so good. And to hear from Emily that she loves my designs makes me believe I did the right thing by going to college and pursuing my dream of fashion.

"I'd love to hire you for our team of designers. You have the eye for what looks good and what's trendy and what will make Livingston Couture a successful business," she says, grinning, and I let out a laugh. She was in Forbes as one of the highest-paid women. Livingston Couture is one of the biggest high fashion companies, but I guess the desire to be better never ends.

"I'd love to be part of your team," I tell her, almost jumping out of my seat. Working for Emily Livingston? That's a dream come true.

"Great," she says. "That's what I like to hear." She smiles. "However, this job opportunity has some stipulations." She clears her throat. "You'd have to move to Paris."

My smile drops. Paris?

"I'd love to have you on my team, but the New York offices are full. Paris fashion week starts later this year, and most of the work for that is done locally. If that's something you can do, I'll gladly give you a place on my team."

I nod, swallowing. “I’d love to move to Paris. But I’m currently still in college, and I’d really like to graduate before that. Would that be possible?”

She studies me for a second before nodding. “I understand the need for an education, especially when you want to get a job in design, but I’m offering you a job right here, right now, and I can’t promise the same opportunity will be available once you graduate.”

I sink a little in my chair. What the hell do I do? I have a dream job in front of me, but I have another dream back home. I want to finish college, live the collegiate life with my friends, and continue having the fun I’ve been having with Grayson. But this is an opportunity of a lifetime.

She must be able to tell I’m debating on what to do because she interrupts all my thoughts by clearing her throat. “I’ll tell you what,” she says. “I’ll give you a month to decide what you want to do. But I’m afraid after that, I need to fill the position, and the offer won’t be available anymore.”

My eyes lift to hers. She needs a month. I can do that. I can make up my mind in a month. “Thank you,” I tell her. “I need to think on it.”

She nods, standing up. “I understand. It was nice to meet you, Rosalie.”

“It was wonderful to meet you, too,” I tell her. She smiles and then leaves.

I have a month. Thirty days to decide what I want to do with my future. I thought I’d have more time. But right now, I have the choice between staying in college and focusing on my designs and maybe starting my own line or being a designer living in Paris.

25

Withdrawals

Grayson

I tuck my phone back into my pocket, wanting to forget about it completely.

I can't just sit here and keep staring at my phone. That's sad. I don't do that. Especially not because of a girl that's been on my mind for the past two days. I keep looking back at our messages, looking at her name, imagining her reactions to my texts.

Who the hell have I become? I'm here re-reading old texts, and she's in New York. She's having fun, and I need to let her do that. Even though all I want to do at this moment is text her, call her, or see her. Fuck. I miss her.

I don't know why. We haven't even known each other for that long, but shit, I miss that girl so much. It's been over a week since I last saw her, and right now, I'm feeling the withdrawals from it.

I wonder what she's doing in New York. Is she scouring for more potential husbands, or did she just crave a trip to New York? I don't know. I never know with Rosalie. She surprises me every day. When I first met her, I thought she was a cookie-cutter good girl, but she's so much more than that.

She's smart, adventurous, and doesn't seem to be scared of anything. I like it. A lot. I like how she hums into my mouth when we kiss and how she tastes like candy. How she seems to love the adrenaline of danger like I do.

I once thought we were completely different, but now I think we're more similar than either of us realizes. I want to know more about her, I want to know everything about her. How she thinks, and what she desires out of life, everything.

I stop myself from pulling my phone out of my pocket and focus on the car instead. Being here clears my head.

"How's she doing?" Mattie asks, handing me a torque wrench.

I tighten the bolts, making sure it's all connected. "Needed a new engine."

"Hmm." Mattie asses me working on the car. I look up, seeing a look of shock on his face. "You're good, kid," he says, leaning against the wall as he watches me.

I've done this so many times I could do it in my sleep, but it's cute that Mattie thinks I'm some newbie wanting to play with cars. I've been working on cars since I was seven. I learned to drive by the age of ten, which probably wasn't the best idea for a kid like me, considering I was a little shit. But fuck, I don't regret it. Especially because I miss those times so much.

"Who taught you?" Mattie asks, throwing me a rag

I catch it and wrap it around my hand to unplug the drain plug. "My uncle." I swallow hard.

"Is he a mechanic too?"

I don't want to fucking talk about this. I can't look him in the eye. I stare down at the car and change the oil, which gives me an excuse to hide behind here a little longer.

"Yeah," I say, feeling like there's gravel in my throat.

"He can't get you a job?"

My jaw clenches. I've been trying to get Mattie to hire me since I came to Redfield, but the bastard won't hire me until I graduate. Figures, some high school dropout wants me to graduate with a degree to work for him.

It's bad enough that my parents are on my case all the time about my grades and making sure I attend school, but even Mattie won't let me work here. It would be a fuck ton easier to make the money I need.

"No, he can't," I tell him.

"Why not? If you're as good as you say."

I inhale, closing the hood of my car a little harder than I anticipated. "Because he's dead," I say, trying to act like it doesn't affect me.

He shakes his head, letting out a breath. "Shit. Sorry, kid."

I shrug because what the fuck else am I going to say? It was my fault. I killed him. Yeah, didn't think so.

He lifts himself off the car. "You heading out of here?" he asks. "I'm about to take my lunch break."

"Yeah. I'm gonna head back to my place."

He nods. "Lock up, kid," he tells me before walking out.

When I'm done, I close the hood of the piece of junk Mattie's letting me work on and lock up the garage, heading toward the back exit. I get on the bike, deciding to leave my car there. I need to feel the air on my skin right now. I have to keep it here since some douchebags tried to steal it before. Knowing Ben Reed, it was probably him. I know Mattie will keep it safe for me here.

I speed home, remembering when I brought Rosie with me to the lake. How she clung to my body, how she trusted me enough to get on the back of the bike with me, and how she loved the adrenaline, telling me to go faster.

I wanted her to feel how I did whenever I took the bike for a ride, like nothing else in the world mattered but the feeling right there in the moment. It's the only thing you can concentrate on. When the wind hits your skin and the sound of the engine roars in the air, you feel alive.

When I pull up to the apartment, Aiden's outside, already dressed and heading out of the front door.

I get off the bike, pulling the helmet off my head. "Where you going?" I call out.

He lifts his head, giving me a single glance, before looking back down at his phone. "Out."

"How informative." I joke.

"I'm going to the library." He grins. "To study."

I snort out a laugh, shaking my head as I walk past him. Yeah, I know what kind of studying he's going to be doing. "Have fun *studying*."

I head to my room, strip off my clothes, and turn on the shower. As much as I love working on cars, I hate feeling grimy, and a hot shower is exactly what I need.

I wrap a towel around my waist when I step out of the shower and use another to dry my hair. My eyes drift to my phone that's laying on the bed. I wonder what she's doing right now.

I finish drying my hair and throw the towel to the floor. I pick up my phone and click on the only name that's been running through my mind all day. She's alone in the big city. I can't help but think of her strolling through the city in that cute little outfit she showed me and not getting hit on.

I'm not jealous, I'm just concerned for her. At least, that's what I keep telling myself as I hear the line ring, and she doesn't pick up.

The line rings for what seems like forever until she answers, and I hear a breathy "Grayson."

I let my eyes drift closed as I let out a breath of relief at the sound of her voice. I miss that voice. It's been way too long since I last heard that voice. "Hey, angel," I say, smirking at the sound of her laugh when she hears my nickname for her.

"Hey."

"Are you busy?"

"No, I just got back home. I've got to say, I miss New York," she says with a sigh.

I smile, crashing down on the bed. "Yeah? How was it?"

She sighs again. "It's my home, so I think I'll always love it. Shopping in New York is always amazing. Ooh, and I had lunch with Emily Livingston." I freeze at the mention of my mother. "You don't know who that is, but she's a famous designer. It went great, I guess."

I clear my throat, avoid the subject, and settle into bed, loving hearing her talk. I honestly think I could fall asleep to her voice. It's so intoxicating, and I wish I could hear it in person right now.

"Did you buy anything?" I ask her.

She laughs, low and breathy. The sound travels straight down to my cock, and I feel it twitch under the towel, but now's not the time. "Yeah," she says. "I'll show you when I get home."

"How was everything with your mom?" I ask her. "Did her attempt to find you a husband work?" I laugh, trying to hide the bite in my tone. When she told me she was engaged back in New York, my heart fucking skyrocketed out of my chest. Joke or not, I didn't like hearing it.

"No," she says with a cute laugh of her own. "We talked, actually. My mother knows that's not what I want. But she got me a meeting with a huge fashion designer, and she wanted to hire me." She sounds so excited. I wish I could see her cheeks turn pink like they do whenever she grins. "But she wants me to move to Paris, and I don't know what to do."

My brows draw together. "You're moving to Paris?"

"Maybe?" she says, more like a question than an answer, and then, she lets out a sigh. "I don't know yet, I mean, I want to graduate college, but this is a once-in-a-lifetime opportunity."

"Didn't you say you wanted to start your own fashion line?"

"Yeah," she says. "I do, but this would be huge."

I hate the thought of her moving to Paris. But ultimately, it's her life. I have nothing to do with it, and I never will. I'm just someone she's using to get the college experiences she's wanted and nothing more.

"Anyway, she said I had a month to think about it, so I still have time."

A month until she decides if she's leaving me forever. Fuck. "When are you coming home?"

"My flight's tomorrow morning, so I'll get there at around noon."

My heart starts to race. She'll be here tomorrow. "I'll pick you up."

"You don't have to do that." She tells me, which makes me roll my eyes. I want nothing more than to see this girl, so hell yeah, I'm going to pick her up from the airport and fucking kiss her the moment my eyes land on her.

"Angel?"

"Yeah?"

"I'm picking you up."

She lets out a breath. "Okay."

I can hear her smile through the phone, and I close my eyes, imagining what it looks like.

All I can think of is when I'm going to see her again. I know this has to end, especially if she moves halfway across the world. And when this inevitably ends, I'll be nothing but an experience to her, but she will always be my angel.

26

I don't want to play anymore

Grayson

I'm restless.

I'm moving on the balls of my feet, waiting impatiently for a flash of blonde to appear at the gates.

I don't know why I'm panicking. It's not like this is the first time I've seen her. It hasn't even been that long since the last time I saw her. I saw her a week ago, which isn't that long, but it seems like it's been an eternity since I last had my hands wrapped in that golden blonde hair of hers or saw that smile that brings me to my knees.

My favorite thing about Rosie is her smile. The way her cheeks glow and her eyes wrinkle, and that beautiful mouth grins wide. I love it, and I can't wait any longer to see it.

I don't even know if she's gotten off the plane yet, and I'm here waiting like an idiot for this girl who's my… what is she exactly? My fuck buddy? That doesn't seem right.

I still as I watch her walk out of the gates, dragging her suitcase along behind her, as she searches around the room for me. I grin. I fucking grin like a madman.

Her eyes find mine, and I somehow manage to smile even more as I watch her try to run in those heels of hers. Why does she wear heels everywhere she goes? I mean, I'm not complaining, they look sexy on her and those legs. I want her naked and those legs wrapped around me, still wearing those heels.

The taps of her shoes get louder as she approaches me, and I erase the distance, striding forward towards her. She drops her suitcase, jumps into my arms and wraps those long legs around my waist as I hoist her up. Fuck, I've missed her.

She wraps her arms around my neck and brings her mouth to mine. I kiss her softly. I kiss her hard. I kiss her like I've missed her. I make up for the fact that we haven't seen each other in over a week, and it's been driving me crazy.

I pull back, brush her golden hair out of her face, and bring one hand to cup her face. "I fucking missed you, angel."

Her cheeks turn the cutest shade of pink as she smiles at me. "Me too," she breathes out.

I don't want to let go, so I crash my mouth back down on hers. I slide my tongue inside, tasting her like I want to taste her body. I kiss her hard and show her how much I've missed having her here with me in my arms.

After a while, I set her back down on her feet, ignoring everyone else around us. I don't care what they think. All I care about is my angel right in front of me. She picks up her suitcase, and I hold out my hand, beckoning her to take it. She wraps her small fingers with mine, intertwining them together, as I get her out of there and head back to my place.

"I've never been in your room before," Rosie says as she looks around my room. She glances at the walls, my bed, my dresser. She's taking it all in, and I'm taking her all in. The image of her on my bed has me grinning as I take off my shirt.

"You have," I tell her. "You just ran out of here before you could see it."

She turns, facing me with pink cheeks. "I didn't mean to interrupt. I just thought you'd be alone." She shrugs, tucking her hair behind her ear. "I should have known better."

My brows furrow. "What does that mean?"

She bites her lip as she looks down. "It means I knew your reputation. I should have figured you'd be hooking up with a girl."

I hate that she believes everything those dumbasses say about me. I thought after everything, she would know that I'm not like that. "We were just kissing."

Her eyes snap up, and she gives me a look of disbelief. "So, you're telling me that if I didn't walk in, you wouldn't have hooked up with her?"

I clamp my mouth shut. She got me there. Brianna and I would have probably hooked up if she hadn't walked into my room, but I'm glad she did. "Okay, you're right." I concede. "But that doesn't matter anymore."

She sits on the edge of my bed, fiddling with the hem of her dress. "I know we're not… you know." She glances up at me for a split second and then looks back down at her hands on her dress. "I just wanted to know if you were still hooking up with other girls."

"No," I tell her, honestly. "The only girl I'm hooking up with is in my bed right now."

She doesn't look up at me. She keeps looking down at her dress. She's not fidgeting anymore, but she still won't look at me. "Really?"

I take a step forward. “Yes, Rosie. Since you and I started this thing, I haven’t been with anyone else.”

“I don’t know if I believe that,” she mumbles. What the fuck does that mean? My jaw clenches as I cross the room. She’s still not looking at me. God damn it, Rosie. Look at me.

I slowly lift her chin to look up at me. “Have I given you any reason not to trust me?”

Her eyes lock on mine, those bright blue eyes shining as her throat moves, swallowing hard, and then she shakes her head.

My shoulders relax a little. “Then why don’t you believe me?”

“Because we’ve only hooked up twice. I expected you to get… busy when we weren’t together.”

I don’t know why I want her to believe me so much. She’s right, we have only hooked up twice, and we haven’t even fucked yet. We aren’t in a relationship, and I could have been with other girls if I wanted to. But I didn’t want to.

“There has been no one else, Rosie,” I tell her. “I…” I swallow the words that are stuck in the back of my throat. My mind is running right now. “I need you to believe me. I haven’t been with anyone else.”

The reason this started was because she came to me looking to lose her virginity, and for some dumb fucking reason, I’ve been trying to prolong it as much as possible.

“Okay,” she says. “I believe you.”

“Good.” I crash my mouth against hers and flip us over so that I'm sitting on the bed and she's standing above me. Her arms encase my neck as she lowers herself to straddle my leg. She hums into my mouth as her hips start rotating on me.

Fuck. She's humping my leg, getting herself off. I groan into her mouth, and she swallows it down. "So needy." I rasp out against her lips. "Grinding on my leg."

She runs her hands up and down my chest and arms. She's exploring me with her hands and feasting on me with her eyes, and I stay still, offering myself up to her. "I love your tattoos," she says, looking at my body with a hunger that I can feel. Her pussy throbs on my leg, and I'm tempted to bring her other leg around so I can press my growing erection to her heat.

"You have a thing for bad boys, huh?" I grin, watching her face light up with arousal as she caresses my skin with her soft fingertips.

She shakes her head. "Not usually." Her eyes look up and find mine, and her arms lock around my neck.

"Then why am I different?"

"Because you're not bad," she says. "Not really."

My confusion takes over my expression. "What does that mean?"

She lowers her head, leaving a soft kiss on my chest. "You're good. You just don't want anyone else to know you're good."

My throat bobs as I gulp. That kiss on my chest. Fuck. "I'm not good, Rosie."

She shrugs. "I think you are."

Isn't that what I want? For her to see me in a way no one else did. And here she is, saying she thinks I'm a good person, and I wish it were true. "You don't know me, angel," I tell her. "Not really."

She knows bits I've told her, but she doesn't know who I am or what I've done. She doesn't know the monster I became at an early age. She doesn't know any of that. And I don't want her to know. I want her to see me as someone who could be good to her, for her.

I cradle her face, running my thumb over her skin. "I'm not like you, Rosie. You're good, kind, a fucking angel." I exhale, loving how she melts into my touch. "I don't deserve you," I tell her. "No one is ever going to be good enough for you, Rosie. That, I can promise."

Her brows furrow a little as she frowns. "You're not a bad person Grayson." Her hand comes to my face as she caresses my face. I let my eyes drift closed at the feel of her hands on me.

"I wish you were right," I whisper.

"I am.," she whispers back, lowering her head to kiss the corner of my mouth.

My eyes open as I see her look at me with adoration. Something in her eyes lights up when she's looking at me, and I feel my chest tense. The way she's looking at me, and the things she's saying...

I squint my eyes at her. "This thing we're doing, these games we're playing." I swallow. "You're not going to fall for me, right?"

I wait for her response. There isn't a flash of emotion on her face. She's frozen, taking in the question until she finally shakes her head.

"No," she says. "You're not who I want." I can't explain what happens to my chest when those words come out of her mouth, but fuck, that hurt. "And ultimately, I'm probably going to end up with some guy who's a member of the country club and who owns a hotel." The corner of her lips raises in a slight smirk. "I just want you to fuck me."

That's good, right? She doesn't want to be with me. She just wants to use me for sex. That's what this whole thing started off as, anyway, so I should be happy that was her answer. And I am. Fucking ecstatic. That's why my heart is racing. Probably.

I laugh at her eagerness as her hips keep moving slowly. "Such hostile words for an angel." My hands drift to her hips, down to her ass, as I grasp it in my hands. "But I'll happily oblige."

"You see," she says, letting out a laugh. "What kind of bad boy says oblige?"

"The kind who went to private school," I tell her, my lips twitching.

She stills. Her hand tightens on the back of my neck. "What?"

I grin. "I told you. You don't know me."

Her eyes scan my face frantically. She even shakes her head, trying to make sense of what I told her. "You went to private school?"

"Yep."

"You… what?" She's confused, which I find so cute. The way her brows draw together, creating a little line between them as she frowns.

I choke out a laugh at her face. "I went to Lynch Prep."

Her frown deepens. "But… that's in New York. You're from New York?"

I nod. "I guess we run in the same circles. Who would have thought?" I smirk at her expression.

"I'm so confused right now," she says with a shake of her head.

"My last name is Livingston," I tell her. I'm done hiding from her. If she wants to know me, I'll tell her. There's no reason for me to keep any of myself from her anymore.

She freezes. "Livingston? As in Emily Livingston. The woman who I had lunch with yesterday. That Livingston?"

"Yep."

"What? How?"

"My name is Grayson Carter Livingston. I just dropped the last name when I came here. I didn't want anyone to look at me differently because of who my parents are."

"Your mother is Emily Livingston. CEO of Livingston Couture," she says to herself.

"You figure stuff out fast," I joke.

"Wow," she says, shaking her head. "You were right."

"About what?" I ask, running my hands on her skin.

"I really don't know you. And here I am, rubbing up on you."

I snort. "Please continue, I don't mind."

"I'm serious, Grayson," she says, lifting herself off my lap and backing away from me.

I groan, running a hand through my hair. "What do you want to know? I'll tell you."

"So, you're rich?"

I shake my head. "My parents are." They might have paid for my tuition, but I'm in no way rich.

"Then why are you a drug dealer?" she asks.

"I'm not." I hate that she still thinks that. "You just assumed it."

"I saw you," she says, not believing me.

I feel my jaw tighten. I would never even touch drugs, not after what happened, never mind sell them to other people. "I wasn't selling *drugs*."

"Then what were you selling?"

I run my hand through my hair, sighing. "Assignments."

Her brows furrow even more. "What?"

I nod. "Homework, assignments, whatever people need me to do." Most of them are athletes with shitty grades who need good enough grades so they can keep playing, which is how I make my money. What I didn't expect was that the rumor would be that I sold drugs instead.

Word got around freshman year that a kid came from a trailer park with an addict for a mother. I took the heat for Aiden, hoping the rumors would die down. Instead, with the help of Ben Reed, word got around fast that it was me. I didn't expect it to turn into this, though.

I lost count of how many people have come up to me asking for drugs. And, of course, it reached the dean, who then called my parents, who now think I'm hooked on drugs. Aiden was right, I should have shut down the rumors, but I couldn't do that to him.

"What?" Rosie asks, shocked.

I shrug. "Turns out I'm not as dumb as everyone thinks."

The scowl on her face smoothes out and is replaced by a frown. "I don't think you're dumb. I just… I thought you were a drug dealer. It's what everyone thinks," she says, taking a step closer to me.

"I don't care what everyone else thinks. I just didn't want you thinking that." I want her to know me. She's the only one who I've wanted to share myself with.

"Well, I don't anymore."

I nod, my shoulders relaxing. "That's good. I like having you know me."

"I like knowing you," she says, taking another step towards me.

I glance up at her, smiling. "I missed you."

She breathes out a laugh. "You already said that."

"I'm saying it again." I won't ever stop saying it. I fucking missed her. "Come here," I tell her.

She takes one more step and then straddles me. I lift the hem of her dress and pull it over her head, revealing her soft skin in nothing but lacy lingerie. Did I mention it's red? It's fucking red. I'm the luckiest guy ever.

I groan, tipping my head back. "Angel, you're killing me here."

"You like?" she asks, grinning.

I let my hands drift to her hips, feeling the lace underneath my hands. "I love," I tell her, squeezing her hips.

"I thought you didn't believe in love," she retorts with a lift of her eyebrow.

I roll my eyes. "Fine. I *really* like it."

"How much?"

"You want me to show you how much I like seeing you in nothing but this lacy thong?"

She nods. I lower my head and find her nipple over the lacy bra and suck it into my mouth over the fabric. She arches her back, letting out a gasp. I bite softly and release her. "Does that answer your question?"

"Nope," she says with a mischievous grin. "I'm going to need more to assess it."

This girl. I shake my head, grinning at her. My hands reach behind and unclasp her bra. "As much as I *really* like this. It has to go."

I pull the straps of her bra down until it falls onto my lap. I throw it onto the bed and lower my head, sucking on her bare nipple. She tastes so good. I almost forget how good she tastes, how good she feels, how good this feels with her.

My mouth leaves her puckered bud, and I bring it to the center of her chest, kissing all over her body. Her neck, her jaw, her breasts, her stomach. All of it.

Her hips start grinding against me, and the heat of her makes me feel dizzy. I play with the hem of her panties, stroking the skin as my hand dips inside.

I find her clit and slightly graze it, enough for her to sigh but not enough to give her the friction she needs. Instead, I bring my fingers down and lower them to find her entrance.

"You're soaked." I groan when I find her pussy dripping all over my hand. I press the tip of my middle finger inside her, hearing her suck in a breath. I slide it in deeper, feeling her tighten against my finger. Christ, she's so fucking tight. My dick twitches at the feel of her squeezing my finger.

"I don't want to play anymore," I tell her.

Her eyes widen, and a slight frown appears on her face. "You don't?

I shake my head, giving her a hard peck on her plump, soft lips. "I want to fuck you."

27

The first time

Rosalie

Yes.

Finally.

Grayson flips me so I'm laying on the bed. "You do?" I ask him.

He nods. "Do you still want to?"

More than anything. "Yes," I husk out.

I reach down to take off my heels, but he stops me. "Leave them on. They're so sexy," he says, running his hand up my calf.

I smile, laying down on my back, looking up at him. My eyes drift to his chest, which is scattered with tattoos. He has a few on his chest and a few on his arms. He's not completely covered in them, but there's also not a lot of bare skin showing. I love them, and they look so hot on him. I never thought I'd like tattoos, but my god, I do.

He reaches for the hem of my panties and pulls them down my legs until I'm completely naked, wearing nothing but my heels. He steps back, his eyes roaming my naked body. "You look…" He shakes his head, "like heaven."

I light up at every compliment that leaves his lips. I try not to let it affect me a lot. I think he noticed the last time I looked at him like I was dying to now. The way he asked if I was going to fall for him made me tense up because I knew I was already on the verge. I've caught feelings for Grayson, of course, I have. How could I not?

But I knew if I told him that, he would stop this. I thought I could do this with Grayson and not catch feelings, but I was so wrong. I miss him all the time, I want to see him every day, but he obviously doesn't feel the same.

He doesn't even believe in love, and I think it would be so easy to fall in love with him, if only he let me. We don't see each other as much as I'd like to, so he obviously has no feelings for me.

I thought he might. He said he missed me. He buys me flowers and looks at me like I'm the only person in the room. But the way he frowned when he asked me if I was falling for him made his feelings on the matter crystal clear.

I'm probably going to get my heart broken when this ends, but for now, I'm enjoying it. I'm enjoying the feel of his hands all over my body, I'm enjoying the compliments and praise he gives me. I'm enjoying him.

He gets on his knees, spreads my legs farther apart, and stares at the spot between my legs.

"You're so wet, angel," he murmurs, running his fingers over my thighs, getting closer to my center. "You're so pretty down here." I let out a moan. I love when he says that. I love the compliments from him, they never get old.

"Can I lick you?" he asks. "I'm dying to taste you again."

I nod, letting out a whimper as a reply. I'm too dizzy to speak any real words.

He dips his head, the tip of his tongue licking my clit, making my hips buck at the contact.

His tongue works me, licking me completely dry. He sucks my clit and leaves open-mouth kisses all over my lower lips.

I can feel myself get wetter the more he eats me until my hips buck against his face, feeling the pressure increase inside my core.

"Grayson." I moan, throwing my head back as one hand clutches his hair and the other fists the sheets.

He dips down, lapping at my entrance, licking up the arousal dripping out of me before coming back up to my clit and sucking it hard. That's all it takes. I clamp my legs around his head as my hips move, and he sucks me until I come so hard, shaking as the orgasm drips out of me.

Grayson doesn't stop. His tongue stays on my clit softly as two of his fingers find their way to my entrance. He slowly slides them both in, it feels slightly uncomfortable, but I'm so wet they slide effortlessly. He groans when he's knuckles deep, and I feel so full. I want to feel him.

"Grayson. Please." I pant, breathless from the orgasm I just had, and the feel of another brewing as he plays with my clit and his fingers are stuffed inside of me.

"What do you want, Rosie?"

"You. I want you inside of me."

"Yeah?"

"Yes." I whimper. "I'm ready. I want you."

His fingers pull out of me, and he stands up above me. "Fuck, Rosie," he whispers, holding my head in his hands. "I want you too."

Not in the way I want you.

He pulls off his jeans and boxers. His cock springs free, and it's right there in front of me.

"Wow." I gasp, staring at his dick. It makes my mouth water, wanting him in my mouth again.

He chuckles as he reaches his dresser for a condom. I gulp. This is it. I'm about to lose my virginity. He rolls the condom on his length slowly, and it makes me throb. I want him so badly.

He walks toward me until he is stretched out on top of me. His lips find mine. He kisses me softly and gently, and I moan into his kiss. I love his lips on mine.

He pulls back and spreads my legs with one hand while the other strokes his dick in languid moves.

"Scoot back for me, angel," he rasps. "Lift your knees."

I scoot back onto the bed, making room for him to join me, and lift my knees until I'm spread out open for him.

He kneels on the bed above me and brings the head of his cock to my entrance. I gasp when I feel it there, and he stills. "You ready?"

I nod, and he pushes inside, slowly stretching me. I let out a breath, feeling him fill me. "Oh fuck." He groans as he fills me deeper.

I wince at the small intrusion of my insides stretching, and he stops. "Shit, did I hurt you?"

"It's okay." I murmur. "Just keep going."

"Are you sure?"

"Yes, Grayson. I want to feel you."

He groans, tipping his head back. "You drive me crazy, Rosie." His hand is wrapped around his cock, and the other reaches down to rub my clit while he continues to push inside of me.

Once he bottoms out, he lets out a curse and groans, closing his eyes. I squeeze my eyes shut too. The feel of him inside me is so intense, I feel so full and stretched, and then he starts moving. He slowly pulls out and pushes in again, and the pain starts to subside as pleasure takes over.

"Fuck, you feel good," he says, speeding up his movements a little. He bends down to kiss me while he moves in and out of me. His pelvis hits my clit, and I moan into his mouth.

His hips thrust, fucking me as he kisses me. I wrap my legs around his waist, allowing him to go deeper until he's so deep he groans. His eyes are focused on mine, and I look up at them as he keeps moving in and out of me.

He smirks, a slight smile forms on his face as he looks down at me while moving inside of me. "Hi," he whispers.

I let out a laugh. "Hi," I whisper back, smiling up at his dark eyes. His face is so close to me. We're looking into each other's eyes. This feels way too intimate, and I love it. Damn it, Grayson. I snap my eyes closed, trying to differentiate between sex and feelings. If Grayson can do it, so can I. I think.

He lifts up onto his knees again and grabs my hips, pulling them to meet his thrusts. I keep my eyes closed, focusing on the immense pleasure building as the room fills with his grunts and my breathless whimpers.

My hand drifts down, and I touch myself, rubbing my clit like I love Grayson doing to me. I rub in slow circles, teasing myself as Grayson fucks me.

"Oh, fuck yeah." He grunts. "Touch yourself, that's it, baby."

I moan, unable to contain the pleasure of his words. He called me baby. He's never done that before.

"I need more," I say breathlessly.

"What do you need?" he asks me, slowing his thrusts.

I shake my head. That's the opposite of what I want. "More. Faster. Harder." I gasp.

"There's a difference between faster and harder, Rosie. Which one?" He asks, still thrusting slowly inside of me.

I need him to speed up. I feel the orgasm cresting inside of me. "Faster," I tell him again.

"You're dripping all over my cock." Grayson grunts, thrusting faster into me, making me throw my head back as he hits a spot inside me that I can feel in my throat.

A gasp gets caught in my throat as he speeds up. "Open your eyes for me, Rosie," he says.

I open my eyes and look up at him, and I'm met with his hooded eyes filled with lust. The sight of him makes my walls squeeze around him, which he must have felt because his eyes drift closed for a minute, and he throws his head back with a groan.

When he opens his eyes, they find mine, and he speeds up his thrusts for a few seconds and then slows down again. I cry out again, and he laughs. "You're close," he says. "I can feel it." One of his hands leaves my hips and drifts to where my finger is on my clit. He places his own on top of mine, adding pressure to it. "Keep touching yourself. I want to feel you come all over my dick."

I nod, quickening my movements, and his hand grabs my hips again. "You want fast?" He asks.

I nod enthusiastically. "Yes." I moan.

He grins. "Fuck, you're sexy," he says, and then he finally speeds up enough to make me cry. He holds my hips in place while he fucks me fast and deep until I fall back onto the bed and cry out in pleasure as I reach my peak.

I feel myself clench around him, tightening the hold of his dick inside of me, which must make him lose control because not even seconds later, he stills and groans as he comes inside of me, spilling into the condom.

He crashes onto the bed beside me as we breathe through the orgasm we both had. He disposes of the condom as I lie on his bed, out of breath but satisfied.

He joins me a minute later and lies beside me on the bed, twisting my head to face him with his thumb on my chin. "How was that?"

I smile. I smile because it was perfect. I smile because it was him. I smile because I never want to do this with anyone but him. I smile because I can't ever tell him that. I smile because I can't cry. "Perfect," I tell him.

He tucks me into his chest, and I bite my lip to keep the tears down. I know without a doubt in my heart that I'm way too deep in this. I know that I'm falling for Grayson, I'm already halfway there.

Unfortunately, he will never feel the same.

What have you done, Rosie?

28

Vibrant pleasures

Grayson

Every sound makes my head snap toward the door. My eyes keep drifting, waiting for her to come out. Jesus, how much longer?

My hands are itching to pull out a cigarette, but I can't do that because I quit smoking for this girl. And now here I am, waiting for her to come out of class so I can spend more time with her.

After we had sex the other day, I kept picturing her underneath me, panting, begging, smiling at me. I wanted it to be good for her, and when she told me it was perfect, it made my chest tense. I didn't want the moment to end. I wanted to keep her there, tucked against my chest, and feel her breath on my skin.

I thought I heard her crying, and I didn't know what to make of it. She cried when I took her driving that very first time, and she said it was because she was happy, so I assumed the same and didn't bother asking her.

And right now, all I want is to see her come out of that door. I can't wait to see the look on her face when I take her to the last place she'd ever expect to go.

The door opens, and my head snaps in the direction of the students leaving class. My eyes are roaming for a blonde in a white dress. She probably won't be wearing that, but I can't help but think of the first time I ever saw her. The image has been engraved into my brain since the first time I laid my eyes on her. The first time I ever saw my angel.

And when she walks out with her head down, looking at her phone, it's like I'm looking at her for the first time all over again. She's not in a white dress though, but that cardigan and blue jeans looks every bit as good on her.

She looks up, and her eyes lock on mine. A large grin appears on her face, and I can't help but smile back at her. There will never be a time when that smile doesn't make me weak.

"Grayson," she says, erasing the distance between us. I love how she says my name with that breathy gasp like she doesn't know if she's imagining me being here. "What are you doing here?" she asks.

"Ready for another adventure?" I ask her. I don't count this as a lesson. I want her to have fun with me, and I want to see her cheeks turn pink when she realizes where I'm taking her.

"Now?"

I nod. "Yeah, you don't have class, do you?"

"No, that was my last class today."

"Then let's go," I say, holding out my hand for her to take it.

She wraps her fingers around mine, and I squeeze. Her hands fit so well in mine, her warmth contrasts my coldness, and I want to relish this moment, feeling her hand in mine.

We walk towards the parking lot, and I get inside my car, driving to the last place she'd expect.

I pull up to a parking lot and stop the car. She looks around, trying to figure out where we are. She looks at me for an explanation when she can't.

I don't give her an explanation but instead open the door for her to get out of the car. She follows me. I can't help but grin. She doesn't have a clue where she's going, and yet, she has that smile on her face like she always does.

I feel a punch in my gut. She trusts me no matter what and doesn't ask me any questions. There is no hesitation; she follows me wherever I go.

I take her hand in mine again and lead us to the store. She doesn't seem to know where we're going, which is surprising considering the name of the store is Vibrant Pleasures, but she'll find out soon enough.

"Holy shit." *Or right now.* She stops as we enter the store, planting her feet on the ground as her eyes widen while she scans the place. I don't know if she even realizes she's squeezing my hand.

I hold in a laugh, trying not to take away from her experience. She wanted to go to a sex shop, right? Well, angel, that's what I'm here for.

"You good?" I ask her, trying to mask the amusement in my tone.

Her eyes slowly turn to look at me, and she swallows. "This is where we're going?"

I nod, unable to take my eyes off her face, her skin pale and eyes wide. "You wanna go look around?" I ask her.

Her eyes seem to widen even more, if that's possible. "You mean… buy something?"

I shrug. "You don't have to, I just thought it would be fun to come here." I'm not going to lie. The idea of her picking out a toy to use is making me hard as a rock. I didn't bring her for that, but it was fun to see the look on her face when I took her here.

Rosie doesn’t know this, but I kept the list. I couldn’t get rid of it. I tried not to stare at it, to imagine what it would be like to experience these firsts with her, even if I’ve done them already. It’s different with her. So one by one, I’m helping her complete her list. I want her to have everything she wants.

I reach for her face, rubbing my thumb over her cheek. “If you want to leave, we can.” I don’t want to make her feel uncomfortable, and I’m not sure if she hates being here or if it’s just shock.

She swallows again and then shakes her head. “No, we’re already here, right? Let’s look around.” Her head snaps to the right, looking at all the toys on the shelf.

She pulls my hand, and I follow, going wherever she wants to go. She brings us to the vibrator section, and I inwardly groan at the thought of her getting herself off with a new toy in front of me. The last time I watched her, I almost combusted, but I’d do it all over again.

She looks at the shelf for a while but then keeps moving, pulling on my hand to follow her, and follow her I do. I can't pay attention to where she's going. I'm too distracted by the hard-on in my jeans right now. I'm trying to exhibit some self-control before I pull down her tight jeans off her body and sheath myself into her.

I brought Rosie here, thinking it would be fun for me, but it’s torture. Absolute torture to endure. Watching her touching the sex toys, wrapping her fists around them, testing them out on her hand. Jesus, fuck. I’m so hard it’s painful.

"Do you want to get out of here?" I rasp, trying to breathe properly.

She gives me a glance, and a mischievous smile bloom on her face. Her eyes dip to my jeans, and her smile widens. She knows I'm turned on, but instead of saying yes and heading to my car, she sighs and turns her head back to the shelf.

This girl is playing a dangerous game. I groan when she picks up an anal plug with a heart on the end and runs her fingers over it slowly. She is torturing me, and she knows it. "This one's cute," she says. "Let's get this."

I freeze. "Rosie. You know that's a butt plug, right?"

She looks at me for a second and then nods. "I know. You ready to go?"

I'm speechless. My mouth waters at the thought of her tight asshole wearing a plug whilst I fuck her, and I freeze. The only way I move is because Rosie tugs on my hand, heading towards the register.

Shit. Is she actually buying an anal plug?

I snap out of all the dirty images of Rosie and hand the woman at the register my card. If she's actually serious about this, I might as well get some lube. I grab the bottle near the exit and add it to the counter.

She narrows her eyes at me, and I ignore it, taking the card back and grabbing the small plastic bag, rushing us to my car.

"Why are you rushing?" she asks as we enter the car.

I start the engine, pull out of the parking lot, and speed home. "Rosie, I'm literally five seconds away from pulling this car over and showing you what that toy will feel like."

"Oh," she whispers. I look to my side, seeing her cheeks blush as she looks straight ahead.

I can't get home fast enough. I'm practically speeding when I finally pull over to my house. I don't even care if Aiden is home right now. All I care about is taking Rosie to my bed.

I pull her into me as soon as we reach my bedroom. I crash my mouth onto hers, and she yelps into my mouth, no doubt shocked by how much I need her right now, but she needs me just as much. She melts into me and wraps her arms around my neck.

I trail kisses down her jaw, neck, and chest as I rip off her cardigan, throwing it on the floor. "You think that was funny?" I ask her, pulling her tank top up and off her body. "Playing with me back at the store?" I bite her jaw, and she gasps, reaching for my t-shirt. I fumble with the buttons on her jeans while she rips my clothes off.

We're a mess of arms and clothes, frantically trying to get closer to each other. Fuck, I need her right now.

I step back when her clothes are off, and she's standing in nothing but white lacy underwear. I haven't seen this yet. I haven't been able to stop thinking about her in that lacy thong since the moment I pulled it out of her bag, which seems like it was a lifetime ago.

I was so stupid, telling her I wouldn't get involved with her like this, and now look at me, dying to get her in the shower and on my cock.

"Angel." I exhale a shaky breath because, right now, standing in front of me with her blonde hair spread across her back, in nothing but her lacy white underwear, she looks like my kind of angel.

I reach for her waist and pull her flush against me, kissing her so hard. I unclasp her bra and pull off her panties, and she mirrors me, pulling my boxers down and off as we stumble backwards into my shower.

The water isn't even on. We're just grabbing onto each other, my tongue inside her mouth as I grab her ass in my hands. When we pull apart, she's breathless, and her eyes are hazy, and I love it.

I grin as I turn the water on, allowing the warm water to run along our skin. Her hair sticks to her back as she tilts her head back, her eyes close as she starts to wash her body. I stare at her. I can't keep my eyes off her. Since the very first day I saw her, I haven't been able to keep my eyes off her.

I pour soap onto a rag and lather my body, and she opens her eyes, watching me as I run the soap all over my body while my other hand wraps around my dick, stroking it while I watch her soap up her body.

I lean forward, catching her nipple in my mouth, and she moans, tipping her head back. I get on my knees, my tongue dragging down her body until I reach the paradise between her legs. Her hands tangle in my hair while I kiss her pussy, soft and slow, not enough to make her lose control, but enough that she bucks her hips and whimpers, letting out those sounds that make my cock twitch.

I grab her hips and twist her body so her sweet ass is in my face, and she gasps when she feels my mouth on her cheeks. She plants her hands on the shower wall, the water cascading down her back. I knead her ass cheeks in my hand, spreading them apart, and dive in, licking that tight hole that's driven me to insanity.

She lets out a mixture between a gasp and a moan as she tries to move away from me, but I grip her hips in place and kiss her asshole until she's breathing heavily and plants her face to the shower wall, her knees buckle as she struggles to stand and I pull back, giving her ass a squeeze.

"I think you're clean enough," I tell her, lifting off of my knees and twisting her around so she faces me. "Ready to get dirty again?"

Her lips part, her breathing unsteady, and then she nods.

We get out of the shower, not bothering to dry off as I push her onto the bed so she's laying on her back, her hair spread out on my bed, and I stare at her, wanting this image to stay in my mind forever.

I reach for the bag and take out the lube and plug and throw them on the bed beside her. "You sure about this?" I ask her.

She nods again and then turns so she's on her hands and knees, sticking her ass out for me. Fuck, I'm not going to last if she keeps doing this to me.

I pop open the lube and cover the butt plug in it. She wanted to experience new things, and she came to me thinking I'd be able to show her everything, but this is new to me. I've never done this before with anyone, so as much as she's experiencing something new, so am I.

I pour some lube onto my finger and bring it to her tight hole. She sucks in a breath when she feels the cool liquid and the pressure of my finger there, and I still, but then she lets out a breath and relaxes. I penetrate her with the tip of my finger, and she moans quietly. The sound makes me shiver. I push in deeper, and she moans louder this time.

Fuck. I squeeze my eyes closed, gripping my cock in my hand, squeezing my shaft until a twinge of pain hits. I need to have some control.

I pull out my finger and bring the toy to her ass, pressing the tip of it against her hole. This one's bigger than my finger, so I go slower, waiting for her to tell me to stop, but she doesn't. She arches her back, allowing the toy to push in deeper, and she falls to the bed. Her chest is planted against the mattress as she moans into the sheets, the sound muffled.

I push the toy in as deep as it can go until the pink heart shines as evidence of the toy shoved in there.

I smooth my hand down her back. "How do you feel?" I ask her, wanting to know if she's uncomfortable.

"Full," she says, the sound still muffled. She turns her head to look at me behind her shoulder. "Fuck me," she says.

Christ. I pull out a condom and roll it on my length, bringing the head to her dripping entrance. She's soaked, and I haven't even touched her pussy yet. I run it up and down her slit, coating my dick in her arousal, and then press the tip into her entrance. She takes me so easily in this position. My dick slips right in with how wet she is. She tightens around me as soon as I start to push in and makes a couple of sexy noises.

"That's it, angel," I tell her, pushing in deeper until I bottom out, groaning at the feel of her gripping me inside of her. I swear she does that on purpose to drive me nuts. "You take my cock so well."

She looks gorgeous like this, her ass filled with a butt plug, her pussy filled with my cock as her face is pressed down onto the bed. My very own angel. I've corrupted her, and I don't regret it.

I fist her hair, pulling it so her head is thrown back, and at the same time, I pull out and thrust back in. She moans so sweetly, and I reward her with a hard thrust.

"Oh God," She moans. "Do that again."

I give her another hard thrust, and she cries my name. Fuck yes. "Is this what you wanted, angel?" I ask her. She nods, whimpering. The sound does crazy things to me. "Tell me. How does it feel?" I grunt, speeding up my thrusts.

She cries out, so enraptured in the pleasure that she doesn't answer me, so I tug on her hair again. "How does it feel, Rosie?" I ask her again.

"So good." She gasps. "Harder."

I give her what she wants and thrust harder. She seems to like it. She might be a little sore afterwards, but right now, she wants hard, so I give her hard. "Such a good fucking girl." I rasp, giving her hair another sharp tug.

Her hair is trapped in my fist, her head is thrown back, and her back is arched. She looks like a fucking masterpiece right now. My eyes drift down to where we're connected, and I love the sight of my cock disappearing inside of her. I spit, watching my spit travel down from the plug to her soaking pussy, and thrust faster, feeling her tighten around me.

My other hand drifts around, finding her clit and rubbing it. She's so close already, and I need to get her there before I lose control. "Come for me, angel. I can feel your pussy gripping my cock inside of you." She moans and bumps her hips back, fucking my cock as I thrust to meet her.

I speed up my movements, feeling the impending orgasm build inside me, and then she stills, falling onto the bed as her orgasm runs through her.

Jesus, I can't take it anymore. I thrust once, twice, and then spill into the condom, feeling her tightening around me, prolonging the orgasm.

Fuck.

I pull out of her and stare down at that pretty ass filled, and I feel myself hardening again. I can't get enough of her. I pull the toy out, slick with lube, and she whimpers as pleasure courses through her while still coming down from her orgasm.

She turns to face me. "Shit," she says, out of breath. "That was so hot."

I agree. I dispose of the condom and place the toy inside the sink. I'll deal with it later. Right now, I need to lie next to her. I would never have figured I would like cuddling after sex. Most of the time, after my hook-ups, they would either leave, or I'd dip out while they were in the shower, but Rosie is different. I need to be near her. All of the goddamn time.

I join her on the bed, grinning down at her sex-tousled hair and flushed face. She's so beautiful, it's crazy.

"Did you like our adventure?"

She laughs, cradling her head against my chest. "If we have any more adventures like that, I might die."

I snort. "Me too."

This all started out as helping her become her own person, helping her figure out who she wants to be, but right now, all I can think of is how long this is going to last because it has to end eventually.

And I don't want it to.

29

Unanswered questions

Rosalie

My eyes drift open, adjusting to the light coming from the window.

I look around, trying to figure out where the hell I am.

A groan comes from my side, and I turn my head, seeing Grayson lying beside me. A smile forms on my face when I think of the day we had yesterday. Our adventure together. I came to him looking for him to lose my virginity, and he's done that, so shouldn't we have ended it by now? He's shown me a lot. How to live life dangerously, how it feels to feel truly alive, and that's all I ever wanted.

But being here with him is all I want now. I want to wake up with him more often. I want him to surprise me with adventures and lessons where I can spend the whole day with him and end the way we did yesterday. I want more time with him.

I reach for my phone on the nightstand and curse when I see the time. I'm going to be late for class. I still need to get home and shower and get ready and—

"Hey." I turn, seeing Grayson laying on his stomach, his face propped up on his arm as he smiles at me.

"Hey," I say back, sitting up and trying to find my clothes from yesterday.

"Are you in a rush to get out of here or something?" He asks, sitting up on the bed.

I shake my head, still looking for my clothes that he threw across the room yesterday. "No, I'm just late for class."

He sighs. "Just stay here. You can skip class one day, Rosie."

I turn to face him. "I already skipped class multiple times. I don't want to be behind on my assignments."

"I'll do them for you," he says, his eyes drifting down my body, which makes me very aware of the fact that I'm standing in his room buck naked.

I snort out a laugh. "I don't think you're used to doing the kind of assignments I have."

He shrugs. "I'll figure it out. C'mon, come back to bed."

I spot my tank top near his dresser and pick it up, pulling it over my head. "Don't you have class?"

He stands from the bed now while I continue looking for my clothes. "Yeah, so?"

I squint my eyes, turning to face him. My eyes immediately drift down to his crotch, where he's sporting an erection. I lick my lips. "I can't have a serious conversation with you when you're naked. Put some clothes on."

"Or," he says, approaching me and tugging at the tank top. "You can get naked and stay in bed with me."

I shake my head. "Clothes."

He groans and steps back. "Fine," he says, picking out a pair of boxers and throwing another to me. He gets dressed while I put on his boxers, and then he crosses his arms. "Go on, talk."

"You're smart," I start. "It's obvious you're good at school, Grayson. Why don't you go to class?"

His jaw clenches. "Because I don't want to."

"That's not the answer I was looking for."

He shrugs. "That's the answer I'm going to give you."

I squint my eyes at him. "Why are you here then?" I ask. "Your mother is Emily Livingston, for crying out loud. If your parents are rich, why do you need money?"

I see his jaw clench again, and he drops his arms, turning around and heading to the bathroom, avoiding my question.

"Grayson," I say, trailing after him.

"Go to class, Rosie," he tells me.

I don't want to go to class. Not now. Not when he's about to finally tell me something real about himself. Ever since he told me about selling assignments, I've been racking my brain as to why he would need to. His tuition is probably paid off, and his parents probably gave him money, so why?

"I'm not going anywhere until you talk to me."

He shakes his head, letting out a bitter laugh. "Why are you doing this? I don't owe you anything. We aren't together."

I flinch, stepping back from him. I know that. He hasn't stopped saying it. But it doesn't stop me from wanting to get to know him, to know everything about him.

"Just tell me," I whisper. "I'll leave right after. I promise. Just tell me."

I knew this had to end sometime, and it sounds like Grayson's already there. I don't want to be a burden on him, I just want to know him.

He sighs, dropping his head forward. "Because I want to get out of here," he finally says. I scrunch my brows, waiting for him to continue. "My tuition is paid, but I don't have any money. You have a trust fund, right?" I nod. "Mine comes with stipulations. I only get access to it once I graduate."

That makes sense, I guess. Most parents wouldn't want their child to get their hands on money and blow it before they even turn twenty-one because they have no idea what to do with it.

"I get where they're coming from," I tell him. "If you don't know how money works—"

He snorts. "I was doing my uncle's taxes by the time I was ten. I've always understood the value of money, how people don't have what we did growing up. That wasn't the problem."

"Then what was the problem?"

"Drugs."

I frown. "Drugs?"

He nods, dropping his head. "My parents think I'm a drug addict, so they don't want me to have access to money because they think I'll shoot up." He lifts his head and looks at me. "The reason I sell assignments is because, if I ever want to leave this shit hole before I graduate, then I need money."

He lifts off the sink and turns his body to face me. "I'm not asking for a million dollars or anything. I don't want that life. I want to start over somewhere new." He shrugs. "Open a garage of my own and work on cars. Away from everything and everyone I know."

I bite my lip, not knowing what to say to him. I have a trust fund, I have financial freedom, and he wants that.

"I don't want to be near my parents," he continues. "If I graduate and accept the money from them, I will always have ties attached to them, and I don't want that."

"I get that," I tell him. I understand what it's like to be a part of that life. You feel entitled to do anything that they ask of you because you took their money. I took their trust and still feel indebted to my mother, which is why I attended that event and talked to the guy she was trying to set me up with.

"Why do your parents think you're a drug addict?" I remember him being so adamant about not taking drugs, and he made me promise I would never do it again. I didn't think anything of it at the time, but now that he's mentioned it, it gnaws at me.

He groans, wiping a hand down his face, and heads into the shower. "Go to class, Rosie."

That's all I'm getting from him, it seems. I don't know what to think when he shuts the bathroom door, and I hear running water a minute later. I find my jeans and tug them on, picking up my stuff and heading out of his place.

30

Secrets come out eventually

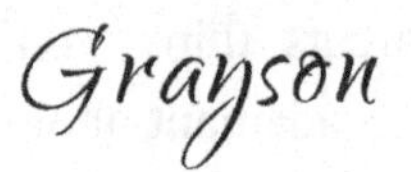

Rosie's avoiding me.

Ever since she left my house two days ago, I haven't heard from her. I text, call, and she doesn't answer. I don't know if she freaked out by what I told her, but she asked me.

I don't want her to know how fucked up I really am. This whole arrangement was about her, so why does she care if I go to class or not?

I panicked when she told me she'd leave and told her the reason why I needed the money. At least it started off that way. During freshman year, I came to Redfield full of anger, wanting to get rid of every memory I had of New York.

But now, I don't know if leaving is what I want anymore. Which is probably why I'm here in New York at my parents' house, having dinner with them. Dinner. That's a foreign concept to me. My dinner consisted of takeout in my car, avoiding being at home as much as possible.

I couldn't take the arguing every fucking day. My father always had something new he resented me for. I don't know why the old man has such a problem with me, but for some reason, he despises me.

I like to think he grew wary of me after what happened. He was his brother, after all, but he's been like this for as long as I remember. Which is why I would sneak out and hang out with my uncle. He ended up being the one person I looked up to growing up.

He taught me everything I know. How to drive, how to change tires, how to change engine oil. His whole life was cars, and whenever I snuck out to his garage, he'd teach me something new.

He took me driving a lot. The longest road trip we had was to Pennsylvania, where he drove us to a mountain, and we sat there, looking out at the view. He gave me my first taste of beer that day.

I didn't think I'd ever go back there again, but when I had Rosie in my car with me, the only place I wanted to go was that mountain. I hadn't been there in over five years, and I was glad Rosie was with me, even if she's avoiding me now.

"Put your phone away," my father snaps, bringing his glass to his mouth and taking a sip of the dark liquid.

I sigh and tuck my phone into my pocket.

"We spend thousands on that school, and for what? You're still the same disrespectful screw-up."

I scoff. "College doesn't all of a sudden make me holier than thou. It's called bad parenting."

His eyes narrow as he points a finger at me. "Don't you talk back to me."

"Okay, why don't we all calm down," my mother says, trying to appease him.

My father grunts. "Don't tell me to calm down," he spits out. "I won't be disrespected in my own house by a murderer."

My jaw clenches, and my fists tighten underneath the table. "I'm not a murderer. How many more times do I have to say it wasn't my fault?"

"Excuses don't cut it, boy. I saw what you did to him," he retorts, lifting his glass and spilling some of the drink on the table. I still remember being frozen in place, watching him die right in front of me. I couldn't move, I couldn't stop it.

"Frank." My mother mutters. He grunts, waving her off. I wish she'd stick up for me. Tell him that it wasn't my fault. Tell *me* that it wasn't my fault.

It wasn't my fault, was it? I try so hard to convince myself that I couldn't help him. But what if I was wrong? What if it was my fault?

"Would you like some dessert?" my mom asks me. "The cook made some delicious cheesecake. Amelia," she calls out, and in comes a maid. A new one since the last time I was here. "Bring out dessert," my mom tells her. "I think we're stuffed from the main course."

Amelia starts clearing the plates from the table. As much as I appreciate my mother for trying to make the situation better, dessert isn't going to suddenly change the fucked-up relationship my dad and I have. I don't understand why he hates me. He always has for as long as I've been alive. There's nothing I can do to change that.

I stand from the table, heading out of the dining room.

"Where are you going? We haven't finished." My dad says.

"To the bathroom," I tell him. "Would you like to check my shoes for needles before I go?"

He grunts, and I take that as my cue to leave. I head out of the dining room and into the downstairs bathroom.

I don't know what I'm doing here. I came here trying to figure out the relationship I had with my parents. My mother asked me to come, but so far, there has been no evidence of them putting what happened behind them.

I stare into the mirror, gripping the edge of the sink as I try to figure out who the hell I am. I'm a product of those two out there. What does that even mean? Will I grow up to be a hot-tempered asshole like my father?

Will I even have kids? I've never thought about it before. A relationship, marriage. Just the thought of having kids terrifies me. What if I end up just like him? What if I become unattached and hate the kid? What if I fuck up his life just like my dad did mine?

The only man I ever looked up to is dead.

Because of me.

Maybe Frank is right. I am a fuck up and a murderer. Maybe Rosie knows that too, and that's why she's been avoiding me.

She doesn't want to be with someone like me, and she told me that herself. I don't want a relationship anyway. So why the hell am I checking my phone again?

I curse at the screen and shove my phone into my back pocket, turning on the faucet and cooling my face off. I head out of the bathroom, debating whether I should leave or go back in there.

"You can't keep bringing this up, Frank." I hear my mother say.

I stand in the corner of the dining room, trying to listen in to what my father will say. She told me to come here to make amends with him, and he's been holding the front door open since I got here.

"I don't have to do anything with the likes of him. He's no son of mine." I roll my eyes. Hearing him say that puts the nail in the coffin. He doesn't think of me as a son. He doesn't want anything to do with me. I just wish I knew why.

"It's bad enough you opened your legs to my brother and birthed that son of a bitch, I don't have to stand by and hear him disrespect me too."

I freeze at the doorway. What?

"Keep your voice down."

"Why?" my father says, slurring his words a bit. "You don't want him to hear how much of a slut you are?"

"Frank," my mother says more harshly.

He laughs bitterly. "I have no need for a wife," he says. "I haven't for a long time. I have other women willing to do your job."

Bile rises in my throat, remembering the times I walked in on him with his assistants. I was crushed knowing he cheated on my mom, and now I know my mom cheated on him too.

This is why I can't imagine a world where love exists. How the hell did two people get married and devote their lives to each other and go behind their backs and betray each other? It's fucking stupid to think that would equate to something as fabricated as love.

"That son of a bitch has his face. He's living evidence of your betrayal to me, to this family, to my legacy," he says. "How am I supposed to forget that?"

I almost snort. His legacy. The one he built with my mother's money. My father's company is nothing but a way to appease himself that he's the breadwinner when we all know she is. My mother has been a famous designer for as long as I've been alive, and I've been nothing but proud of her.

But the same can't be said for my father. I always felt like he was jealous of her success, that he felt emasculated by her wealth. But maybe it was more than that. Maybe it was the affair she had.

"You promised me you would let it go. I can't keep doing this with you," my mother replies.

"I can't forget it. He's a reminder of your betrayal. That asshole is nothing but a disappointment. I was willing to raise him as my own, but then he went and murdered my brother."

My jaw clenches, and my palms itch to go in there and throw a fucking punch in his face.

I don't need to be here. I stumble backwards into the statue behind me, causing the dining room to fall silent.

"Grayson?" My mother calls out.

I step into the dining room, seeing my mother with a red face and my… father? Uncle? Frank, with a disgusted expression I've been on the receiving end of my whole life, at least now I know why.

"What the hell were you doing?" Frank asks. "Were you eavesdropping?"

"About how Uncle Gary was actually my dad? Yeah, I heard that."

"Bout time you knew," he spits back, taking a sip from his whiskey.

I snort out a laugh. "Now I know why you never liked me."

He gives me a glance, repulsion painted on his face. "You have his face," he says. "I'm surprised you didn't figure it out. Never took you for a dumb fuck."

Frank and my uncle didn't share a lot of similarities. Frank was rich, my uncle was not. Frank has a receding hairline, and my uncle had a full head of hair. They might not have been similar, but they were still brothers. They shared DNA. I ignore his statement. I'm not dumb. I know that. He knows that. I don't even bother replying to him as I turn to face my mother. "Did he know?" I ask her.

"Grayson," my mother starts.

I shake my head. I don't want to hear any excuses. "Did he know?" I ask her again.

She lets out a breath, a sympathetic look on her face. She shakes her head. "No, he didn't know."

I nod. "So, it was just a coincidence that I spent so much time with him. That he wanted to teach me about cars and hang out with me?"

She nods. "He loved you so much," she says with a hint of a smile. "Maybe he suspected. But your father and I agreed to keep it between us."

"You knew?" I ask Frank. I guess it's redundant to call him my father. He never felt like a father, and now I know he isn't even my father biologically.

"I walked in on them," he says, avoiding my eyes and taking a sip of his drink.

"He's my dad?" I ask my mother. It feels surreal. My father.

She nods.

"He was, and then you killed him." Frank retorts.

I feel my fists clench at my sides. "I didn't kill him."

He narrows his eyes at me. "What else do you call standing there watching him while he dies?"

I didn't kill him. It wasn't my fault. I didn't know what to do. I panicked. "I was thirteen," I say through clenched teeth. I was only a kid. I was a fucking kid.

"That doesn't excuse your actions."

"I came to you," I yell across the room. "I asked for your help." I run a hand through my hair, feeling my whole body burn with anger. "If you weren't too busy fucking your assistant, you could have helped me!"

He stands from the table, slapping the table with force. My mother jumps in her seat. "You killed him. That's on you. Don't you forget it," he yells back.

"Frank. Don't talk to him like that," my mother says from her seat.

"That screw-up was a cokehead anyway. No one misses him."

My face heats, and I go blind with rage. I stalk towards him and grab his collar. "He was your brother," I seethe.

"He was a fuck-up," he spits out. "Just like you."

I shake my head, hating those words that come out of his mouth. Sure, he had problems with drugs. But he was the best man that I ever knew. He was my father, and I didn't even know it. And I lost him.

I feel someone tug my arm and turn my head, seeing my mother. Her eyes are filled with tears as I see her mouth 'Grayson' over and over at me. I can't hear her, though. My ears are ringing with hate for the man in front of me.

My fist makes contact with his cheek, blood sputtering out of his mouth.

I push him against the wall. "Fuck you," I breathe out.

I let him go and turn, heading out of this fucking house and leaving this life behind me.

My mother can keep living her fucked up married life with that psychopath and leave me alone.

My father is dead.

And I don't have a reason to come back here anymore.

31

Sleepless nights

Grayson

I can't sleep.

I can't shut my brain off for five fucking minutes.

My uncle, or who I thought was my uncle, was actually my father. And he's dead.

The urge to escape has never been bigger. I don't even know if I still have access to the trust or not. I have no idea what I'm going to do. I practically have no family, no one to turn to, and no money.

The shit I sell around campus isn't much, especially when some people don't pay up what they owe. What I have saved up is nowhere near enough to move as far away from here as possible and open up my own garage.

And I can't even count on the trust fund to get me out of here anymore. My golden ticket to freedom has been taken away from me. So, what do I do now? Do I keep attending school, hoping for an opportunity where Mattie lets me work for him once I graduate? Or do I leave with the money I have and do… what am I going to do?

I thought I had everything set up. Graduate, get money, leave. But now all of that is gone, thrown out the window.

Fuck. I just want to sleep. I want to forget about this and close my eyes. But I can't. I twist and turn in my cold ass bed, wanting to grab onto Rosie, but she's not here.

She hasn't answered my texts since she left the other day, and I don't know what to make of it. Is she done with me? Is this over? I knew it had to happen eventually, but not now. I'm not ready. I fucking need her.

Fuck this. I can't stay here any longer. I'm going to burst a vein if I keep thinking about it. I pick up my phone, swiping away the texts from my old hookups. I don't want any of them. I want a blonde with blue eyes and a sexy mole on her upper lip. I want my angel.

I open our texts, groaning at the absurd amount of unanswered texts I sent to her. I send another text and stare at the screen, anticipating her reply, or at least three dots, just anything, really. I need to know she's not done with me.

But there's nothing, of course. I'm not going to let her ghost me. If she wants this to be over, then she needs to say it to my face. I can't handle not knowing where we stand. And I don't want to let her go, not just yet. I don't know when I'll be ready to end this between us, but I know it's not now.

I throw on my jeans and a clean shirt and head out of my room. I race down the stairs, halting when I see a sleepy Aiden standing in the kitchen.

"Where the hell are you going? It's two in the morning," he grunts, filling up a cup with water.

I shrug. "For a drive."

"You going to see Rosie?" he asks.

"What?" I laugh, trying to sound like I don't know what he's talking about. Is it obvious that I'm lying? It must be because he turns around and raises his eyebrow at me, clearly seeing through my bullshit.

I don't appease him, though. "I have no idea what you're talking about," I tell him, hoping he'll drop it.

He scoffs. “I *heard* you. She screamed your name so loud, I thought you were dying.”

I close my eyes. Fuck. “You heard?” The day I brought Rosie home, I didn’t know if Aiden had been there, and I hadn’t cared. My mind was filled with Rosie and nothing else.

He grins, nodding. “You call her angel. That’s cute.”

I groan, running a hand down my face. For fucks sake.

“What happened to ‘I can control myself?’ I knew that was bullshit.”

I choke out a laugh. “Fuck you.” Yeah, I was full of shit when I said that to him. I thought I could, but I was only fighting with myself. That girl had me from the very beginning. I knew I couldn’t hold back if she kept asking and begging me so sweetly. I was fucking putty in her hands.

He shakes his head, sighing. “I told you it wasn’t a good idea.”

“I don’t need you telling me to stay away from her. You’re not my dad,” I say, narrowing my eyes.

He shrugs. “Not sure about that. I get called daddy pretty often.”

I snort out a laugh, wiping a hand down my face. I’m too tired for this shit. “It’s fine. I’ve got it under control.”

“Yeah,” he says. “Heard that last time.”

I sigh. “Are you going to keep grilling me, or can I leave?”

He grins. “Yes, son. You can go.”

I scoff, not bothering to reply to him, and head out of the house.

What will she do when I get there? Will she kick me out and say we’re done? I’m not ready for that. Maybe I should head back home. Maybe living in denial is better. I don't have to acknowledge that she doesn't want anything to do with me.

I pull up to her apartment, sit in my car, and stare up at her building. She's probably asleep. I don't want to wake her, but I need her so much right now.

Maybe it's just a psychological effect of quitting smoking. I traded one addiction for another, but right now, I need a hit of the feeling I get when Rosie smiles at me or looks at me or whenever she's near me.

I need to smell that sweet perfume she wears. I need to taste those strawberry lips. I just need her.

I head inside, sighing when I see Sergio the Grouch at the concierge again. I ignore him and make my way to her apartment.

I stand in front of her door for minutes, which seems to drag on. I don't know what to expect when she opens up the door. I want her to smile and pull me in for a kiss.

I knock, hearing shuffling on the other side of the door. She opens the door, and I let out a breath of relief at the sight of her in front of me. Jesus. What has she done to me? It's like I can't breathe when she isn't near. I don't even know how to function without her anymore. What the hell is this?

"Rosie," I whisper, but I don't know what the hell to say next. She's standing in front of me, looking absolutely beautiful. She's in those cute little pajamas. Her hair flows down her back, and she doesn't have a speck of makeup on her gorgeous face. Her mole is on full show. But she's frowning. I didn't know what I'd expect, but it wasn't this.

She doesn't look happy to see me at all. Her brows are drawn together as if she's confused, and a slight frown is on her face. I want to wipe it off and replace it with one of those addicting smiles instead. I want her to smile at me.

"Grayson?" she asks. "What are you doing here?"

"I uh…" I mumble, running a hand through my hair. "I came to see you."

"You did?" she asks, raising her eyebrows.

I nod. "Yeah, you didn't answer my texts."

She shakes her head, and I deflate. This is it. This is when she'll tell me we're done and she never wants to see me again. Fuck, I knew I should have stayed home.

"I thought you didn't want to see me again," she says.

"What?"

She wipes her eyes. "The other day. I told you I would leave if you wanted me to. I thought that's what you wanted?"

"What?" I say again, shaking my head. "Rosie, I never wanted you to leave. I told you that stuff because I wanted to. Because I trust you. Because I *didn't* want you to leave."

"You don't?" she asks, widening her eyes.

I shake my head, taking a step closer to her. "Angel," I whisper, cradling her gorgeous face. "I've been driving myself crazy thinking you were done with me." She gasps a little as I run my thumb over her plump, pink lower lip. "Are you done with me?" I ask her. God, I want to kiss her.

Her lips are parted by my thumb. She looks up at me with those baby blue's staring into my soul. She looks like a dream. She shakes her head, and I grin, lowering my head and planting a soft kiss on those full lips of hers.

She melts into me, wrapping her arms around my neck, and I pick her up, holding her ass in my hands and wrapping her legs around my waist. I've missed this so much. I've missed her so much. I shut the door with my foot and head to her bed.

I sit her on the bed, trailing kisses down her neck. I start to lift her tank as she lets out a yawn. Fuck, I'm such an asshole. She's tired. She needs sleep, and I'm fucked up out of my mind wanting to forget everything and be with her.

I stop myself and lay her back down on the bed, propping her head on a pillow. I lower my head and press my lips to her forehead. "You're tired. I shouldn't have come here."

"You don't have to leave," she says, yawning again.

I let my eyes drift closed. I don't want to leave. Ever. "Lie down, Rosie."

She lies her head on the pillow, and I strip off my clothes, getting into bed beside her. I brush her hair away from her face, and she turns to face me. "Are you going to leave?" she asks, sounding a little sad.

I couldn't leave this bed for all the money in the world. There's nowhere else I'd rather be. "No, Rosie. I'm not going anywhere," I say, pulling her into me and my shoulders relax the moment she wraps her arms around me and cradles her head into my chest.

"I went to visit my parents," I whisper.

She lifts her head and pulls back a bit. "You did? In New York?"

I nod, brushing her hair out of her face and rubbing the strands between my fingers. "I killed my uncle."

"What?" she says, her eyes widening.

"At least, I thought I did. I thought I killed him. This whole time, I blamed myself."

She tightens her hold on me. "What happened?"

I sigh, staring up at the ceiling. "I used to hang out with my uncle. A lot. He was fun and nothing like my parents. He wasn't rich, and he definitely didn't have maids or any of that shit. He lived by himself in an apartment over his garage, where he worked on cars." I look down at her. "That's where the obsession started, I guess," I say, smiling down at her.

She squeezes my hand, urging me to continue. I tilt my head back. "He taught me how to drive and fix cars. He taught me everything I know. But he suffered from addiction." I swallow the lump in my throat. "He smoked weed, he drank, he did coke, even heroin. He was an addict, and I was just a kid. I didn't know what to do."

I was only eight when I noticed he wasn't himself. When he woke up at four in the afternoon, and his eyes were red. "I hated what the drugs were doing to him. He never hurt me, never gave me drugs. He would kill me if he knew I smoked, but he was a mess, Rosie." My voice cracks, and I clear my throat. "He looked like shit. Barely slept, barely ate, and he was broke and in so much debt from the drugs."

I blink away the wetness in my eyes and swallow. "One day, he told me to get a tool he needed for the car he was working on, and I went upstairs. I left him. Fuck, I wish I hadn't. But I did. When I got back… He'd done drugs all his life. I didn't know. Fuck, I didn't know."

I tried to ask Frank for help that same morning. I went into his office, wanting him to help his brother, but instead, I walked in on him and his assistant. He yelled at me to knock before coming in, and I left. He didn't help me, and in the end, I couldn't help my *dad*.

My voice is shaky, and if it weren't for Rosie squeezing my hand, I'd think I was back there. I had a few episodes right after it happened where I would see myself back there again, witnessing it like it was the first time.

"I didn't take long so he must have barely snorted the line, because when I came back he was out. Down on that hard concrete floor. His mouth was foaming, and he was spasming on the floor, and I did nothing. I watched. I was frozen in place, watching him die. I panicked. Only after he stopped, I grabbed my phone and called the police, but it was already too late. He was dead."

She tucks her head into the crook of my neck, leaving a soft kiss there. "It wasn't your fault," she whispers against my chest.

Those words make me feel like a ton of bricks have been removed from my chest. I've never heard anyone say that before. Not even my mother.

"He was my father," I whisper. "My mother ended up confessing that she cheated on my dad, or I guess, my uncle. Fuck." I breathe out. "This is so confusing."

She tightens her hold on me. "I blamed myself for years," I tell her. "I lived with the burden that I didn't help him. When he needed me, I didn't help him." I drop my head, looking down at her. "I watched my dad die."

Her eyes drift closed, and she wraps her arms around me, holding onto me. Fuck, this feels good. Being here with her. I don't ever want to leave. "It wasn't your fault. You're good, Grayson. You're a good person."

Every day I spend with her, I start to believe it a little more. Someone as good as Rosalie wouldn't want to be around me if I was so horrible, right?

"Is this what this is?" she asks, running her soft fingertips over the ink on my arm. Her eyes lift to look up at me as she continues caressing my skin.

I swallow and give her a curt nod. She looks back down, leaning in to kiss his birth date tatted on my skin. "He would have been so proud of you," she whispers against my skin. "Thank you for telling me."

Something thick builds in my throat. "I…" I take a breath and swallow down whatever I was about to say and say something smart instead. "Are you thinking of moving to Paris?" I haven't brought it up since she told me about it. But I can't stop thinking about it. She might move away. I won't see her ever again.

She lets out a breath, closing her eyes. "I don't know. Your mother is a wonderful person. It would be a dream come true. But I hate the fact that she's making me choose between two dreams."

I nod. "Yeah, I'm not the biggest fan of hers right now either." I should have talked to her about Rosie, but she doesn't know that we know each other or that we're… involved.

Rosie yawns again, struggling to keep her eyes open. "I'm sorry I woke you, angel. Go to sleep." I kiss her forehead, tucking her head into me.

"I'm sorry," she mumbles.

"For what?"

She lifts her head, and those blue eyes shine as she looks at me through hooded eyes. "You came looking for sex, and I can't give you that. You wanted a distraction, to have fun, and instead, I'm half asleep."

I sigh, closing my eyes when I feel her breath on my skin. "It's okay, Rosie. Get some sleep," I say, relaxing into her as she holds onto me.

The fucked-up thing is that I wasn't even thinking about sex. I was thinking about what we were doing right here. I wanted her arms wrapped around me as she tightens her hold on me until we fall asleep.

She feels right tucked next to me, her head fitted against my chest. She feels like she was made for me.

And I'm scared as fuck of what that means.

32

The L-word

Rosalie

I'm met with three angry faces. Well, not really angry, more like disappointed. "No." They all say at the same time.

My shoulders slump. "Why not?"

"Because you'd be working for someone else."

Gabi nods. "And all your designs would be under someone else's name," she says.

Leila puts her hand on my shoulder and frowns. "This isn't what you wanted, Rosie."

I sigh. I've been trying to rack my brain with what to do for the past two weeks. I was given a month, so time's running out, and I need to make a decision. I need to know if this job is the right thing for me to do or if my friends are right.

"It's going to be a long way away until I launch my own brand."

"Yeah, but you wanted to go to college, right?" Madi asks.

I nod.

"Then do that," Leila says. "You wanted this for years, Rosie, and now you want to abandon it?"

"Yeah, but Paris—"

"Will still be there when you graduate," she finishes.

"But the job offer won't be," I tell her.

"You don't need that job offer," Gabi says. "That was the first one, and there will be plenty more if you want it. But you want to create your own line with your own designs and your own name," she says.

That's true. I do want that. I want to create and design the clothes and be in charge of the whole operation, I do. But working for a designer like Emily Livingston would also be beneficial to my career. It would allow me to learn new things about the business that I wouldn't be able to do on my own.

"You wanted an inclusive line, right?" Leila asks. I nod. One of the most important things to me as a designer is to create high fashion for all body types. "You won't be able to do that if you work for someone else," she says.

I close my eyes. I'd love to live in Paris and work for a fashion designer, but I'd love to have my own line too. "You're right," I say on an exhale.

"So, does that mean you're staying?" Gabi asks.

I shrug. "I don't know. I think so." I only have two weeks to decide, but I think they're right. I can always try again once I graduate if I still want it, and if not, I can start creating my own line.

"Please stay," Leila says. "You're only eighteen, and this is our freshman year," she says. "We have four more years left. Let's make the most out of this."

That's the biggest reason I don't want to move to Paris. College. Being here with my friends and living the college life I always wanted. "Yeah," I say, nodding. "I want that."

"Good," Gabi says, exhaling and dropping her head back on the couch. "Any more life-changing news we should know about?" she asks, popping a chip in her mouth.

"Like Grayson?" Madi says.

My eyes flash towards her, looking towards where she's sat at the kitchen table. "What about him?"

"Really, Rosie?" she says.

"He's fine," I say with a shrug.

"That's it?" Gabi asks. "You drop a bomb on us, saying you're hooking up with him, and then leave us with nothing?" She shakes her head. "Where's the details? I want them."

I choke out a laugh. "I didn't tell you guys anything. You guessed."

She grins back at me. "And you just confirmed it."

I close my eyes. "Damn it."

"So now that the cat's out of the bag, what's going on with you two?" Gabi says.

I shrug. "I don't know."

She furrows her brows. "You don't know?"

"It's complicated," I say.

"Ah," Gabi says. "How well I know those words. Let it out, Rosie. Tell us everything."

I sigh. I might as well tell them. "I asked him to take my virginity."

"Wait, what?" Madi gasps.

"Yeah, you're a virgin?" Gabi asks, her brows raised.

Madi glares at Gabi. "That wasn't what I was shocked about," she tells her.

"I was," Gabi replies. "Look at her," she says, gesturing to me. "That girl oozes sex appeal."

"Uh… thanks? But technically, no. Not anymore," I say, unable to contain my grin.

"So, he did it?" Leila asks. "He took your virginity?"

I nod. "Yeah, it was… perfect."

Gabi snorts. "Lucky. My first time was on an old futon in his parents' basement. He smelled like cheese."

"Cheese?" Madi asks. "Why would he smell like cheese?"

She shrugs, taking a chip out of the bag and shoving it into her mouth. “His parents were cheese mongers. The whole house was a rat’s dream,” she says.

“Well, you love cheese,” Madi says, pointing down to her cheesy puffs. “So, it couldn’t have been that bad.”

“I love eating cheese, that doesn’t mean I want to smell it when he was deflowering me.”

Madi snorts. “I can’t believe you just used the word deflowering.”

Gabi grimaces. “Me neither,” she says, pulling out another chip.

“Okay, enough with the cheese,” Leila says, turning to face me. “So, what happened?”

I smile, remembering the gentle way that he held me and the way he stopped to make sure I was okay. It was everything I hoped for and more, and it was perfect because of him. “He took it slow,” I tell them. “He didn’t want to do it at first, he said he didn’t want to complicate things. So, he helped me in other ways.”

“What do you mean other ways? Anal?” Gabi says. Madi rolls her eyes, and Gabi’s mouth parts open. “What?” she says, shrugging. “It was a genuine question.”

“With life,” I say, instead, wanting to keep that night between Grayson and me.

“Huh?” Madi asks.

“I asked him to show me the ultimate college experience. Grayson Carter was the complete opposite of me that I could think of, and I wanted to know what it was like to live his life, to not have responsibilities, to let go, and have fun.”

“We could have shown you that,” Leila says.

"And you did," I tell her. "In a way. But being with Grayson was different. He showed me his life, his world, and I loved it." I smile, remembering every lesson with him. I loved going on adventures with him. I loved spending time with him in general.

"And him," Leila says.

"What?" I snap out of my thoughts and face her.

"You love him," she says. "It's all over your face."

"I don't know," I admit. "How do you even know you're in love?" I'm not a cynic like Grayson. I believe in love, and I love spending time with him. Everything in me needs to be with him, talk to him. Is this love, though?

"It consumes you," Gabi says. I look at her and see her staring into space, her throat moving as she swallows. "Everything reminds you of them. Everything you do makes you want to share it with them, and you want to spend every minute with them to the point where you can't imagine your life without them. Nothing in this world makes the pain of not having them around better. No matter who you date, kiss, or sleep with, it will never erase your feelings for that person, for what you wish you could have, but ultimately know will never happen." She blinks and then turns to face us, a weak smile on her face. "That's what love feels like."

We all stare at her as she swallows.

"Jesus, Gabi," Leila says. "Speaking from experience?"

She shrugs. "Something like that."

I think of what Gabi just said. How it consumes you, and you want to spend every minute with that person. That's what I feel for Grayson. The way he makes me feel is like there are a million butterflies in my stomach, but he also makes me feel like I have nothing to worry about whenever I'm with him.

I feel like I can be myself with him. Whenever I'm around him, I can be me, and he won't judge me. He doesn't want me to be anyone else other than myself. I love who Grayson is. He's a good person, although he tells himself the opposite, he's nothing like what people said and everything I hoped he would be. He's the kind of man I want to be around all the time, and I can never get enough of.

"I'm in love with Grayson." I breathe out.

"Hell yeah you are," Madi says. "You blush every time you talk about him. Granted you've only talked about him once, but I can see it all over your face," she says grinning.

"I'm in love with Grayson," I repeat.

"Uh… yeah?" Madi says.

I squeeze my eyes closed. "I'm in love with Grayson." It doesn't matter how many times I say it or admit it to myself, I can't make sense of it.

"Are you okay, Rosie?" Leila asks.

"Maybe she's processing it," Gabi says.

"No. I can't be in love with him," I say.

"Why not?" Gabi asks.

I exhale. "He said he wanted this to be casual. No feelings, no relationships." And I promised him I could do it. I was so sure, but I never stood a chance.

"You never know," Madi says. "He could change his mind."

I shake my head. "You don't understand. Grayson doesn't believe in love. He'll never be with me. He won't ever feel what I feel." I drop my eyes. "He'll never love me back."

"I know the feeling." Gabi mumbles.

"What do I do?" I ask them.

"Maybe you should tell him," Leila says.

"No." Gabi intercepts. "She can't do that. He'll freak."

I frown deeper. He will?

"You're not helping," Leila says to Gabi. "You never know. He could feel the same."

My eyes drift closed. "He doesn't." No matter how much I want him to, he doesn't love me, and he won't ever love me. It doesn't matter that I'm in love with him. He doesn't believe in it and doesn't feel the same about me.

"Then you have to cut it off," Madi says.

My head snaps up. "What?"

"You're going to hurt even more if you drag it out and fall more in love with him. And then, when it ends, you'll be crushed." She gives me a sympathetic smile. "But if you end it now, you can get over it, Rosie."

"I don't want to do that," I say, almost whispering. "I don't want this to end with Grayson. I don't want to be away from him. I want him near me all the time."

"I know," she says. "But it's the only solution."

I stare at my phone on the table, thinking of the last time I tried to avoid Grayson, and he still showed up at my place, wanting to see me. He trusted me enough to tell me about his uncle and his father. He let me in. I want more of that, and I don't want this to end.

I also want him to love me, and he can't do that. If I can't be with him, the least I can do is help him. He wants to leave Redfield and his parents, and he needs money to do that. He might not have any, but I do.

If I can't tell him how much I love him, I can show him instead.

33

What did she just say?

Grayson

The chair scrapes against the floor when I take a seat at the island. The delicious smell seeping into my nose as soon as I enter the kitchen. "What you making?" I ask Aiden.

He turns and faces me, laughing as he shakes his head. "It's almost two in the afternoon. Did you just wake up?"

I shrug. "I was tired." The lie rolls out of my mouth so easily. I barely slept, I tossed and turned all night, unable to shut my brain off. My uncle was my father. Everything I knew was a lie.

I still can't wrap my brain around it. I can't get over the betrayal. I'm on my own now. I have no one. I couldn't even get out of bed long enough to go to class yesterday, so sue me for wanting to stay in bed all day on the weekend.

What I really want to do is go to Rosie's again. That night, I slept like a baby with her arms wrapped around me and her head tucked into my chest. I can't sleep without her. I could go over there, but it doesn't seem like she wants to see me anymore.

She isn't answering my calls. I thought I made my feelings clear last time. I want to keep seeing her, but apparently, she doesn't want the same. It was a dumb thing to tell her what happened.

She doesn't care about my life or any of that stuff. She got what she wanted from me and is done with me. She deserves someone better, someone nice, someone that will treat her well and make her the center of their world. God, I wish I could be that someone. I think I could make her really happy.

"Smells good," I tell him, grinning when he pulls out a bowl and fills it with his mac and cheese, sliding it over to me.

I don't know where the hell he learned it from, but dude can cook. "Where did you learn to cook?" I ask him while shoving a spoonful into my mouth.

He fills another bowl for himself and sits on the other end of the island. "Myself," he says, digging into the food.

I don't push him on the subject. Everything Aiden has told me about his life was on his terms, whenever he wanted to tell me. So I stay silent and enjoy the food. I feel for the guy. I want to make sure that he's okay, but he clams up whenever I ask, so I let it go.

My phone lights up with a notification from my bank, and I inwardly groan. What now? I drop my spoon when I open up the app, seeing $50,000 has been added to my account. What the fuck?

I lift myself off the stool, staring at my phone, wondering where the hell the money came from.

"You good?" Aiden asks.

I don't bother looking at him. I see the payment came from New York, and I narrow my eyes, heading out outside and calling her.

She picks up on the second ring. "Grayson. Honey, it's so nice to hear from you."

"What the hell, mom?"

There's a pause. "Grayson? Is everything okay?" she asks.

"Why?"

"Honey, what's wrong?"

Is she trying to play it off like she didn't do this? "Is it some sort of bribe or something?" I ask her. "I don't need your money."

"Honey, what money? What's going on?" she asks in a panicked voice.

"The money you deposited into my account. 50 grand, mom, really?"

"Grayson, I didn't put any money in your account. I have no idea what you're talking about."

I still, my brows furrowing. She wouldn't lie about this. She'd have no reason to. "You didn't send the money?"

"No," she says. "Grayson, 50 thousand is a lot. What have you gotten yourself into?" she's quiet for a second, and then her voice cracks. "Are you doing drugs?"

I close my eyes, groaning. "No, mom. I told you I've never done drugs. Do you not know me?" I have never once touched the stuff. When I saw what it did to my uncle and how it ended his life, I never wanted to touch them.

I remember Rosie asking me for drugs and how I wanted to tell her what had happened. I didn't want the same thing to happen to her. When I walked in on her paranoid and hyperventilating, it was like it was happening all over again, and I couldn't stop it. The thought of losing her almost crippled me. I couldn't get off the floor when I saw her curled up there, needing me and begging me to help her.

"Honestly, Grayson, I don't. You changed after what happened."

"Can you blame me? I let him die, mom." This was the first time we have talked since dinner last week. I think knowing he was my father makes me want to talk about him.

"I don't blame you, honey. I blame myself."

I freeze, my eyebrows scrunching. "What do you mean?"

She's quiet for a second, but then I hear a sniffle. "I always wondered if what happened between us… He was a good man, Grayson, you know that. But the drugs, the drinking… I wonder if it was because of me."

"Mom," I say, shaking my head as I hear the words come out of her mouth. "No. You can't blame yourself. Uncle Gary loved you, he never said a bad word about you. He was just… he needed help, mom. I should have helped him. I should have done more."

"You did everything you could for him, honey," she says, her voice cracking.

"Not enough." I could have done more. I could have done… something.

She sighs. "I should have never kept this secret from you. I'm so sorry for doing that to you."

I swallow, about to say the words I never thought I'd say. "Did you love him?" I don't have to say which 'him' I mean. She knows.

"Yes," she breathes out. "I loved Gary so much. But ultimately, I was married to your dad. I didn't want to change that."

He's not my dad. My dad is dead.

"But I'm done with that," she says.

"What do you mean?"

"I'm divorcing him, honey," she tells me. "I always thought I was doing the right thing. Staying with him to give you a family. I wanted him to treat you like a son. But he never did. And now that you know the truth, there's no reason to keep pretending anymore. I should have never subjected you to a lifetime with that man, knowing he would never love you like a father should love his child."

My throat clams up, a tight feeling in my chest. "Mom?"

"Yes, Grayson?"

"I'm sorry."

"For what, honey?"

I blow out a breath, wishing I had a cigarette right now. "For being a disappointment."

She sighs. "Don't believe those words Frank told you. You were never a disappointment to me. You're my son. I love you, Grayson."

Fuck. I feel the tears start to rise, so I clear my throat. "Yeah. Listen, I've got to go."

I hang up, blinking away the wetness in my eyes, and focus on my phone. If it wasn't my mother, then who the fuck sent me that money. I call my bank, waiting for the music to end and for someone to pick up the phone.

Finally, the line picks up. "Hello, this is Mary speaking at National Bank. How may I help you today."

"Hi, this is Grayson Livingston. I recently received a deposit, and I'm wondering who sent it. I can't see the sender."

"One second, let me check that for you." A pause and the sounds of a keyboard clicking echoes on the other end. "Yes, it was sent anonymously."

I curse silently. "Can you just tell me who it was?"

"I'm sorry, sir, we can't discuss other customers' details," she says.

"I don't want details, I just want a name. I want to uh… thank them."

"Let me see what I can do for you." Another pause and more keyboard clicks, and then she clears her throat. "Okay, I have here on record that a Miss Rosalie Whitton deposited the money into your account. Does that help, sir?"

What the fuck?

"Yes, thank you," I say as I hang up the phone.

Rosie? Why the hell would Rosie send me money? I walk back into the house, grab the keys from the counter, and head out of there. I don't care if she doesn't want to see me anymore. I at least deserve a reason for giving me money. Is this a parting gift?

I race to her house, barely stopping the car before I step out of it, seeing her stand outside her apartment building, looking so beautiful in a white dress. My favorite. Fuck.

She lifts her head and smiles when she sees me. Her smile is so wide, making me forget why I'm here in the first place. I can't help but get weak when I see that smile that makes me want to pull her into me and kiss her, but I'm mad at her right now.

"What the hell, Rosie?"

Her smile disappears, and a frown replaces it, and I instantly want to kick myself for removing that beautiful smile from her face.

"Grayson?" she asks, frowning as I step closer to her.

"Why?" I ask.

"Why what?"

"I know it was you that deposited the money into my account. I want to know why."

She narrows her eyes. “I told them I wanted to remain anonymous.”

“What the fuck is going on? Is this a repayment for taking your virginity? I banged you good, so you pay me? I’m not a prostitute,” I snap.

Her eyes widen, and she steps back. “No, I just…”

“You what? What the fuck was that for?”

“I wanted to help you.”

“Help me?” I repeat.

“Yes. You needed money. I had some, so I helped you.”

I laugh bitterly. “I don’t want your daddy’s money, princess. I didn't need your help, and I never asked for it. You came to me asking me to make you the complete opposite of who you are, remember? I don't need to be your charity case.”

Her lip trembles, and I clench my jaw, fisting my hands to avoid pulling her into me. “I don’t need you. I don’t need a needy girl wanting to cling onto me like a wet dog,” I say, reciting Aiden’s words.

I don’t know why I’m doing this, why I’m hurting her. Why I’m saying these things I don’t mean. Maybe it’s the sleep deprivation, but whatever it is, I’m being a complete asshole to her right now, and I know it.

I don’t want to hurt her, even if I’m mad that she did this without asking me first, without realizing that I’d hate for her to give me her money, I can’t hurt her.

“I didn’t cling to you,” she says, her voice breaking.

Oh fuck, don’t do this to me. I might break if I see her cry. I want to take it all back. I didn’t mean a single word that escaped my mouth.

“Why, Rosie?” I ask her, my voice softening.

She looks down at the ground and shakes her head.

"Why?" I ask her again.

"Because I love you!" she yells, lifting her head in time for me to see a tear fall down her cheek.

I flinch backwards. What the fuck did she just say?

34

Broken hearts club

Rosalie

"You're lying."

I feel another teardrop on my lip, tasting the salty evidence of Grayson breaking my heart. I wanted to help him, and he came to me, angry as if I had attacked him.

"What do you want me to say, Grayson?" I'll do anything he asks me to at this point. He wanted to know why I helped him, and I told him the truth. I love him. I helped him because I love him, even if he doesn't love me.

He's frantic, running a hand through his hair as he stares at me with shock. "Tell me you're lying."

I shake my head, using my hand to wipe my tears. "I can't do that."

He laughs bitterly. "You don't love me," he says. "It's impossible. Love isn't real."

I'm sick of him saying that. I'm tired of him trying to invalidate what I feel for him, for making me think I'm crazy for being in love with him. "You can't dictate my feelings," I tell him. "I love you, Grayson," I say again, my voice cracking. "I'm in love with you, and that's why I helped you. Because even if you don't want to be with me, I still want you to be happy, whether that's here or in another state."

His jaw clenches when he hears those words come out of my mouth. He shakes his head, avoiding eye contact with me.

"Whatever you feel, it's not love. You're attracted to me, maybe even like spending time with me, but that's not love. There's no such thing!"

"I love you," I tell him again, feeling the tears fall freely now. I never thought he'd be the one to make me cry.

"No," he snaps. "You don't. What you feel is lust, but you're too inexperienced to know the difference." He laughs bitterly, running a hand down his face. "I knew this would happen. You're too naïve for your own good. I'm the first guy to stick it in you, and now you think you're in love."

Every word he says digs into my stomach like a knife. *Too inexperienced. Too naïve.* "I love you," I say again, my voice so quiet it's barely a whisper.

"Stop," he says, pinching his nose. "Stop saying that."

I take a step closer to him, wrapping my hand around his. "You don't feel anything for me at all?" I ask him. "Nothing?" He doesn't need to be in love with me today. I just want to know I'm not alone in this and that he has feelings for me, no matter how small. Anything. I just want something.

He swallows as he looks down at our hands. Mine wrapped in his as I intertwine our fingers, trying to make him feel the bolt of electricity I feel whenever I touch him, whenever I'm near him.

He curses and pulls away from me, and I know. "No," he says. The knife twists deeper. "I don't." He steps back, and his jaw clenches.

"Nothing?" I ask again, my lip trembling.

He looks to the side, his jaw clenched. He can't even look at me. "I told you. I warned you that if you couldn't handle it, we wouldn't do it."

"I didn't know I would fall in love with you."

He looks at me again, and his mouth opens like he wants to say something and then closes again. "I told you not to catch feelings. I never wanted to hurt you. Never." His jaw clenches again. "This is all on you. I'm sorry." And with that he turns and walks away.

"Wait," I call out. He doesn't turn. He keeps walking towards his car. "So that's it? We're over?"

He steps inside and shakes his head. "We never happened."

He closes the door and speeds off, leaving me standing alone and heartbroken.

35

Angel wings

Grayson

"What the fuck are you doing?" Aiden yells.

Jesus Christ. My head throbs as his voice ripples through the air. He's been doing that a lot recently, getting involved in things that have nothing to do with him.

"Drinking." I spit out. "You got a problem with that?"

He narrows his eyes at me, staring down at the bottle in my hands. "Since when?"

I snort. "I've always drunk. I'm not a Mormon."

He shakes his head. "Grayson. You drank one beer, two max. Never a full bottle of whiskey before." His face twists in disgust. "You're bordering on alcoholism."

I don't want to hear him anymore. I groan, burying my head in my hands. "Shut up."

"I'm trying to help you out here."

For fucks sake. My head snaps up. "I don't need your help," I yell. "Why does everyone think I need help? I didn't ask you or her for anything." Do people just automatically assume I'm a helpless fuck up?

"Her? Rosalie?" he asks.

I don't want to talk about it. I ignore him, taking a drink out of the bottle, feeling the liquid burn in my throat.

"Is this about your parents?"

I wave a hand. "Yeah, sure." I don't want to go into details about how he was right and give him a reason to gloat.

"That sounds convincing," he says wryly.

"Listen," I say, looking up at him. "I don't want to talk about my feelings or whatever bullshit you're trying to do, so why don't you fuck off and go find a girl to fuck?"

"Jesus Christ," he whispers. "What the fuck happened to you?"

I look away, feeling my jaw clench. Rosie happened. She told me she loved me. She had to ruin a great thing we had with feelings. Why did she do that? Fuck, this is all my fault. I knew I shouldn't have gotten involved with her, especially since she was so innocent when she came to me.

Aiden was right. She mistook what we had for something else, and now she thinks she loves me.

Fuck, I'm such a dickhead. I ruined that poor girl. I didn't want to hurt her. I hated seeing that look on her face, the tears spilling down as she looked at me and kept repeating, 'I love you' over and over again.

Every time she said it, it was like a knife digging deeper and deeper into my chest. It fucking hurt knowing I could never say those words back to her. And when she asked if I had feelings for her, I didn't know what to say.

The way she wrapped her hand around mine made my skin burn, making me gasp for air like I always do whenever she's around me. It clouded my judgment and made my brain foggy with emotion, ready to tell her yes, that I had feelings for her. But then I blinked and thought rationally, and I knew that I didn't, not in the way she was asking me.

I love being around her, having her near me, seeing her smile, the way she talks, her laugh, everything about her, but

I don’t love her. I couldn’t love her because it wasn’t real. I like her, sure, but there was nothing more to it.

“Dude, just get out of here,” I mumble, bringing the bottle to my lips and taking a swig.

“I’m not going anywhere. Not until you tell me what’s going on. You’re scaring me.”

“Don’t worry, I’m not like your junkie mom.” I bite my lip. What the fuck is wrong with me?

He squints his eyes, shaking his head. “I know you’re hurting right now with whatever is going on that you won’t tell me. But let me remind you that my fists still fucking work, whether you’re crying or not.”

“I’m not crying.”

“You will when I kick your ass,” he threatens.

I laugh. “Go ahead. At least then you’ll leave me alone.”

“I told you I’m not leaving. You’re my best friend, even if you’re acting like an asshole.”

I groan. “Fuck. I just want to be alone. Why won’t you get that?” I want him to leave, to let me rot away in peace without hounding me for questions I don’t want to answer. “Why are you still here?”

“Because I love you, man.”

“Jesus Christ.” I laugh. What the hell is wrong with everyone?

“Tell me what’s going on and how I can help you,” he says.

“You can’t. No one can help me.” I feel like I have a massive hole in my chest, and nothing can fill it. This bottle stinging my throat doesn't fill it, despite every sip that I take.

“I can try.”

I snap my eyes to his. “Can you bring my uncle back to life?”

He frowns. “He died?”

I swallow. “When I was thirteen.”

“Is it his birthday or something?”

“Nope. Just celebrating the fact that I’m alone,” I say, holding out the bottle and bringing it to my lips once again.

Aiden sighs. “Ok, you have to start talking because I have no idea what’s going on.”

“He was a drug addict.” I hear him hold his breath, and I can’t help but laugh. Yeah, he didn’t see that coming. “And he overdosed when I was thirteen.”

“Shit.”

“Yeah. It gets better,” I say, swallowing another sip. “I visited my parents this weekend. Turns out he was my dad.”

He’s quiet for a while and then clears his throat. “So, you’re drinking because?” he asks.

I glared at him. “Isn’t that reason enough?” He said he’d leave, and yet he’s still here. I just want him to go.

“Yeah, but you hated your dad, right? Didn’t seem like you’d care that he wasn’t your real dad. So why are you bummed out?”

I sigh, closing my eyes and tipping my head back on the couch. I’m not going to spill my fucking guts to him. I just needed a drink, no real reason to it.

“Nice tattoo,” he says, gesturing to my arm.

I look down, staring at the plastic wrap around my arm, and swallow hard.

“Angel wings, huh?”

I close my eyes, cursing under my breath. It was a dumb move, but I couldn’t get her out of my mind. She’s already deep in my body, might as well have her on it. I don't reply. Instead, I take another drink from the bottle.

"Fine. You don't want to talk about it? I'll leave."

"Thank God," I mumble.

He grabs the bottle from my hands. "And I'm taking this with me," he says, holding it up.

I get up from the couch. "You can't fucking do that." Honestly, who does he think he is? He might be a hot shot on campus, but he can't just take my fucking drink.

"I can if I think you'll drink yourself to death," he says.

I scoff. "That's not going to happen."

He shakes his head. "Wake the fuck up," he says. "You drank half a bottle already." I look at the bottle in his hands, seeing it's half empty. I drank all that? "What you need is a shower and figure out why you're really drinking right now."

He walks away, and I groan, sitting back down on the couch where I slept last night. I reach inside my pocket, take out a cigarette, and light it up. I'm not with Rosie anymore, so I can smoke again any time I want.

I bring it to my lips and… I can't do it. I can't smoke because every time I bring it to my mouth, I think of the look on her face when I kissed her. Fuck.

I throw the whole pack in the trash and head into the kitchen. I open the cabinets looking for a drink. I don't give a fuck what it is as long as it takes some of this pressure from my chest away.

I curse when I can't find anything. I guess Aiden went through and got rid of everything. Dickhead.

I head upstairs, wanting to get a decent night of sleep. I haven't slept well in days. I can't get into my bed because my sheets smell like her. I can't keep torturing myself by sniffing the remains of her perfume. I'll never get her out of my mind then.

I rip the sheets off my bed and strip off my clothes, getting in the shower. I lather my body, closing my eyes, remembering her soapy hands running down my body, her soapy tits in my mouth, the way her legs trembled when I ate her out. Fuck.

I snap my eyes open, looking down at where my hand is stroking my cock at the thought of her. What is wrong with me? It's not like she was my girlfriend. We fucked twice, big deal. I've fucked many girls on campus way more than that. Why is this one girl affecting me this way?

I can't even take a shower without thinking about her. I can't sleep without being reminded of her soft hands wrapping around my body and her body nestling into me. I can't smoke without seeing her face wrinkled in disgust. I can't do anything because of her.

I might have hurt her.

But she fucked me up even more.

36

Step 5: Acceptance

Rosalie

I pull the sheet over my head when I hear the front door close. Leila has been in and out of my apartment ever since Grayson and I broke up.

Technically we didn't break up because, according to him, we never happened. But we happened. At least to me. He was my first kiss, my first time, my first love. He was my first everything. He showed me how he lived, he showed me freedom, and I loved the version of myself that was happy with him.

I felt like I could be myself with him without feeling like I had to impress anyone. There were no rules, restrictions, or expectations. He took me as I was and made me fall for him.

The last connection I have to Grayson is the bank notification of the money being returned to my account. He's done with me. He wants nothing to do with me, not even my help. And now here I am in bed on a Friday, heartbroken over a boy who never even loved me.

Not to mention I missed class this whole week. I can't even get out of bed and get in the shower. I can't stop thinking about the time he filled the bath up and took care of me when I was high and delirious. How could he not feel anything for me when he treated me like I was everything?

He completely ruined every other guy for me. How the hell can I find someone who measures up to him and looks at me like he did? How can I find someone who will whisper sweet nothings in my ear and call me angel? How am I supposed to believe that love is real if Grayson did all of that and doesn't love me?

"Hey," Leila says, walking into my bedroom.

I groan and ball up under the covers, wanting her to get the message that I don't need an intervention, or a pep talk, or whatever she's here for. I just want to wallow in my misery of being a stupid, naïve, inexperienced girl who fell for Grayson even though he warned me not to.

"How are you feeling?" she asks.

I bury my head into the mattress, groaning again.

I feel the bed dip as she sits on the edge. "Listen, Rosie. I'm here for you. Whatever you need, I'm here."

I don't respond. I squeeze my eyes shut, feeling my lip tremble as tears spill out of me. I don't want anyone here. All I want is Grayson. But I can't have that.

She sighs and stands up. "C'mon. You've stayed in bed all week. I think it's time to get up and move on."

I roll my eyes and pull the sheets down, looking up at her. "I don't want to move on."

She frowns a little and shakes her head. "Rosie, you can't stay depressed forever."

"I'm not depressed," I tell her. "I'm just sad. I'm allowed to be sad."

She nods and then scoots closer beside me. "What happened with Grayson?" she asks.

That day after Grayson broke my heart, I came upstairs and buried myself in the sheets, still smelling his body wash, and cried myself to sleep. And when the girls came over, they found me in bed crying and asked what had happened. I didn't tell them. I just told everyone to leave and let me cry it out.

I don't know how much longer I'll feel like this. Leila might be right. It may be time to move on. Ever since I started this with Grayson, I knew how it would end. I just never expected to fall for him and have him tell me he feels nothing for me at all.

Am I stupid? Because I saw how he looked at me, how he smiled at me and took care of me, and I'm supposed to believe that meant nothing?

"Maybe I should rethink Paris."

She narrows her eyes at me. "Is this you wanting the job offer, or you trying to run away?"

I sigh, tipping my head back. "I told him I loved him," I whisper. Of course, I want to run away. How can I stay here and see him around campus?

"You told him?" she asks. I nod, squeezing my eyes shut. "And what did he say?"

"That he doesn't feel the same. That he feels nothing for me at all," I say, my voice breaking.

"That's bullshit," she says. "There's no way he feels nothing for you, Rosie. He called me, angry as hell, telling me that you could have died. He said, 'what were you thinking giving her drugs? That was so stupid of you. If you were really her friend, you wouldn't have done that.'"

"He said that?"

She nods, her face dropping as a frown forms on her face. "I'm so sorry, Rosie. I would never have thought that would happen." She swallows. "I don't have much experience with weed. I just thought edibles would be easier for you. I should have written a note or something."

I shake my head. I don't want her to blame herself. "It's not your fault. You texted me."

"Yeah, and that wasn't enough. I should have known your phone would have died or—"

"You couldn't have known that," I say. "I don't blame you, and you shouldn't blame yourself."

"I do," she says, her eyes welling up. "I honestly can't apologize enough."

I reach out from under the covers and squeeze her hand. "I love you, Leila. You did nothing wrong. You helped me with something I asked for. It's not on you, plus I'm okay."

"Yeah," she says, smiling as she looks at me. "Yeah, you're okay."

I smile. "I can't believe he yelled at you." I think this is the first time I'm smiling in a week, and it's about Grayson. The thought of him yelling at my best friend about my safety makes me want to laugh, but then I think of everything that happened, and that empty feeling returns.

"Yeah," she says, chuckling. "And by the way, how did he get my number? You know I hate giving people my number," she asks, raising her brows.

I bite my lip. "I'm sorry, he must have gotten it from my phone," I say, shrugging.

"It's fine," she says with a sigh.

"Why do you hate people having your number, by the way?"

She shrugs. "I just don't want someone to get a hole of it. People get too clingy. I strictly only do one-night stands," she says.

I furrow my brows. "Doesn't that get lonely?" I ask her. I couldn't imagine sleeping with a new guy every night. It sounds horrible to me. I'm so glad I felt comfortable with Grayson before he finally took my virginity. It was a complete game changer, being able to trust him with my body.

"It works for me," she says, shrugging.

I sigh. "The one time I try to hook up with a guy, and I fall in love."

"It wasn't just about the sex though. It sounds like you hung out and talked. Of course, you'd get attached."

She's right. It wasn't just about the sex. I trusted him and liked him and then gave my body to him. I should have known this would happen. "Then why didn't he?" I ask. If he liked being around me too, why didn't he get attached?

She looks defeated as her shoulders slump. "I don't know," she says. "But I don't believe he feels nothing for you, though."

I sigh and look away from her. "Trust me, he doesn't."

She finally stands up from the bed and pulls the curtains open. "Okay, get up."

I snap my eyes closed and bring the sheet back over my head. "What are you doing?" I ask her, my eyes struggling to adjust to the light I haven't seen in seven days.

"An intervention," she says. "You've wallowed enough. Now it's time for step two."

"Which is?" I ask her, popping my head out from under the sheets, squinting from the light flowing into the dark room.

"Get back out there," she says, standing with her hands on her hips.

I shake my head. Nope, not yet. "Isn't there some steps in between that?"

"Well, you missed denial, anger, and bargaining, and went straight to depression, which means the next step is acceptance."

I shake my head again. "I'm not ready for that."

"And you never will be if you stay in bed all day," she says.

I pull the covers over my head, snuggling into the mattress. "But it's so comfy here," I say.

"I bet," Leila says, ripping the covers off the bed, leaving me in just the sheet. "But how about we go out tonight?" she says. I groan, turning over and burying my head in my pillow. "C'mon. The girls are going to the bar later tonight. You can get dressed, look sexy, and try to move on."

None of that sounds appealing to me. "I just want to sleep," I tell her, the noise muffled by the pillow.

"You can sleep all you want after we go."

I look up and squint at her. "Can I eat a whole tub of ice cream?"

She smiles and holds up two fingers. "Two. But you need to get your butt off this bed first. You in?" she asks.

I pout. "Do I have to?"

She nods. "It's the only way you'll start to get over him, Rosie."

All I know is that I don't want to feel like this anymore. I don't want to sit and cry over Grayson and think we did and realize it was all a game to him. A favor and nothing more. "Okay."

"What was that?" she says, lifting her eyebrows in shock.

I roll my eyes, throwing my pillow at her. "I said okay."

She laughs, grinning, and I laugh along with her. Maybe it won't be so bad. "Let's go," she says, pulling my arms up and off the bed. "You need a shower," she says, wrinkling her nose. "You stink."

"I do not," I say, defensively.

"Rosie, te quiero, but you smell of misery and desperation," she teases, shoving me out of my room. "C'mon," she says, trailing behind me. "Let's find something hot for you to wear."

37

Dance the pain away

Rosalie

I don’t want to be here.

I want to go back to bed and bury myself in my sheets until I can get Grayson’s smell out of my mind. I love the girls, and I appreciate everything they’re doing to try and make me forget about the hollow feeling in my chest, but right now, I would prefer to be alone.

I don't want to move on or meet anyone new. I just want to be alone in my misery and focus on how I'm to blame for how I'm feeling. That I was dumb enough to fall for a guy that specifically told me not to do that.

“You want another drink?” Leila asks.

I shake my head, fiddling with the straw in my empty glass.

“Maybe she wasn’t ready yet,” Gabi says.

“I wasn’t,” I mumble.

“She doesn’t need to get under a guy today,” Madi says. “She just needs to get out of that apartment and hang out with us. She needs to see that Grayson isn’t the only guy that exists. There’s plenty of guys who’d be interested in her,” she says.

I glance up, meeting her eyes. “I don’t want anyone else,” I tell her. Because the truth is, even if there were a row of guys standing outside waiting for me, I wouldn’t even glance their way. I want Grayson. I love Grayson, and I can't have him.

"Right now," she says. "You're hurting. I get that, but you've got to accept the fact that you and Grayson aren't going to happen."

I shake my head, feeling the tears spring in my eyes. "I love him, Madi," I tell her. "How am I supposed to get over that? I can't just turn those feelings off."

How did I even get into this position? I wish I hadn't gone to that party or played Never Have I Ever, or gone to Grayson's house begging him to take my virginity.

"I know, Rosie. I know," she says.

"Just hang out with us tonight," Leila says, putting her hand on my shoulder. "I promised you a tub of ice cream when we get home."

"Two," I say, holding up two fingers.

She smiles. "Okay, two," she agrees. "But that warrants at least a walk to the bar."

I sigh. "I don't want another drink."

She nudges me on the shoulder. "Who said it was for you?" she says, a smirk on her face.

The others start laughing, and I choke out a laugh, too, lifting out of the booth. "Fine," I say. "What do you want?" I ask her.

She shrugs. "A beer is fine."

I look down at her glass, still half full. I don't even think she wanted another drink. She just wanted to give me an excuse to not sit in the booth sulking all night.

I smile down at her, silently thanking her, and then turn, heading for the bar. I see Aiden at the counter once again, and he smiles when he sees me walking towards him, and I give him a tight-lipped smile.

I want to ask him. Should I ask him?

"Hey, Rosalie," he says, flashing that grin that makes girls fall to their knees.

"Hey," I say, leaning against the counter and sliding over the cash. "A beer, please."

He snorts. "You don't really look like the beer type," he says, lifting his brow.

I laugh. "It's not for me," I tell him, turning my head and pointing at Leila, who's now in the corner of the room, talking to some guy. "It's for my friend over there."

"Does your friend have a name?" He asks.

"Leila," I say. I turn around, and his eyes are still on Leila. "So, that beer?" I ask.

His eyes turn back to me, and he shakes his head, snapping out of it. "Yeah, sure. Coming right up," he says, grabbing a glass and filling it up.

I chew on my bottom lip, staring up at him. Should I ask him? I mean, he is his roommate. He would know how Grayson is doing or if he's dating other girls.

Maybe I shouldn't ask him. I don't want to hear that he's moved on already and is perfectly happy and really never felt anything for me. That would shatter me even more.

The more I wait, the more I battle with myself. "How's Grayson?" I blurt out.

He pauses, his eyes widening as he looks at me. "Uh…" He says, scratching the back of his head. Oh god, what is he about to tell me?

I sigh. "Never mind," I say, looking down at the glass sitting on the counter.

He curses and then sighs. “He’s a mess, Rosie.”

I look up at him, and his brows are furrowed. “He is?” I don’t know how I feel about that. I don’t want him to be hurting, but why would he? This is what he wanted.

Aiden nods. “He’s a wreck. I don’t exactly know what happened between you two, but—"

“Oh, no,” I interrupt, shaking my head. “Nothing happened between us,” I say, feeling the bitterness of those words on my tongue. Technically that’s what Grayson said.

He raises his brow. “Rosalie. C’mon.”

He knows.

“He told you?”

Aiden shakes his head. “I heard you,” he says, his lips twitching.

My brows scrunch together. “Heard me what?” My cheeks heat as I catch on to what Aiden is telling me. “Oh.”

“Yeah.” He laughs.

I bury my face in my hands, trying to hide the embarrassment I feel from Aiden hearing me and Grayson have sex.

“I don’t know what happened between you two,” he repeats. “He hasn’t exactly said your name, but I can only imagine it has something to do with you, with how you look right now.”

“Is it that obvious?” I ask him.

“Yeah,” he says. “You look just as bad as he does.”

“Wow.” I scoff. “Thanks.”

He laughs. “You still look hot, don’t worry. I see the same look in your eyes that he has in his.”

I shrug. “He ended it.”

“Yeah,” he says, nodding. “I guessed as much.”

"So I don't know why he's upset. He got what he wanted." I say, feeling a twinge of pain in my chest. The thought of Grayson feeling a fraction of what I'm feeling is unbearable to me. Even if he doesn't love me, I love him, and I don't want him to hurt.

"I don't think so," he mutters, sliding the drink over to me.

"Thanks," I say, handing him the cash, and he waves me off.

"Tell your friend it's on me."

I laugh. "Will do," I say, picking up the glass and heading back to the table. I set the drink down in front of Leila, who's got her eye on the guy she was talking to earlier.

I hand her the money, and she frowns. "The drink is for me," she says. "I'm paying for it."

I shake my head, a smile on my face. "It wasn't me," I tell her, pointing over to Aiden, who's looking our way. "It was him."

She turns her head, looking at Aiden, who smirks at her and turns his head away from her direction. "Oh," she says, taking the drink from me and taking a sip.

She glances at Aiden once more, who's not looking over anymore as he talks to a girl at the bar, and then turns to look at the guy who she was talking to earlier. How is it so easy for her to be attracted to a guy and forget about him the next day?

I wish I could do that. I wish I could forget Grayson, but part of me also doesn't want that. It wants to remember every good memory I had with him. How it felt to ride with him on the motorcycle, how he made me feel when he sped up his car, how his lips tasted, how he smiled at me and called me angel, how so deeply in love I am with that man.

I always knew I'd never end up having the kind of love I wanted and dreamed of. I've been preparing to be set up with a country club boy ever since I could walk, so I thought, what's the harm in having fun? But what I didn't know was that I'd fall deeply in love with him, that it would consume me and make me see everything so differently. The way he holds me, the way he smiles at me, I want that forever.

I want to find something like that for the rest of my life. And I want it with someone that feels the same thing as I do. Unrequited love is a bitch. My heart hurts all the time. It physically feels empty. It's as if a part of me is missing. A part of me that doesn't want to be mine.

I tip my head back and sigh. I just want to forget it all. The next thing I know, someone's grabbing at my arm, and I twist my head, seeing it's Gabi. "C'mon," she says. "Let's dance."

I groan. "I don't feel like dancing," I tell her.

She fake gasps. "I feel offended," she says, putting her hand over her chest dramatically.

I laugh. "I thought Madi was the actress."

She shrugs and then tugs on my arms once more. "C'mon. It's the only thing I'm good at. If I can't cheer you up, then I feel I've not done my job."

I roll my eyes. "Fine," I say, standing up and letting her lead me to the middle of the bar.

She takes hold of my hands as her hips move along to the beat, and she smiles at me. I stand awkwardly in front of her, and then her eyes snap to mine, and she frowns. "You're not dancing."

"No one else is dancing," I whisper to her, looking around at the guys staring at us with a grin on their faces.

She glances around and then shrugs. “So? Don’t live for them. Live for yourself.”

I freeze in place. Gabi notices and frowns a little. “What?” she asks.

My lips raise in a small smile. “Grayson said that to me once.”

Her brows raise. “He did?” I nod, remembering our trips and how he always wanted me to be myself. “Huh,” she says. “Maybe he’s not a complete asshole.”

I frown. “Yeah.”

She pulls me towards her, and I yelp. She smirks as she squeezes my hands. “No more thinking of Grayson.” Her hands leave mine and drift to my hips. “Dance,” she whispers, and I chuckle, moving my hips underneath her hands until she lets go, and we’re both dancing alongside each other to some 90’s hip hop song.

It feels good. To let go. To dance like truly nobody’s watching, even though they definitely are. I don't focus on any of them. My eyes stay on Gabi as we dance, and she laughs, closing her eyes and moving her hips to the music. I copy her moves, throwing my head back and dancing to the music.

I step back and bump into someone. I snap my eyes open. “I’m so sorry.” I blurt out, turning around and staring at a chest. I look up, and I’m met with a pair of blue eyes looking down at me as he smiles.

“My bad,” he says, chuckling. “You were lost in the music. I should have known better.”

“Yeah,” I say, laughing nervously. “I wasn’t paying attention.”

“I was,” he says. “And you’re stunning.”

My face drops. I turn my head to the side, see Gabriella smirking at me, and then turn back to the guy. He's cute. Tall, light brown hair, blue eyes. But he's not Grayson. The way he calls me stunning does nothing to me. It's nothing compared to how Grayson looks at me or calls me angel.

I give him a smile. "Oh, thanks," I say.

"No worries," he says with a chuckle, flashing his smile. "Wanna get a drink?"

"Uh… I'm with a friend, so…" I turn to Gabi, and she nods, mouthing 'go.' I sigh and turn back to the guy, who's waiting for an answer. "On second thought, I'd love a drink."

He grins and leads us to the bar. Aiden sees me once again, and his eyes travel from me to the guy, his brows furrowed, but I look away from him and turn to the guy beside me.

"I'm Rosalie, by the way," I tell him, sitting on the stool.

He smiles again, his pure white teeth flashing at me. "Andrew," he says. "What would you like to drink?"

"A margarita is fine." Everything reminds me of Grayson. The first time he brought me here and bought me a drink. A margarita. He let me get drunk and carried me home. God, I miss him.

He nods and turns to Aiden, who I'm avoiding glancing at. "A margarita for the girl and a scotch on the rocks for me."

I see from my peripheral Aiden dipping his chin and moving away to make the drinks, sliding them over to us when he's done. He doesn't say a word, which I appreciate. It might be a little too early to move on, but I have to try. I don't need to kiss him or even like him. I just need to talk to other guys.

"Thank you," I say, taking a sip of my drink as ice sloshes around in his.

"My pleasure," he says, grinning and looking down my body.

What do I even say to him? Do we have to do small talk? God, I hate small talk. It was so easy speaking to Grayson. I didn't have any first-date jitters. I never felt like I ever had to impress him.

I didn't have anything to be scared of. He always made me feel comfortable and like there was nothing to be ashamed of. So why can't I talk to this guy?

We sit in silence as we sip our drinks, and I try to think of what I can talk to him about. But before I can open my mouth, he stands from the stool and holds out his hand. "Will you dance with me?" he asks.

"Uh…"

He shakes his head. "I couldn't keep my eyes off you earlier, and I'd love to be the person you were dancing with instead."

That sounds almost… sweet. I nod. At least dancing doesn't warrant talking. "Sure. I'd love to." I say, taking a final sip of my drink and standing up, taking his hand.

The music changes to a slow song as we head to the middle of the bar, and he puts his hands on my waist. I drift mine up to his neck, giving him a tight-lipped smile. This feels so wrong. It shouldn't be his skin under my hands. It shouldn't be his neck I'm holding on to. It shouldn't be his hands on my waist.

But I lean in, dropping my head on his shoulder as he tightens his hold on me. I close my eyes, imagining it's Grayson. My friends probably wouldn't approve of that, but it's the only way I can stomach being here right now.

I imagine it's Grayson's hands on me, I imagine it's his neck I'm holding onto, I imagine it's his dark hair that I tangle my fingers in, I imagine it's his dark eyes I'm looking into. Oh shit.

It is.

My eyes are staring into Grayson's. I'm looking at Grayson. He's staring back at me with his jaw clenched, and his eyes are darkened, fire burning in them.

I gulp and hold onto Andrew as we continue staring at each other, none of us daring to break eye contact.

Why is he looking at me? Why is he here? Is he going to pick some girl up and bring her back to his bed? The bed where he took my virginity. The bed where we slept together. The bed where I wrapped my arms around him.

No way. I spin us so I'm no longer staring at Grayson, and I continue dancing with Andrew.

38

Does this song ever end?

Grayson

What the fuck is she doing with that guy?

I shouldn't be asking that, and I definitely shouldn't be imagining all the ways I can break that asshole's face. I was the one who ended it with her. I was the one who couldn't tell her the words she wanted to hear. I was the one who said we never happened.

Which is complete bullshit. We happened, and we were fucking good. I shouldn't have said that to her, and I shouldn't have ended it. But hearing her say those words to me with her sweet, breathy voice on the brink of tears as she begged me to love her back, I couldn't do it.

The reality is I like her a lot, so fucking much, but what she wants from me, I can't give her. No matter how much she thinks she loves me. She doesn't, and she'll understand that sooner or later. She'll know what I did was for the best, and then she'll forget all about me and move on.

Hell, she might even take that asshole home tonight and get over me by getting under him. I hate the thought of that, but she's not mine anymore. No, she was never mine, to begin with.

She'll forget about me sooner or later. She's probably starting to, but I'll never forget her. I'll never forget my angel and how sweet she sounds when she laughs or even says my name. *Grayson*. One word, and I'm weak. One fucking word, and I fall to my knees. She has no idea what she's done to me. I have no idea how I'm going to get over her.

It's like as soon as she stepped into my life, she became the thing that was missing. That sounds dumb. Fuck, What the hell am I even thinking? I sound like one of those delusional girls. Jesus. I need a fucking drink.

The only reason I'm here is because Aiden called me telling me he needed a ride home, even though his shift doesn't end for another two hours, which I didn't know until I got here and my eyes met hers.

He probably set this up, which wouldn't surprise me. I should go home. I should leave and come back when the bar closes. I shouldn't be looking towards her blonde hair and his hands on her body.

My jaw is so tight, it fucking hurts. I tear my eyes away from them as I tap on the counter, getting Aiden's attention. "Get me a scotch."

He chokes out a laugh. "Bro, relax your face. Jesus."

I glare at him. "I don't need beauty tips. I need a drink."

He shakes his head, filling up a glass with the dark liquid. "You need to talk to her," he says, sliding the drink to me.

I take a sip of the drink and shrug. "What is there to talk about? It's over. It was a hook-up, and it's done." Even as I'm saying those words, I know it's not true. Nothing about us was a hook-up. We were so much more than that.

He narrows his eyes at me. "You don't act like this over any hook-up."

I haven't mentioned anything to Aiden about Rosie. He doesn't know that what happened between us was so much more than fucking, even if he suspects it. He doesn't know that she was perfect, so sweet, so beautiful and I fucked it all up. I fucked her up.

I take another swig of my drink and look over my shoulder, where they're still dancing. Her head is laying on his shoulder. The sight makes the tight feeling in my chest increase tenfold. I don't want some other guy making her happy. Making her smile and laugh and being the cause of that sweet sound coming out of her mouth.

I don't want that asshole's hands on her hips, feeling her body under his hands. Feeling how good holding her is. Jesus, how much fucking longer are they going to keep dancing, "Does this song ever end?" I huff out.

Aiden laughs, and I flip him off. He sighs and leans on the counter. "What happened between you two?" He asks.

I fucked up. "Nothing." I spit out, knowing it's bullshit.

He scoffs. "C'mon. I'm not stupid."

I groan. I know how he is. He's not going to let this go. "Jesus. Fine." I spit out. "You were right. She got attached; she told me she loves me." I say, craving the burn from the whiskey in my throat.

His brows draw together. "So?"

I lift my eyes to meet his. "So? Didn't you hear what I said?"

He nods. "Yeah, but why's that a bad thing?"

I laugh bitterly. "Because she doesn't love me," I tell him. "I don't know what she feels for me, but love isn't it."

"And you don't love her?" he asks.

"Of course not." I down the rest of the glass. "Love isn't fucking real."

He laughs. He actually laughs, shaking his head. "Tell me you don't believe that."

I shake my head. "You do?" I ask him, staring up at his face. It looks like he's about to laugh again.

"Believe in love?" he raises his brow. "Uh, yeah?"

"Christ," I mutter, running a hand down my face.

"Hey, can I get a beer over here?" someone mutters.

He sighs, lifts himself off the counter, and starts filling a glass with beer. "Grayson. if you don't think love is real, then what is it you think you feel for Rosalie?" He asks me.

"I don't feel anything for her." I force out, hating how my throat seems to constrict as the words come out of it.

He serves the guy at the end of the bar and then comes over to me again. "Listen. When you want to be honest with me, then we'll talk. I'm not going to stand here and listen to this bullshit."

"It isn't bullshit," I say. "Yeah, we had fun, but now it's done."

He stares at me for a while and then shakes his head, narrowing his eyes at me, "You said that shit to her, didn't you," he asks, crossing his arms over his chest.

I shrug. "Not those exact words."

He grimaces. "You're a dumbass."

"What?"

"You're a fucking dumbass," he says. "You've been lost without her. Drinking, sleeping all day, acting like you've got a stick shoved up your ass all week. You can't even look at her with another guy without feeling sick. And you think you don't love her?"

"I don't."

He gestures with his head behind me to Rosalie. "That girl said she loves you, she felt comfortable with you and told you how she feels, and you said 'it was fun, but now it's over' to her face," he says, frowning at me. "You broke her heart."

Fuck, don't I know it. I did everything I possibly could to avoid that situation. I didn't want to hurt her. "I told her not to get attached."

He crosses his arms, glaring at me. "Was she just a fuck?"

This guy is begging for my fist. "Don't fucking talk about her like that."

"Was your whole interaction purely sexual?" he asks me again.

I look away, remembering everything we did together. How I showed her what makes me feel alive, how I took her drinking for the first time, dancing with her, taking her to the lake.

"Not exactly. We did other stuff," I tell him.

"Like?"

"Like shit I don't want to tell you," I spit out. I don't need to tell him everything that happened between Rosie and me. It was between us. It was ours.

He laughs. "You're head over heels in love with that girl."

I swallow, shaking my head. "I—"

"Love isn't a made-up concept, Grayson. It's when you can't stop thinking about someone. You want every day with them. You trust them. You love everything they do. You love everything about them."

I picture her smile and how my chest tenses every time she smiles at me. Her laugh, her voice, how sweet and breathless it is. Her face, that gorgeous mole that I can only see when she doesn't have makeup on. How she gets excited about everything, how she feels in my arms when she cradles her head into my chest.

Aiden's voice snaps me out of a Rosalie montage in my head. "If you don't feel that way for her, then fine. You don't love her," he says.

Shit. He's right. I do feel like that for her. I can't even sleep when she's not near me. Every time I think about how I'm never going to see her again, never going to kiss her again, never going to hold her again, I struggle to breathe.

"Fuck," I curse, running a hand through my hair.

He grins. "You're welcome."

I love her. Of course, I fucking love her. I want every moment with her. I want to wake up with her, go to sleep with her, share every day with her. I want to teach her everything and share all of her firsts with her. I want to hear her laugh, I want to see her smile, I want to make her happy because she makes me happy just by being around, by being herself.

I want her.

I love her.

"I'm going to get my girl back."

39

Kiss in the rain

Rosalie

My head drops, looking down at the ground. We've been dancing for what seems like forever. Technically it's only been three songs, but it's three songs too many. Andrew seems great, but I'm just not ready. Maybe I'll take his number, but I don't know when I'll ever be ready.

I didn't think I'd feel this defeated after things ended with Grayson. I didn't think I'd fall for him and be heartbroken all in the span of twenty-four hours. How long do heartbreaks last anyway? Is there a timeframe when it starts feeling easier to imagine your life without them?

"You're so hot," Andrew whispers in my ear, and I'm glad he can't see my face right now because the disgust on my face would put him off. For some reason, when Grayson complimented me, it made my face light up, it gave me butterflies and made me smile, but when Andrew does it, it sounds… wrong.

"Uh, thanks," I say.

"Do you want to come back to my place later?"

My throat bobs as I struggle to find the words to tell him no. I don't want to go anywhere but to bed tonight. I have a date with two giant tubs of ice cream and Bridget jones.

"Um..." I mumble and pull back to look at him. Maybe dancing with the guy for over five minutes made him think this was leading somewhere I definitely didn't want it to go.

"I don't think so," someone behind me says, and the next thing I know, I'm being dragged away.

"What the hell?" Andrew mutters from behind me.

I spin my head, seeing Grayson grabbing my hand as we walk out of the bar. Grayson?

He pushes the door open as we head outside, the cold night air hitting my skin. He spins me around and presses me back against the brick. He stares down at me, tongue darting out to lick his bottom lip. "What was that in there?" he asks.

"Grayson?" I whisper, looking up at his dark eyes. Am I imagining this? I thought he'd never want to speak to me again after what happened.

He closes his eyes and tips his head back, a small smile forming on his lips. "Christ, I've missed that," he mumbles.

"What's happening right now?" I ask him.

"Were you trying to make me jealous, angel?" he asks, his fingers meeting mine. I shiver under his touch. Angel. He called me angel again.

I almost smile, almost throw my arms around him and pull him into me, but I have no idea what he's doing. I don't know why he pulled me outside, why he's calling me angel, or why he's asking if I was trying to make him jealous. I would never do that to him. I didn't think he'd care. After all, he was the one who ended it.

"No," I say, shaking my head. "We're not together anymore. Actually, we were never together, right? So, there's no reason for you to feel jealous."

He frowns. "Don't say that."

I shake my head. "I would never do that to you. I don't want you to hurt like I'm hurting."

I look up at him, and his eyes trace my face, his throat bobbing as he swallows. His hand cradles my face, and he tilts his head down. He leans in, and his lips meet mine, fast and hard like he's punishing me for something, but I take it. I open my mouth and let his tongue inside, tasting him for the first time in over a week. Oh god, I've missed him so much.

But I still have no idea what the hell is going on. I pull back on a hum. "What are you doing?" I ask.

He smiles with that sweet smile, and his thumb runs over my lip. "Taking back what's mine," he murmurs, meeting my eyes.

I suck in a breath, my heart thumping inside my chest. "What do you mean by that?" I ask him.

"It means I'm an asshole," he says, his brows furrowing. "It means I'm an idiot for not realizing it sooner." He leans down until our breaths mix, and his lips almost touch mine. "It means I love you."

I stop breathing. All the air is stuck in my chest as I process the words that just came out of his mouth. He loves me?

"But… you don't believe in love," I somehow manage to say.

"I didn't," he reaffirms, shaking his head. "Until you."

The way he's looking at me is so intense. His dark eyes burn into mine, and I can't look away. "What?" I say, shaking my head, a little dizzy.

He swallows. "I love you, Rosie. I love you so much, I just didn't fucking know it." He laughs bitterly, shaking his head. "I don't know what I thought love was, but fuck, I love you. Of course, I love you. I can't stop thinking it, saying it. I want to say it all the time. I almost did a few times," he admits.

"I honestly thought I was just caught up in the moment, but my mind knew it before I did. Everything I feel for you screams love," he says, running his thumb over my cheek. "I want to be with you every day, all the time. It feels like I can't breathe when I'm not with you," he says, shaking his head. "Seeing you in there, with some other guy's hands on you, made me realize that I couldn't let you go. I knew if I didn't accept my feelings and tell you, I would lose you forever, and I won't let that happen. I couldn't live with myself knowing I let the best thing that's ever happened to me out of reach."

I can't contain it. I smile so wide at the man I love, who loves me back. My heart thumps so loud I'm sure he can hear it. "Grayson." I breathe out.

He groans. "Fuck, you have no idea what you do to me. I want you. Today, tomorrow, and the next. I want you forever. If you'll have me, I want to be yours. Completely yours, and I want you to be mine."

I nod, I don't stop nodding, and he laughs, but he doesn't stop there. "I want to wake up with you, go to sleep with you, go on adventures with you. I want to buy you flowers every single day."

I laugh. "That seems a little excessive—"

"I'll do anything for you, angel. Everything. I will be the best for you. I will do everything in my power to make you happy. Whatever it takes, I will do it."

"You mean that?"

"I mean every fucking word," he says, taking my hand and placing it over his chest. "You are the only girl that makes my heart beat this fast. The only girl I dream of kissing. The only person I trust undoubtedly with everything."

"I trust you too." I breathe out. His heart beats under my touch, and I gasp.

The corner of his mouth lifts. "I told you. It's only you that does that to me. You've fucking ruined me, Rosie."

I look down at where his hand is covering mine, pressed against his chest. I miss him so much. I miss having his hands on me, touching him, kissing him, and he's here telling me he loves me. I don't know what to make of it.

"You hurt me," I whisper.

"I know," he says, frowning. "I will apologize for pushing you away every single day of my life. As long as you'll have me, I'll never make you regret being with me. I love you, Rosie. I love you. I love you," he repeats, making me laugh, tears filling my eyes. "If you don't want to be with me… fuck, I don't know what I'll do, but I'll know that it's your decision, that it's what you want. I need you in my life, but if you don't feel the same way then…" He trails off, looking to the side, his jaw clenches as he closes his eyes and breathes out, running a hand through his hair.

My eyes fall down and catch on his arm. I freeze. My whole body stops moving, I stop breathing. "Grayson," I whisper. He looks down, seeing what I'm seeing, and places my hand on his arm, allowing my fingers to explore the tattoo. "Angel wings?" I ask.

He nods. "You were inside my head, Rosie. Every day, no matter how hard I tried, I couldn't get you out. You were already a part of me, and I never wanted to forget you, so I needed you on my body too."

He drops his head, his eyes darkening as his hand clutches my face. "You made me believe in love, Rosie. I was in denial, I didn't want to believe it. I just… love hasn't worked out well for me before. My parents, my uncle," he says squeezing his eyes shut.

He blows out a breath and opens his eyes. "I'm so scared to lose you. To me, you are the definition of love and I'm so sorry, angel. I'm sorry it took me so long to figure my shit out and realize how crazy in love I am with you."

I look up at him and swallow. His dark eyes burn into mine, his hair falls over his face. I reach up and brush his hair out of his face and stand on my toes. "I love you, Grayson."

He smiles, his dark hair falling back onto his face as he bends down to pick me up. He grabs my thighs, and I tighten my legs around his waist as he holds me up. "Fuck, I love you too."

Our lips meet, and I smile into the kiss, which he returns as he laughs into my mouth. We're smiling together as we kiss, and it's perfect. He's perfect, and he loves me. I tighten my hold around his neck as he presses me into the wall.

I hum into his mouth when I feel wetness on my forehead, along with another and another. We break apart as we look up, rain falling on us, heavier now.

He grins. "Looks like you got your kiss in the rain."

I can't help but smile. "Just fucking kiss me."

"Such hostile words from an angel," he repeats his words from our first time. "But I'll happily oblige," he says before our lips meet again, and the warm feel of his lips and tongue contrasts the cold rain falling on my shoulders, drenching us.

I've never felt happier in my life.

EPILOGUE

To do list: Completed

Grayson

"You're still coming this weekend, right?"

I laugh at my mother's eagerness. She hasn't stopped asking me to come over since she found out about Rosalie and me dating. At first, she couldn't believe someone like Rosie was with me, which I didn't know what to make of. I guess I thought the same when we first got together.

It still surprises me that someone as beautiful and good as Rosie is with me. I'm the luckiest guy ever. Especially because tonight, I get to take her on a date.

"Yes, mom. We'll be there." I tell her. "I've got to go. I love you."

"Love you too, honey."

I hang up the phone and knock on her door, waiting for her to open it. It's been too long since I saw my girlfriend. Fuck, girlfriend. That word makes me shiver, but not in the way it used to. In a way, that makes me shake with anticipation to see my gorgeous girl.

The door swings open, and I'm socked in the chest. "Holy shit."

I look down her body, her long blonde hair flows down her back, and on her body is a sexy, little black dress hugging her figure. I've never seen her in black.

"What have you done to my angel?" I ask her.

She grins. "You like?"

I erase the distance between us and lean down. "I love," I rasp, tipping her head back. "And I love you," I whisper before kissing the living shit out of her.

Her lips are so sweet, she's always so sweet, but tonight she looks like a provocative dream. Her lips part with a gasp and I use it to my advantage and slide my tongue inside her mouth, tasting her, savoring her, drowning in her. I can't get close enough. I want to crawl inside her skin where she keeps the pure sunshine beaming inside of her.

My hand finds her thigh, lifting the dress as I raise my hand on her thigh, feeling her supple skin under my touch. I groan into her mouth when my hand travels high enough to her hips, where I don't feel any panty lines. She's not wearing any fucking underwear.

"This date will be over sooner than planned if we keep this up."

She pans her hands on my chest, feeling the material of the shirt. "That's fine by me."

I laugh, leaning in and kissing the top of her head. "God, I love you."

"I'll never get tired of hearing it." she lets out a sigh of contentment.

"Good, because I'll never get tired of saying it." I pull back and tighten the hold on her hand, squeezing it. "I got you something."

"You didn't have to get me anything," she says, and then she smiles. "What is it?" I can't help but laugh. I figured out pretty quickly that her love language is gifts. I love seeing the look on her face when I surprise her. It doesn't matter what it is, she lights up every time, and I love it.

I pull out the flowers I bought for her earlier and hand them over to her. She gasps and takes them from me, and I feast. Tracing her features with my eyes, seeing how her eyes light up and her cheeks turn pink as she grins. She's so happy, and that's all I want. I want to make her happy. I want to be on the receiving end of those smiles for the rest of my life.

Because nothing feels better than seeing Rosalie smile. It's so warm, so beautiful. It's my angel.

"Grayson," she breathes, making me smile from hearing my name alone. "They're beautiful."

"They're orchids," I tell her. "White orchids. They remind me of the first time I ever saw you."

She looks up at me, lips parted in shock, and she gulps. "I think these are my favorite flowers."

I laugh. "I thought you said you didn't have any favorites."

"I didn't," she says. "Until you."

"You like them?"

She nods. "I love them. Thank you."

"You don't have to thank me, angel. I want to make you happy," I tell her.

"You do." She wraps her arms around me, flowers in one hand, the other around my neck. "So much." She pulls back, and her eyes fall onto my lips before looking back up at my eyes.

"Ugh." We turn at the sound of Leila walking out of Rosie's room. "Look at you… in love." She shakes her head. "I'm leaving before I throw up."

I try to hide my laughter in the crook of Rosie's neck, but it doesn't go unnoticed.

"I can hear you," she says, narrowing her eyes at me before leaving the apartment.

Yeah, I guess she's not my biggest fan ever since I called her and pretty much scolded her for giving Rosie pot brownies, but I can't help but want her to like me. She's Rosie's best friend, she's important to Rosie, which means I want to be on her good side.

I had to bribe Gabriella with candy to get her to stop ignoring me. She wanted to punish me for breaking Rosie's heart. Believe me, I torture myself over that fact often. I hate that I hurt her, that I made her believe that I didn't love her when I know now that if I had to be without her, I'd be a miserable man unable to carry on without my angel.

At least Madi likes me. She's cool, didn't give me shit about it, just warned me that if I broke Rosie's heart again, I'd have to deal with her. I promised her that I would rather die than hurt her again.

"You ready?" I ask Rosie.

She nods, flashing me that beautiful smile of hers. "Let's go."

Once again, she's so excited even though she has no idea where we're going. I have a surprise for her. I kept the list. Maybe I shouldn't have, but I couldn't stop thinking about it. We only have one thing to cross off. Skinny dipping.

I've done it before. Senior year of high school, but I barely remember any of it. It was boring, disappointing. But this time, it's different. It's with Rosie. I'm experiencing another first with her. I want to rewrite my whole history with her. I want to make all of her experiences my own.

I want to do everything with her. For the rest of my life.

THE END

Acknowledgements

Rosalie and Grayson were so fun to write. I honestly had the best time writing their story and their characters.

I related a lot to Rosalie and found comfort in her character as I was writing her. Grayson made me fall in love with him, all he ever wanted was love and Rosie finally gave him that.

I hope you all enjoyed reading Never Have I Ever as much as I loved writing it.

I would like to thank all the people who supported me and continue to support me. This release wouldn't have been as easy without you. Your support and love makes me so happy and keeps me motivated.

Thank you to my best friend, Anoopa, who has had to put up with endless nagging during the writing process of my book. Even though she doesn't show it, she's probably sick and tired of me by now, but thank you nonetheless. I love you.

And thank you reader, for picking up my book and giving me a chance as an indie writer.

Please leave a review if you enjoyed the book and be on the lookout for the next book in the Campus Games series!

About the Author

Stephanie Alves is an avid reader and writer of smutty, contemporary romance books. She is English / Portuguese and she loves happy endings, whether it's in a book or a romantic comedy. All of her books are available to read on Kindle Unlimited.

You can find her here:

Instagram.com/Stephanie.alves_author

Stephaniealvesauthor.com

Made in the USA
Monee, IL
21 February 2025